The Boy Who Came Walking Home

The Boy WHO CAME Walking Home

Peter Scott

Down East Books

DEDICATION

To my Mom

ALSO BY PETER SCOTT

Lost Crusade

Something in the Water

"Home is the place where, when you have to go there,
They have to take you in."

Death of the Hired Man
Robert Frost

Design by Phil Schirmer

ISBN 0-89272-617-2
Library of Congress Control Number: 2003105203

Printed at Versa Press Inc., East Peoria, Illinois

2 4 5 3 1

Down East Books
P.O. Box 679
Camden, ME 04843

For book orders and catalog information,
call 800-685-7962, or visit www.downeastbooks.com

CHARACTERS
IN ORDER OF APPEARANCE

Virgil Coombs, age twenty-nine. Lobsterman. Husband of Gladys. Brother of Walter, Ava, and John Coombs. Father of John Ulysses Coombs. Uncle of Henry.

Gladys Coombs (née Wedge), age twenty-four. Wife of Virgil, above.

Henry Coombs, age sixteen. Son of John (deceased) and Rachel Coombs. Pitcher for the Stonington Quarrymen and corporal, U.S. Army.

Ava Coombs, age thirty-seven. Sister of Walter Coombs. Spinstress matriarch of Coombs Cove. Archenemy of Tessie Wedge.

Rachel Coombs (née Bowen), age thirty-three. Widow of John Coombs. Mother of Henry.

Steve Robbins, age eighteen. Corporal, U.S. Army. Master of the internal combustion engine.

Tessie Wedge, age forty-five. President of the Barter Island Rebekahs, treasurer and secretary of the island church, Mistress of Morality and Comportment on Barter Island.

Claire Schuyler, age sixteen, aka the "little Dutch girl." Student in Stonington. Friend of Steve Robbins and, especially, of Henry Coombs.

Amos Coombs, age twenty-three. Husband of Clytie, father of Leah. Lobsterman. Nephew of Walter, Ava, et cetera. By disposition sheepish but determined.

Maggie Bowen, age twenty-one. Cousin of Rachel Coombs, sister of Clytie. Barter Island schoolteacher. In private a suffragette; an admirer of Emily Dickinson and Margaret Sanger.

Ruth, age twenty-one. College friend and former roommate of Maggie in Bangor. Maggie's correspondent.

Leah Coombs, age six. Daughter of Amos and Clytie. The apple of Cecil Barter's squinty eye.

Clytie Coombs (née Bowen), age twenty-three. Wife of Amos, mother of Leah. A diabetic baker of confections, and a virago of hefty proportions.

Cecil Barter, age nine. Son of Cecilia Barter. Student. Young admirer of Leah Coombs. Kitten killer.

Walter Coombs, age thirty-eight. Lobsterman. Bachelor brother of Ava and John.

Dr. Henry Banks, age thirty-nine. Stonington physician, connoisseur of country cooking.

John Ulysses Coombs, age six months. Son of Virgil and Gladys Coombs.

Reverend Nathaniel Sharpesdale, age forty-four. Pastor of the Barter Island church, with the lead role in Tessie Wedge's morality play.

Cyrus Weed, age fifty-five. Tessie Wedge's factotum.

Fuddy and **Skippy**, age seven. Dim schoolboys.

Huldah Cain, age seventy-six. Burnt Island prophetess whose familiar is a seagull.

Major General Hodges, age forty-nine. U.S. Army. Commanding officer, Camp Devens, in Massachusetts.

Major Abner Small, age seventy-eight, of Penobscot, Maine. Civil War veteran. Nurse for Steve Robbins, and wayfinder for both Steve and Henry Coombs.

Coombs

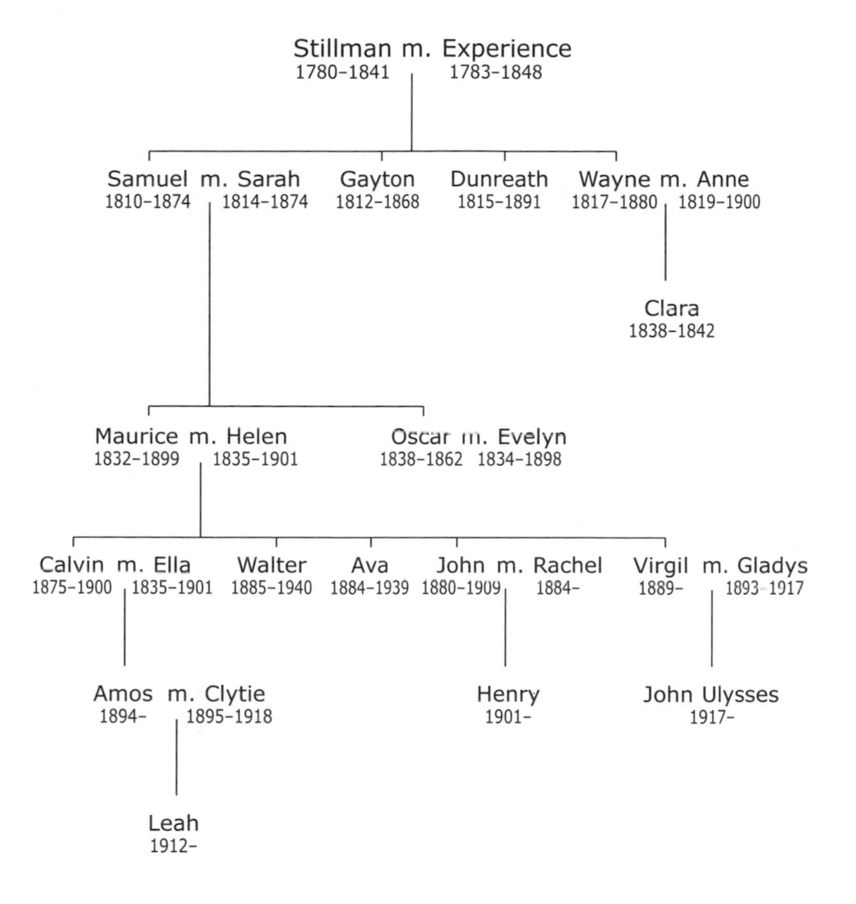

Stillman m. Experience
1780–1841 1783–1848
Samuel m. Sarah
1810–1874 1814–1874
Gayton
1812–1868
Dunreath
1815–1891
Wayne m. Anne
1817–1880 1819–1900
Clara
1838–1842
Maurice m. Helen
1832–1899 1835–1901
Oscar m. Evelyn
1838–1862 1834–1898
Calvin m. Ella
1875–1900 1835–1901
Walter
1885–1940
Ava
1884–1939
John m. Rachel
1880–1909 1884–
Virgil m. Gladys
1889– 1893–1917
Amos m. Clytie
1894– 1895–1918
Henry
1901–
John Ulysses
1917–
Leah
1912–

Part One
1917

"I spy Kaiser at the door.
We'll get a lemon pie,
And we'll squash him in his eye,
And there won't be a Kaiser anymore."
Children's ditty, 1917

Chapter 1
A Frail Net

"I'd like to see Henry play ball. I would. But I've got no use for Stonington. If Stonington was bait, I'd swim past it."

Amos Coombs, July 4, 1917

When people asked Virgil Coombs why he needed to wear a clean shirt every day, he said, "I just do." Everyone on the island knew that when the young Virgil sold his first crate of lobsters, he'd sent away to Sears for seven cotton shirts—four khaki and three blue—and had worn a clean shirt every day since. Everyone also knew that he insisted on washing and ironing them himself on Sundays, when Gladys was in church—a fact that the men met with skepticism, and the women thought was some sweet. Part of the fun of it for Virgil was not knowing which color would come out of the dark closet when he reached in for a clean shirt each morning. The only person who ever pressed him on the subject of fresh shirts was his nephew Henry, who pestered Virgil for an explanation for everything he did.

"You might as well ask Irville why he has to squat every time he lights his pipe," Virgil had said. "Why don't you ask him that?"

"Because I don't care about Irville," Henry had replied. "He's not my uncle."

"I know that," Virgil had said. "Reach me some more bait bags. I wear a clean shirt because my father did." Virgil wore oilskin cuffs to protect the sleeves of his shirts when he was handling bait. "And the women like it."

If Henry had not rolled his eyes, Virgil might have gone on to explain that he hated to stink of bait, which was true, and may even have told him about the excitement of not knowing what color would come out of the closet in the morning, but that surely would have resulted in those rolling eyes, and really pissed Virgil off, so he let it go.

On that morning in August 1917, when Virgil and Henry set out from the cove for Stonington, Virgil was wearing a blue shirt, somewhat worn in the elbows. He stood on the deck of the *Gladdy C.* with his hands in his pockets, watching Henry row toward him in the old peapod they called *Friggit*. Behind Henry, across the still cove and beyond the stretch of meadow, both Virgil's own house and the family house, where his brother and sister lived, were framed in full sunlight on the rise. He saw his sister Ava cross her dooryard toward his house with a pitcher of something, going to look in on his wife Gladys, who lay as limp as a cloth doll in her bed. Virgil's attempts to hoist Gladys's spirits with words—"The baby will be healthy this time, and so will you"; "The third time is good luck"—were wearing so thin that only a trip to see Dr. Banks in Stonington in hopes of getting some new medicine would do.

Henry brought the peapod alongside and dropped his ball glove and spikes onto the washboard. He was wearing his high rubber fishing boots and the uniform of the Stonington Quarrymen, for whom he pitched, the tall Number Sixteen. As Henry tied off the peapod, a school of harbor pollack, swimming in disrupted ribbons, wandered into the cove and, finding the water too warm even for them, shifted and swam beneath the *Gladdy C.* to get back to deeper water.

"It's about time," Virgil said. "Are you ready?"

"I'm standing here waiting on you," Henry said, adjusting his new Boston-style ball cap.

As they slipped out of the cove and Virgil came aft to be ready to catch the breeze, Henry sat on the transom punching the pocket of his glove with his fist.

"Why don't we go under power?" Henry asked. "I could use some time to warm up before the game." He threw a few roundhouses to loosen his pitching arm.

"You'll get there in plenty of time," Virgil said. "It's a fair day for a sail. There's no need to waste gas until we get into the harbor. When we get there, help me remember to buy that atomizer for Gladys, will you?"

Behind them Henry's mother stood on the high granite ledge in front of her house, which was now visible among the trees. When she saw her boy's arm go round and round, she thought he was waving good-bye, and she waved back, unnoticed, wishing him luck.

"I will, if you help me remember to get a haircut," Henry said. "I promised Mother."

As the *Gladdy C.* rounded the northern head and sailed out from under the lee of the high island into the open bay, Henry went forward to crowd on more sail, and Virgil sat at the tiller breathing in the bright afternoon. In the wide bay a three-masted schooner—a granite hauler by the rough looks of her—was making her way north toward the Goss quarry on Crotch Island. Beyond her, and as far as Mount Desert Island that rose up in the north, the blue expanse was alive with skittering white summer sails. They passed within a hundred yards of Chester Grindle, another Barter Island lobsterman, who was emptying a trap with one hand and with the other shaking out a bait bag for a diving, squabbling crowd of gulls. When Chester looked up and saw Henry standing at the mast of the *Gladdy C.* in his red-trimmed baseball uniform, he gave Henry the thumbs-up and shouted words of encouragement that were lost on the breeze. Henry returned the gesture and waved his cap.

Virgil remembered another morning very much like this one, eight or nine years before, when Henry was still in knickers and Rachel still in mourning for her husband, his brother John. She was wearing a straw hat held in place with a pink ribbon tied in a bow under her chin, and loose strands of her chestnut hair streamed in the breeze. Virgil remembered that she was sitting on a low stool in the cockpit, her suitcase at her side for a weekend visit with her people in Stonington. Henry was wearing a sailor suit—a middy shirt and a blue scarf—and Rachel was scolding him to sit still, not to soil his clothes on the washboard. Virgil did not remember warning them to watch for the boom as he prepared to come about near Bill's Island, but he did remember Rachel's hand holding Henry's head down and her ducking as the boom passed over them. He remembered moments later Rachel's sudden cry of horror, and Henry screaming in pain and terror as he danced beside the mast, tugging at his left hand, which was pinned at the wrist between a mast hoop and the mast.

Virgil had thought he remembered letting the sail go and standing helplessly at the tiller, one arm outstretched toward Rachel as she climbed onto the cabin, lifted the boy off his feet, and freed his hand. But some time later, how long Virgil could not remember, at supper in Ava's kitchen, he had been surprised and a little perplexed to hear Rachel tell Ava that it had been he, Virgil, who had climbed up and freed Henry's hand from the hoop. Rachel said he had sat on the edge of the cabin roof with Henry sobbing in his arms while she reefed the sail. She said Virgil had kissed Henry's chafed wrist and rocked him until he was quiet.

"Oh, no," Virgil had said. There had been a tiny dab of chocolate icing on Rachel's upper lip. "No, it was you that took him down and held him, not me, Rachel."

Rachel had held his eyes in hers for a long second, willing him to her gently. Ava, who had not liked the way they looked at each other, had asked Henry who it was that had picked him off the mast, but Henry had only shrugged his shoulders and said he didn't remember any of it.

"Maybe it never happened," Ava had said. "Maybe you both dreamed the same thing, only differently. It doesn't really matter, does it?"

At the time Virgil had thought that it did matter, and he had known by the look in Rachel's eyes that she thought so, too, but now, as they approached Stonington and he watched Henry sharpening his spikes, he thought that it probably did not.

Virgil did not bother to crank up his engine when they came into Stonington harbor. All but one of the fifty or so boats of the Stonington fishing fleet were out, their skiffs and peapods waiting peacefully on their moorings for their return. A steamer smack was tied up at Caldwell's dock, taking on lobsters by the basketful for the restaurants in Boston. As Virgil slipped through the array of skiffs, nudging one here and there, he passed a solitary lobster boat moored in the middle of the harbor; her captain, a man Virgil had seen before but whose name he did not know, stood stock-still on his deck, in jacket and tie and bowler hat, with mustaches that drooped to his chin. Virgil raised a hand in greeting, but the man, who was looking right at Virgil, did not respond, did not even nod—one of those Deer Island men who had no use for men from Barter Island.

Though they could see a few people busy among the buildings on the waterline, the rest of the town—Opera House, hotel, and brightly painted houses perched helter-skelter on the steep granite slopes of the hills that embraced the harbor—seemed asleep in the sunlight. On the town wharf three young men Henry's age, none of whom Virgil recognized, were untangling a huge net and feeding it onto a spool that a fourth boy turned slowly, singing the dirty ditty about Valparaiso Sue from Peru.

"Hello, Henry," the farthest one cried. "You give 'em hell today, you hear. We're looking for a no-hitter."

Henry asked Arnold if he was coming to the game.

"Damned straight we are," the boy replied. "Soon as we get this son of a bitch stowed."

Of equal height, exactly six feet, with the same fair freckled complexion, and the same way of walking with a backward lean as though their torsos were only reluctantly following their long legs, Virgil and Henry looked more like brothers than uncle and nephew. They usually walked side by side keeping the same easy pace, but today Henry, his spikes tied together and slung over his striped shoulder, strained ahead, eager to get to the game and see his friends.

"For Christ's sake," Virgil said. "I'm going to work up a sweat trying to keep up with you. Why don't you go on ahead. I've got to see the doctor first anyway."

When he rounded the corner by the livery Virgil stopped so suddenly in the lane that his torso caught up with his legs, and he stood staring in helpless wonder at a brand-new radiant blue four-door touring car, polished so bright that he had to squint to see it.

"Would you look at this," Virgil said. "Jesus wept."

Henry stopped and grudgingly joined Virgil, eager to get him out of the middle of the road where someone might see him standing there staring gap-mouthed at a Christly car like it was a naked mermaid drying her hair in the sun.

"It's a Maxwell touring car." Henry used a patronizing tone that Virgil did not like one bit. "It's been here since last spring." Henry pushed his uncle gently toward the car to break his spell and get him out of the road.

"I can read." Virgil pointed at the name MAXWELL in chrome script on the radiator. As he made a slow appreciative inspection of the car—the running lamps on either side of the windshield were made of sterling silver and cut glass—Virgil remembered that a short year ago Henry had begged him with tears in his eyes to talk his mother out of sending him to Stonington for high school. When Virgil had refused to intervene, saying that his father would have wanted him to finish school, the first Coombs boy to do so, Henry had turned his back on Virgil and had not spoken to him for a week. Now, after a year in the town, the bashful boy who'd once clung to Virgil when they came up for some errand was treating him like a country bumpkin. Virgil thought to say something to Henry to put him in his place, but instead he asked him whose car it was.

"It's Doctor Small's," Henry said. "I thought you knew about it. Charles Scott is running a scow from the mainland across the reach that will hold two automobiles as big as this. At once. Doctor Wasgatt has a Buick runabout up in Deer Isle that they say could do forty miles an hour if there was a fair stretch of road on this island to try it on. There will be, I'll bet, and soon." Henry reflected for a moment. "It'll be a hundred years before you see a car like this down on Barter Island."

A sputtering engine and a low metallic moan turned their heads to Stevie Robbins, who had pulled up behind them in his flivver. Stevie, the boy with a genius for internal combustion engines and an ability to make any machine move forward, sat large and upright in his contraption, his left elbow leaning on the door that read CAPACITY: 5 GALS in white paint.

"Hullo Mister Coombs, Henry," Stevie said. "You want a ride up to the ball field?" Stevie was the big third baseman for the Quarrymen, a hard man to get by on your way around third to home; he was wearing his uniform, with the cap pulled down over his ears to hold his hair in place. His flivver—a patchwork of old Model T parts stripped to little more than frame, windshield, and seats—shivered in anticipation of another passenger.

Henry said thanks and, finding the passenger door wired shut, stepped in over it. DANGER: 1000 JOLTS.

Virgil imagined himself riding up the steep hill in the backseat of Stevie's machine—a kitchen chair bolted to the floor—and said he would walk. As he watched the boys drive away, laughing at something said, Virgil thought that he saw Henry riding away from the cove, from Barter Island and him, to a different world where he, Virgil, would be a confused and helpless stranger. Henry kept laughing and did not look back. A lone herring gull alighted on the leather top of the bright touring car, lifted his tail feathers slightly, moved his birdie bowels, and released a generous white offering onto the windshield, which made the gull, and Virgil, feel a little better.

On Main Street, Stevie cut back on the throttle to ease past the iceman's skittish team.

"The old bastard said if I spooked his team again, he'd come after me with an ax, and I believe him," Stevie said. "Cigarette?" He flipped up the windshield and scratched a kitchen match across the dash to light Henry's, then his own. "She's up there already," he added, "sitting in the front row behind home plate with her little sister."

"How the hell do you know that?" Henry asked.

"I was just there. I came down to get you," said Stevie.

"They haven't started yet, have they?" Henry asked. "It's not one o'clock yet."

"No, hell," said Stevie. "Half the players from both teams haven't showed up yet. You told her you're going to quit school and join the army."

"Jesus," said Henry. "That was supposed to be a secret. Damn her. If that ever gets back to my mother . . ."

"It won't," said Stevie. "She only told me. I don't think she believes it anyway."

When they passed Miss Tessie Wedge in front of the pharmacy, Henry held his cigarette out of sight.

The road past the Opera House to the school and ball field above was steep, but dry and packed firm. Stevie adjusted the needle valve and throttle and started the climb, leaning ahead into the hill.

"Give her too much too fast and she could flip over backward," Stevie said.

As the flivver strained for the crest of the hill it slowed to a walk, and steam with a taste of hot metal and oil poured back over the boys. When Stevie eased it over the top of the hill, Henry looked back down at the town and harbor below, and the high broken spine of Barter Island in the distance; he flipped his cigarette into the road behind and turned his eyes and mind on the ball game, and the audience behind home plate.

Virgil saw Tessie Wedge on the sidewalk ahead of him and muttered "Oh shit" under his breath. Miss Tessie, his wife's maiden aunt (Virgil would not call her Aunt Tessie as Gladys did), was dressed for a day of shopping off-island in a double-breasted moire jacket with leg-o'-mutton sleeves that had been fashionable for ladies when Virgil was a boy, but were matronly to all but Miss Tessie in 1917. Virgil thought that she must have come up from Barter Island on the mail boat, and he hoped that he could get past her with a sentence or two. Miss Tessie, who believed that conventionality, as she saw it, was morality, had been waging silent combat with Virgil's older sister Ava for twenty years, and had long been vocal in her disapproval of her niece's marriage to a Coombs. Miss Tessie's family lived on the west side of Barter Island; in her mind, her niece Gladys was a princess held captive by a family of troglodytes in a remote cove on the far side of the mountain. She adjusted her face in the shade of her wide hat to greet Virgil. Virgil tipped his hat.

"Hello, Miss Tessie," Virgil said.

Though she had passed forty, Tessie Wedge had hardly weathered at all. Her complexion was still too pretty to powder; her hourglass waist and full bosom still drew wistful stares from men who did not know her.

"Good afternoon, Virgil," said Tessie Wedge. "What brings you to Stonington in the middle of the day?" *When you should be taking care of your poor wife or hauling your traps.* "How is my poor Gladys? I feel bad that I haven't been over to see her lately; it's been so busy you know."

"She's still quite weak, and bedridden," Virgil said. *As you well know.* "That's why I'm here, to see if Doctor Banks can give her something to make her comfortable."

"Poor dear," said Tessie Wedge. "She was the prettiest girl in the Penobscot Bay." *Until you wore her down with one pregnancy and miscarriage after another.*

"Is," Virgil said. "She *is* the prettiest girl in the Penobscot Bay."

Tessie Wedge smiled seraphically. *She's a Wedge, after all.*

"Good afternoon, Miss Tessie," said Virgil.

"And to you, Virgil. Tell Gladys, please, that I will be over to visit shortly. We've missed her this past month in church." *Where you haven't set foot since you were married.* "Enjoy your baseball game."

The little that Virgil knew about baseball he had learned from Henry in the last couple of years. He could not remember ever playing baseball as a boy, or even having seen a game, though he had a vague memory of a scene such as this one—hiding behind his mother's vast skirts from a crowd of angry shouting strangers somewhere off-island, perhaps here in Stonington. Watching Henry practice his pitching at home with a bait basket as his target, Virgil had learned about breaking balls, sliders, inshoots, fastballs, and brushing a batter between the belt and the letters to keep him from crowding the plate; he still did not understand what "bunching your batters" meant, though, or why anyone would choose to bunt when he could lay into the ball and score a home run.

This afternoon he sat on the far end of the top row of the bleachers, where he could see the whole spectacle. When Rachel was with him, he sat in the same corner with her between him and any strangers who might decide to sit close by; today he put his hat on the plank next to him to make it look like he was saving that seat for someone. Rachel smelled of bath soap and often got so anxious for Henry, with all those people watching him alone on the mound, that she clutched Virgil's sleeve. Today the spectators milled around on the baselines, in places three-deep; as late as the third inning (Virgil had yet to learn top from bottom) people continued to arrive on foot, and in wagons and buggies. The people who had come from Deer Isle gathered on the third-base line behind their Mariners, who wore dark blue uniforms and Chicago caps; the fans from Stonington collected behind their Quarrymen. Behind the backstop—a framework of peeling spruce poles covered by a worn-out gillnet—the bleachers were packed shoulder to shoulder, with the exception of the gap occupied by Virgil's hat. As these were the only two teams in the Penobscot League that hailed from Deer Island, many of the spectators and a third of the players were related somehow to members of the opposition, and as a consequence the rivalry was as bitter as bad blood, which was often shed by the flashing spikes of a base runner, to everyone's satisfaction.

Long tall Henry dropped the resin bag, hid the ball in his glove, glanced over at the runner on third base, nodded to the catcher, and released a fastball that went low and inside. On the Fourth of July the Stonington Quarrymen had lost to the Mariners by one run, and had lost by the same margin three weeks later; now, in the fifth inning, they were tied three to three with two outs and a man on third who danced around with his arms held out from his sides. Henry lined up another pitch. Virgil held himself with his arms across his chest. He was amazed that Henry could be so calm, surrounded by so many people watching him, shouting at him every time he threw the ball. At times like this, Virgil's pride in the boy, which grew an inch every time he watched him play, caused his hands to tighten the vise grip they had on his knees. Virgil wished Rachel was with him.

The hog-bodied Mariner batter knocked Henry's next pitch over the head of the right fielder to roll among the picnickers in the tall grass near the wagons. Virgil shut his eyes to block out the roar from the Deer Isle fans, and thought his heart would break for Henry as the runner crossed the plate and the batter stopped at second. The Quarrymen on the bench threw their hats down into the dust; the five girls sitting behind them in Stevie's flivver hung their heads. But in the next two pitches Henry threw strikes, one slider after another, and Virgil's hands relaxed on his knees. The batter, a skinny boy whose cheeks were cratered like the face of the moon, tipped Henry's fastball over the head of the umpire, where it ripped its way through the flimsy gillnet and was caught by an astonished fan in the fifth row. Henry struck the boy out and retired the side with only one run given up, but this was only his second strikeout of the game. On the sideline the Quarrymen's coach talked to Henry with a solemn hand resting on his shoulder, then waved to another player to warm up. Henry sat down on the end of the bench by the water pail, drank half a dipper, spilled the rest in the dust at his feet, and leaned forward, forearms on his knees. Watching Henry, Virgil did the same; he wanted to go down and say something to comfort Henry, but thought that he should not.

The pitcher who relieved Henry gave up five runs in the next three innings, which made Virgil feel better for Henry's sake and wonder why the coach did not put Henry back in. The Deer Isle fans were getting louder and louder, here and there dangerously personal; a new green touring car, which

Virgil thought must be the Buick from Deer Isle that Henry had mentioned, honked its croaky horn every time a Quarryman swung and missed. With her little sister in hand, a girl of Henry's age, in a blue bonnet and snow-white pinafore, eased her way through the Stonington crowd and stood behind Virgil, who sat sulking on the end of the bench. She was a pretty, pink-cheeked blond girl with long dancing curls; Virgil thought she must be the Dutch girl that Henry denied he was sweet on. Virgil could not remember her name. Henry did not know that the Dutch girl, Claire, was behind him until her little sister tapped him on the back. He looked over his shoulder, saw Claire's smile that was meant to reassure, and turned back to the game without a word or the slightest lift of his glum expression.

When the Quarrymen came up to bat in the bottom of the ninth, they were down by six runs. The taunts from the Mariner fans—"I hope you catch lobsters better than you catch fly balls, Teddy!"—were chafing the nerves of the Quarrymen raw. The Mariner fans roared and honked and hooted when their red-faced pitcher struck out the first batter. Grim Henry was next up; he pounded the plate with his bat and glared at the pitcher. On the second pitch Henry connected for a hard line drive, which the second baseman snagged and held aloft in his glove for the adoring multitude. Henry threw down his bat. Virgil shook his head at Henry's display of emotion, and watched as the Stonington crowd began to slip away in two and threes.

When the game was lost, Virgil put on his hat and waited in his seat in the sun for the Deer Isle fans to settle down. He thought that he would like to knock the spit out of the bastard who kept squeezing that car horn. When the Stonington crowd had dispersed, leaving only a few consoling clusters of family and friends gathered around the bench, Virgil went down to say a few words to the players he knew and collect Henry, thinking that the ride home was going to be a goddamned grim one.

Gladys Coombs rose slowly from deep in a laudanum dream. When she surfaced she found that she was still on her back in bed, and that the sun had just gone down behind the mountain, shading her house and the cove. Gladys did not need to sit up and look out the window to know that it had been Rachel's footsteps coming up the cove road that had summoned her from her dream. Rachel was carrying something that made one gravelly footstep louder than the other; someone else would have thought that a woman who walked with a hitch in her stride was approaching, but Gladys knew the footsteps were Rachel's. She had come home from work early, as she had promised she would, and Gladys thought that if it was a basket of food from the church ladies that she was carrying, it must be quite heavy and Rachel must have found someone to give her a ride over from town. She heard Rachel and Ava talking quietly in Ava's dooryard; she could not make out what they were saying, and she did not strain to hear.

When Rachel opened the kitchen door and whispered her name, Gladys spread the counterpane over the litter on the bed and turned on her side facing the far wall, feigning sleep. The medicine had eased her pain, but when she was awake, she had to suffer the terrible pressure down there. The veins in her legs felt as if they would burst, and even when she held her thighs together, it felt as if the baby was pushing down on a wet bag full of pudding that was about to burst. Gladys wanted to open her eyes and tell Rachel about the pressure, how it felt, but she thought that it would make her feel even dirtier to hear herself describe it. She could no more bear to complain to Rachel than she could bear to watch Ava when she came to take her soiled underclothes from the hamper on wash day.

Gladys listened. Rachel set something heavy on the kitchen table, and with the faintest rustling unpacked it. She put something into the icebox, then pulled out the drip-catch tray and emptied it into the sink. For a long minute Rachel stood still. Gladys did not have to look to see her, in her working frock with the cuffs and collar still clean, a full skirt, and the apron behind which she hid her hands when not alone; she was standing by the sink, as straight as a trellis, going over the kitchen with an eye for things that Ava had not done. Gladys thought that she had not been able to watch her morning glory open in the morning sun for nearly two weeks, and she felt sorry for herself. A pair of raucous crows, or perhaps three of them, drifted in a loud dispute over the house, setting Rachel in motion.

The women on the west side of Barter Island said that Rachel held her head too high. They said that she dressed smart and kept herself trim and handsome (though plain) because she was trolling for another husband. In weak moments, in the store with her Aunt Tessie and too many times at the Nitsomsosom Club, Gladys had agreed with them, and had hated herself for doing so. She knew that Rachel kept herself and her house neat and proper to set an example for Henry and out of respect for her lost husband, who had kept himself and everything he owned looking like it had just come out of a bandbox. Gladys often envied Rachel for her ruddy complexion and good health; usually she was consoled by her own pretty reflection in the mirror, but when she was sick abed as she was today, she did not dare to look at herself.

Rachel walked softly through the dim parlor and into the bedroom, bringing with her the sweet smell of fruit pie and something roasted in basil. Gladys lay on her side breathing as a sleeper would; the baby kicked once and pushed with its shoulder. Rachel carried the breakfast bowl and cups from the bed table into the kitchen and returned to place a vase of fresh flowers, which Gladys guessed would be purple loosestrife from the edge of the bog—her favorite. Rachel opened the far window to let the draft from the kitchen door draw out the dank air.

Gladys felt Rachel standing at the bedside, and she could smell the damp towel that she set on the bed while she moved the catalogs from the chair. The touch of the washcloth on her temple and forehead was as cool and soft as early morning.

"I'm going out to your yard to pick up some of the early apples, if the deer haven't gotten them," Rachel whispered. "To make us some applesauce."

Rachel refolded the towel for a cooler surface, and caressed Gladys's neck behind her ears like her mother used to do when she had the fever.

"Don't worry, dear, you'll be all right soon," Rachel said. "The baby is going to be fine. You both will. God will provide."

Outside, Rachel set the basket down under the Jonathan trees. A few hundred feet uphill from the house, she was framed in the upper half of Gladys's open window. Gladys pulled herself up onto the pillows to watch her. Moving made her want to pee, and increased the pressure. She lay perfectly still to let the laudanum catch up again and take her mind off her body.

Rachel held her apron gathered in one hand, collecting apples for the basket. When she moved farther uphill, the slanting sunlight touched the top of her head and made her bundled auburn hair glow like torchlight. Rachel inspected each apple, rolling it over in the grass with her toe before she bent over; she hated being stung by bees. When she had gathered the good ones from beneath the far tree, she came back and lowered her apron to let them tumble slowly into the basket. Under the tree closest to the window, Rachel reached for an apple that looked just fine, but when she picked it up, she found that the underside was brown and rotten, split open and oozing. She held it up to the window, where she had sensed that Gladys was watching, and made a sickly face before dropping it onto the ground. Gladys smiled, almost happy, and when Rachel lifted the basket and held it at an angle so that Gladys could see that it was more than half full, Gladys raised a pale, grateful hand in reply, and closed her eyes.

"Look," Virgil said. "I know you're pissed off, but that doesn't mean you can't lift a hand to help out."

"What?" Henry snapped.

"The spring line for one thing, if you don't mind," Virgil said. "I'm going to see if I can get this engine to go."

Virgil lifted the canvas cover from the little engine and folded it carefully. The moorings in the harbor that had held sleepy skiffs and peapods earlier in the day now held dozens of fishing boats, all but a few tied down and washed down, their crews gone ashore. The Conary brothers, the last to come in, were hauling in their sail; aboard a sloop nearby, a boy no more than twelve was bailing the bilge while his captain scrubbed the washboard. A gray-bearded man in a muffin cap, rowing on his knees to better see where he was going, made his way through the maze of boats whose bows pointed to the sun as it sank toward the distant Camden Hills. Henry took off his striped shirt, rolled his cap and glove up in it, and tucked the bundle out of sight.

The *Gladdy C.* was powered by a temperamental Palmer two-cycle make-and-break engine that Virgil and his brothers, who would soon be under power as well, had installed in the cove that spring. Virgil cranked the flywheel, got no response, fidgeted with the choke, and tried again, to no avail.

"It's not getting any spark," Henry said.

"I know that." Virgil wiped his brow; he hoped that the Conary brothers were not watching.

"Amos says if you back the flywheel half a turn first, she'll catch," offered Henry.

"*Amos* says? What the hell does Amos know about this engine, or any engine?"

"Just give it a try," Henry said. "Here, let me. You choke it."

Henry backed the flywheel, then cranked forward furiously with all the power of his pitching arm. The engine coughed, sputtered, then caught as Virgil adjusted the choke. Henry did not need to say anything; he stepped back and looked at his uncle as if he had just struck him out.

"Jesus wept," said Virgil.

Clear of the crowded harbor, Virgil steered close to the Crotch Island quarry to watch the chuffing steam crane lower a block of blue granite the size of an outhouse into the hold of the unkempt schooner that they had seen coming in that morning. Astride the bowsprit, smoking a stubby pipe, a black-haired boy struck a worldly pose for Henry, who turned aside lest the boy see envy in his face.

Virgil shut down the engine and they raised the mainsail for home, alone on the open bay with a congenial pair of harbor porpoises that swam off their port bow. The wind, chilly now, had backed around to the northwest and stiffened; Virgil thought that they would be home in plenty of time for him to wash his shirts and fix a small supper for Gladys if she wanted one. Henry sat as far forward as he could, sulking in his undershirt, and Virgil thought to suggest that he put his shirt and cap back on against the chill, then remembered.

"You didn't get your hair cut," Virgil said.

"No," Henry said. He did not turn around. "It doesn't matter."

"Don't pout, Henry. Coombs men don't pout. All it was was a baseball game," said Virgil, though he suspected that it was more than the game that was bothering Henry.

"Leave me alone, would you?"

The *Gladdy C.* slipped around the northern head of

Barter Island into the lee and the shadow of the mountain; Virgil let out the sail and let her run with the breeze and the going tide.

"I talked to Stevie after the game," Virgil said. "I told him that if he ever wanted to sell that flivver I'd buy it from him. He said—"

"The hell you did," Henry said.

"The hell I didn't." Virgil hauled on the sail.

"What would you do with a car like that down here?" Henry asked.

"Why, I'd drive it around, what do you think? You could drive it, too; we all could."

"Drive it where?" Henry stood up at the mast as they turned into the cove. "Drive it back and forth on three miles of dirt road?"

Henry snorted; he waved toward the houses in the darkening cove ahead.

"East Jesus," he said ruefully. "No, not even east Jesus, but a long haul from it, so far from the real world that the nearest big city is a tiny town on an island that's still miles from the mainland where the biggest event of the year is a baseball game played on a field where a foul tip almost kills somebody because the backstop is a jury-rigged frame of rotten goddamned gillnet!"

Virgil shook his head sadly. He had thought that his offer to buy the flivver and bring it down to the island would please Henry, but instead of thanks he got a raft of bitter crap, and he did not understand why.

Virgil patted his shirt pocket to check for the little bottle that Dr. Banks had given him for Gladys, and, finding it, he remembered that he had forgotten to buy the atomizer she wanted so badly. He thought to chide Henry for not reminding him, but Henry would only say that *he* had not reminded *him* to get his hair cut, either, so Virgil let it go.

"You could've at least given her a smile," Virgil said. "After she braved that crowd to come and see you on the bench there. She's some pretty. She the one they call the little Dutch girl? What's her real name, anyway?"

Henry did not answer.

CHAPTER 2
Family Matters

"Who the hell is Margaret Sanger?"
Walter Coombs, August 23, 1917

Rachel stood with her hands in the pockets of her smock, watching for the mail boat at the little window of her office on the top floor of the cannery. Without a hint of breeze all day long, the sweet, fishy steam that arose from the vats below lingered in the upstairs offices. It rolled up the staircase in billows, and seeped up through the cracks in the floorboards. It wrinkled the pages of her ledger, fogged the window, permeated her clothing, even her petticoats, and curled her hair until it hung in damp, stinking ringlets. It was the kind of day she hated at the cannery, but today Maggie Bowen was coming home, and she had said in her last letter that she would be wearing her hair in a bob. Rachel peeked at the watch pinned to her smock, and rubbed a new hole in the foggy pane.

Rachel and Maggie were cousins,. both Bowens, and twelve years apart; Maggie had been the flower girl in Rachel's wedding. When Maggie was a girl, she'd stood apart from her fellow students in the schoolyard during recess, or had stayed at her desk to read. She was polite, even amiable, but she did not join the other girls when they gathered in ribbons and curls to whisper and giggle outside the schoolhouse; she walked home alone. Some said that she was shy, others that she was a snob; the truth was that she preferred the company of older females—Rachel, whom she visited often, chief among them. After John died, Maggie walked over to the cove from town after school to have tea with Rachel at least twice a week. Only thirteen, Maggie had the sense not to try to console Rachel in her grief, or to express even the slightest pity; instead she played with little Henry in the dooryard or read to him by the front window, while Rachel, tired from a long day at her new job at the cannery, took care of her house and started supper. When they talked over tea, Rachel urged Maggie to go on to high school in Stonington and, if her family was willing, to go on to teachers college, or better. She told Maggie that when she was her age, she had been afraid to leave home, Barter Island, and board with strangers for two years, and she regretted it. Rachel remembered that there had been a spray of white lilacs on the table when she had covered Maggie's soft hand with hers and made her promise that she would continue her schooling, and Maggie, without a blink, swore that she would.

When Maggie left for Stonington, Rachel gave her a Waterman fountain pen and a box of stationery, saying that she hoped that she would put them to good use.

"I'll write every day," Maggie had said.

"Well, not every day." Rachel had laughed. "But I'll answer every letter you write, I will."

Maggie wrote on Sundays and Wednesdays, and twice a week Rachel carried her letter home to relish by lamplight when Henry had gone to bed. Maggie wrote about the family she boarded with: "frugal Methodists who read only the Bible and hymnals" but who left her alone in her "cozy garret." She wrote about the moving pictures she saw at the Opera House on Saturdays, the nosy girls in her class, the raggedy children of the poor mill workers whose shacks she passed going to and from school, and her love for Emily Dickinson, with whom she agreed that the New Testament was a "merry book." Rachel replied with island gossip, the adventures of Henry, news of Maggie's sister Clytie and her parents (who did not answer Maggie's letters), and a weekly package of gingersnaps.

While she was at teachers college in Bangor, Maggie came home only twice: once to witness her teenage sister's hurried marriage to Amos Coombs, and two years later to help care for her ailing father and within two weeks help bury him in the plot behind his house, in which Amos and Clytie now lived. From Bangor, Maggie sent Rachel newspaper clippings about the suffrage movement, playbills from Charlie Chaplin pictures, amusing articles from Collier's and the Saturday Evening Post, and, later, well-worn copies of Margaret Sanger's Birth Control Review. She wrote to Rachel about her new friend Ruth, with whom she boarded, the young men she met who were no more than "posturing boys," her loneliness (in spite of Ruth), her secret fears, and the longings that only Rachel could understand. Rachel's replies offered comfort; she told Maggie of her own loneliness, her secret desires, and her own foolish fears. Rachel kept Maggie's letters in shoe boxes under her bed, a box for each of the five years containing twelve monthly bundles tied in thin ribbon, and she knew that Maggie had kept hers.

"Someday," Rachel had written, "we'll sit in our rockers on the porch and read them aloud and laugh till we weep at how tender we once were."

Amos Coombs braked his wagon down the hill into town, thinking that the light drizzle would surely turn to rain before it was done. As the wagon seat tilted forward on its springs, Leah gripped her father's shirtsleeve to hold them back. Below them in the thorofare between Barter Island and Kimball's Island, the mail boat was making her slow way toward the town landing, her smoke a black ribbon against a pewter sky. When they reached the bottom of the hill and crossed the creek by the sweets shop, the mail boat had pulled ahead of them.

"Stop, Daddy, stop!" Leah yanked at Amos's sleeve. "You said we could get candy. My licorice."

"We'll stop on the way home, dear," Amos said. "Look, there's the mail boat coming. We need to hurry to get to the landing. I'll bet that's your Aunt Maggie on the deck there. Wave to her."

Leah did not wave, nor did Amos. But the woman in the straw hat standing at the stern of the mail boat waved to them, until Amos, who knew that it was Maggie, waved back.

"Wave to her, dear," he said. "She sees you. You'll hurt her feelings."

But Leah, who at five could already imitate perfectly her mother's obstinate set of jaw, tucked her clenched hands under her arms and locked her gaze on the nag's brown rump.

A sudden gust of steam from the pressure cooker in the open side of the cannery and the angry shouts of strangers within made Amos's horse dance to the side and Amos grip the reins anxiously lest the nag do something to draw attention to him or, worse, make him look foolish in front of the west-side people they passed on the way through town. In the wide door at the front of the cannery, Rachel pinned her hat in place and stepped out into the road, so eager to get to the town landing that she did not notice Amos's wagon until he hailed her.

"Come ride with us," Amos said, and pulled to a stop next to her.

"Thank you, Amos," Rachel said. "Good morning, Leah. Don't you look nice today?"

Leah smiled and smoothed her skirts.

"Oh, look at me," Rachel said. She held out her arms to show that she had forgotten to take off her smock. "Wait one second, will you Amos?"

A chubby boy with a barrel hoop in each hand sprinted past the waiting wagon, with a smaller boy in angry tears chasing him.

"You said we couldn't stop," Leah said.

Amos put his arm around her little shoulders and drew her to his side and said: "Here she comes now."

Rachel tucked her skirts beneath her and settled next to Leah on the seat. She did not ask Amos why Clytie had not come to meet the boat because she did not want to hear Amos have to lie.

"Isn't this exciting, Leah?" Rachel said. "Your Aunt

Maggie's coming home to live with you, and to be your teacher when you start school."

"She's not going to stay with us forever," said Leah. "She's going to find a place of her own as soon as she can, or she'll board around like the other teachers do."

Rachel looked at Amos over Leah's head and asked him with her eyes just whose words the little parrot was repeating, as if she needed to ask at all. Amos said he was glad he had thought to bring a canvas to cover Maggie's luggage; it was going to come around to rain sure enough.

The Barter Island town landing was a long, rugged wharf, built wide enough for a small freight wagon to turn around on it, with a float and gangplank for landing passengers and a block-and-tackle hoist for freight.

Amos pulled up in the road on the rise above the landing. Rachel lifted Leah down from the wagon, whispered something in her ear, and, with her hand in the girl's, led her in a skipping descent of the hill as the mail boat slipped in to the float and tied off. Amos watched them from his wagon seat, thinking that if Clytie tried to skip down a hill like that, she would build up so much momentum going down—all that weight on those weak little feet—that she would bowl over the passengers and plow through the packing crates before she tumbled off the end of the wharf and into the water.

At the top of the gangplank, pressed against the rail by the departing passengers, Rachel watched Maggie on the deck below while Leah examined the two boys who had run past them on the road and now stood nearby on the wharf. The smaller boy, Cecil Barter, had his barrel hoop back—he was standing in it—and he also had a fat red upper lip, which he licked tenderly from time to time. Cecil was eight years old, and Leah was afraid of his voice.

When Maggie came up the gangplank, Rachel wrapped her in a long, silent embrace, then pulled her and Leah to the side to make way for the captain with the mailbag on his shoulder. Maggie knelt to talk to Leah and saw Amos approaching; beyond him was the wagon, her father's, hitched to an unfamiliar horse, and empty. She told herself that she was not surprised that her sister had not come to greet her, but she was. Amos offered her a hand at arm's length in greeting, avoiding her eyes as he always had, and asked for her luggage.

"I've got two trunks," Maggie said. "Rachel and I can manage one of them—it's just clothes—but the other is quite heavy. There's the heavy one now."

Two sturdy young men in overalls struggled up the gangplank under the weight of a single trunk, which they carried not with the handles but with two hands each beneath.

"What you got in here, miss?" the larger one asked. "A horseshoe collection?"

"Here, don't set it down." Amos squatted between the two men and offered his shoulder. "Set it here."

The men hefted the trunk, held it steady while Amos adjusted it on his shoulder, then stood back in slack-mouthed awe as Amos rose and started up the steep hill.

"Books," Maggie said. "My library."

She and Rachel each took a handle of the second trunk.

"I'd tip you a nickel if I had one," Maggie said to the young men.

"We wouldn'tve taken it if you did, miss." The larger of the two touched the brim of his grimy cap, while the other watched Amos negotiate the hill under the trunk.

Rachel and Maggie rode on the back of the wagon, their legs dangling, Rachel's in motion when she laughed. Amos stopped at the cannery, and he and Leah watched as Rachel lifted Maggie's hat to see her bobbed brown hair and muss it with her splayed fingers.

"Wait till Miss Tessie sees this," Rachel said.

"She'll want to bob hers, too," said Maggie.

Rachel and Maggie parted with promises to see one another soon, and Rachel watched from the doorway of the cannery as Maggie resumed her seat on the back of the wagon.

"Aren't you going to come sit up here?" Amos asked. He held his palm out flat to feel the drizzle for rain.

"I'm getting off at the schoolhouse," Maggie said. "I've so much to do. I want to get started. I'll walk home later."

"It's going to rain," Amos said.

"I don't think it is," Maggie said. "Even so, I'll enjoy the walk. It's been a long time since I walked home from town."

Virgil brought the *Gladdy C.* around the head and into the cove and saw what he had been living in fear of for over a week. Ava stood waiting on the wharf, bare-headed, her blouse open at the collar, squinting in the wet breeze. The tide was going, but there was still enough water in the cove that he could sail into the wharf; as he approached and

Henry went forward with the gaff, Ava shouted.

"Don't even bother to come in," she said. Amplified by the ledges that rose on both sides of the cove and the surface of the water, the everyday authority in her voice was increased, as though she spoke from a lofty pulpit.

"Go now Virgil, and go quickly," she said. "It's going to take surgery to save the baby and a miracle to save Gladys. Where's Walter?"

"He's just south of York's Island," Virgil said. "Is she—"

"Just go, Virgil," said Ava. "Henry, take the peapod and bring Walter in. Don't let him tell you that he has to finish hauling his string. I want him right now."

Henry waved in assent and scrambled to starboard to gaff *Friggit*.

Ava turned and strode through the meadow, passing the cow who lay chewing her cud under the cover of the two big rock maples. Ava thought that she would like to be sitting on the stone wall beneath the trees without a thought in her head, God knew she would. She should have known before dawn that morning, when she had heard the pitiful sound of Virgil's voice through the open windows, that he would give Gladys an especially heavy dose of laudanum before he went out to haul his traps. How many times had she warned him, through all three of these horrible pregnancies, that the laudanum slowed Gladys's heart and sapped her strength, making her so stupid that she could neither feel nor heed her own body's warnings? But Virgil had never been able to bear another human's suffering. When he was a boy, he could drown a litter of puppies, or without blinking cut the throat of a pig he had raised—even, she had always suspected, with a little pleasure; but when their sister had had the croup, he had slept and even eaten in the fish shack, where he could not hear her helpless cough, and when Gladys had cried out during the first miscarriage, Virgil had wept in frustration and pain at the kitchen table. Why they put themselves through such suffering time and again, Ava thought she did not know. She did know, of course, but she did not understand. She thought that it must be the delight that she had seen in both of their faces each time that Gladys learned that she was pregnant—hopeful in spite of what they knew and refused to believe, hopeful until the fear set in. Perhaps tonight it would be over, she thought. Perhaps Virgil would get back with the doctor in time and Gladys would deliver safely. More likely, she thought, there would be a wailing and gnashing of teeth in the cove tonight.

Henry knew that he would have to row a good mile into the wind, so he stayed close to the shore for as much lee as he could get and hauled on the oars with all his heart and weight, pulling with the running tide. Henry was a wiry boy, with little bulk to his upper body, yet he had never lost a rowboat race to anyone on the island, and this was a great source of pride for him. He found Walter's Friendship sloop off Green Ledge and yelled as he approached, but his voice was carried astern by the wind. When Amos saw Henry coming, he straightened over the trap he had been picking and held up a huge flapping lobster in each hand, grinning, Henry thought, like an idiot on a picture postcard. In school the boys had called Amos "Hammy" behind his back because of his broad face and flushed complexion.

"We got nearly seven pounds from that one trap," Amos shouted. "We're dogging 'em, Henry."

Henry spun the peapod around and rowed backward, pushing his way toward the *Grampus*. Walter, who knew too well that Henry had come with a summons from Ava, did not look up from the pair of claws that he was pegging on the barrelhead.

"Virgil's gone to Stonington to get the doctor," Henry said. "Ava wants you to come in right away."

"Christ," Walter said. "Well, I'm going to finish hauling this string first. I've got two more traps on it." He lifted his bowler hat and wiped his brow with the gray sleeve of his long johns.

"She said you'd say that. She said to tell you to come right now."

"Why? What the hell does she want me to do?"

"I don't know," Henry said. "How the hell do I know what she wants? The baby's coming."

"Don't get smart with me, goddamn you," Walter said. He marched to the trap that Amos was tying shut, and Amos stepped back out of his reach.

"Goddamn her, anyway." Walter shoved the trap overboard. "Are you coming with us, or are you going to row back?"

Henry answered by coming alongside. With his back to Walter, Amos took the peapod's bowline; he stretched his mouth and popped his eyes in mock terror, and Henry nearly laughed aloud.

The old lobster that Walter had left unplugged on the

barrelhead reared up on his spiny legs and waved his terrible war claw in the air, reaching for an enemy or a clumsy finger to crush. Walter grabbed him from behind, pinned his claws with one hand, pushed wooden plugs into the joints of his claws with the other, then tossed the flailing monster into the barrel with the rest.

When Amos offered timidly to take Walter in to shore, then come back and finish hauling the rest of the string, Walter did not reply. Nor did he speak when Henry rowed him ashore, but sat with his arms crossed over his bullish chest and stared at the horizon over Henry's shoulder.

"He's more than just pissed off." Henry climbed aboard the Grampus, where Amos was covering the sail. "He's about to blow."

"He's not so much pissed off as he is scared for Gladys," Amos said. "You know how tender he is about her; he always has been. This time he's more worried than ever; Ava is, too, and for good reason, I would guess."

"Mother said she never should have gotten pregnant again," said Henry. "She said she should have known better."

"She told you that?"

"I heard her telling Ava last winter," said Henry. "I was on the staircase."

Amos scooped up a bucket of water, and scrubbed then rinsed his oilskin apron.

"I'd pray for them, if I thought it would do any good," he said.

"If you knew how," said Henry.

Henry doused the washboard with the bucket and leaned over to fill another. A few feet below the surface, the eelgrass was bending seaward with the last pull of the going tide. On the sandy bottom, his grandfather's mooring chain, long disused, lay rusting in a scribble where it had sunk years before.

"Did you see in the *Messenger* where there's been a second draft for Hancock County?" Henry asked.

"I didn't see it, but I heard about it. Maurice Greenlaw is on it." Amos pointed at the washboard with the brush for another bucketful, which Henry delivered. "We don't have to worry about it; I've got a wife and kid."

"I'm going to enlist," Henry said. "I'm going to join the army."

"Oh, bullshit," Amos said. "With us in it already, the war will be over before you finish school. Even then, you won't be old enough; you've got to be eighteen. Give me a bucket on the bulkhead."

"I can pass for eighteen right now, easy. I'm going this fall. Rodney Stinson lied about his age and he got in."

"For what?" Amos asked. "To get out of school? You've been reading too many of Colonel Triplett's adventure books. This isn't a charge up San Juan Hill we're talking about; it's trenches and bombs and gas and mud and blood. Pure misery."

"What the hell do you know about it?" Henry lifted the plank and watched while Amos swept the deck gurry into the bilge.

"I can read, can't I?" said Amos. "I'm telling you, you don't want any part of this war; it would be too much for you. You finish school."

"The hell it would." Henry's stroke on the bilge pump

quickened. "I'm good for it, Amos, and you know I am."

"Maybe you are," Amos said. "Ease up on that thing; you're going to bust the gasket. Maybe you are. But I don't know. What about the training they put you through? They say some fellows, even rugged ones, can barely get through it. They've got to make you tough. They've got guys whose only job is to beat you up every five minutes. Even at night. They wake you up and stomp mudholes in your chest. They stab you in your leg with a bayonet to get you used to what fighting the Hun will be like."

"Oh for Christ's sake," Henry said.

"Well, what about your mother, what about school, what about that little Dutch girl in Stonington that Virgil teases you about?"

"Mother will be all right," Henry said. He did not say that Claire, the "little Dutch girl," had held his hand against her breast and with tears in her eyes had promised to wait for him. "And look, I'm tired of everybody talking about me finishing school. Walter didn't. Father and Virgil didn't. You didn't. I don't know why I have to. I'm going to join the army. I am."

"If you don't understand about finishing school, then it won't do any good for me to say anything," Amos said. "I'm not going to worry, because I know you won't dare to enlist."

"The hell I won't." Henry threw out his chest, his hands clenched at his sides. "You just wait and see, damn you."

"I will," said Amos.

Though the idea of going alone to Stonington, perhaps even to Bangor, and then God knew where among nothing but strangers, scared Amos half shitless, he thought how sweet it would be to stand on the mail boat in a uniform and bravely wave good-bye, even sweeter to get away from the stifling kitchen where Clytie grew fatter and meaner by the month. He hung his apron on the bulkhead next to Walter's and gaffed and dragged a lobster crate aboard, thinking with satisfaction that he had called Henry's bluff.

"This crate won't take too many more," Amos said. "Get that empty one, would you? I have to get home. I've got chores to do."

"Not so many now, I'll bet." Henry had begun to cool down. "Now that Maggie's living with you."

"No, not so many," Amos said. "Maggie's some helpful, at least when Clytie will let her be. She cleaned all the windows with vinegar and newspaper, polished and swept the parlor cleaner than it's been in years. She'll go to work on the kitchen soon, if she can drive Clytie out of there long enough. Maggie offered to do the cooking. I wish she would. Clytie boils everything, even whole chickens. She's boiled the paper off the kitchen walls, just setting there eating cupcakes and crullers and swelling up like a loaf of bread that's rising."

"Christ," Henry said.

"I know it," said Amos.

Chapter 3
A Truant Disposition

"Maggie Bowen didn't take the schoolteacher job down here so she could come back home, and it certainly wasn't for the money. She's got her own reason; you'll see."

Tessie Wedge, August 30, 1917

Perched uncomfortably atop a lobster crate whose planks sagged under his weight, Dr. Harry Banks leaned against the bulkhead of the *Gladdy C.* and felt his spirits sink with the sun behind the Camden Hills across the bay. Another night on Barter Island. Another night in a cramped and stuffy house with fretting, or, God forbid, weeping women. Not a night in the island's little village, where he could take a spacious room in Mrs. Turner's boardinghouse, but in Coombs Cove, on the far side of the island's mountain spine, the cold and lonely weather side of the island. How they withstood the dark, frozen winter months out there—trapped in their little houses and sheds by the frightful sea, by ice and snow and the remorseless winds—he did not know. He thought that if he had to endure a winter in one of Barter Island's isolated coves, they would have him chained to the cellar floor by New Year's Eve, and he would probably be glad of it.

Virgil leaned forward from the tiller and teased the choke and throttle for more power, but the little engine that they called a "one-lunger" only persisted in the steady chuffing sound that gave it its name. When he had surprised Dr. Banks that afternoon as he was leaving his office, Virgil had been frantic—spitting pieces of sentences, nearly dancing in anxiety on the sidewalk—but now he had lapsed into a solemn, wordless daze, and responded to Dr. Banks's occasional attempts at conversation as though from deep inside a cave.

Behind Virgil, the last rays of the sun burnished the striped underbelly of the high clouds that approached from the northwest.

"It's a mackerel sky," Dr. Banks offered. "We'll get wet tomorrow."

"It'll breeze up first," Virgil replied.

Well. There, Dr. Banks thought. We have mined the mystery of existence and come up, yet again, with the weather.

The doctor wiped the salt spray from his spectacles with his handkerchief and stood to look around as they approached the island. Off their starboard bow were the harbor and town, above which the white spire of the island church pointed toward heaven on the wooded mountainside. He caught a whiff of wood smoke—birch—from a kitchen stove, and thought that someone must be baking a pie.

On the eastern side the open sea was evening blue, and there was a slight but distinct autumn chill in the air.

Barter Island was remote and forbidding, Dr. Banks thought, yet it was the most beautiful place he had ever visited, even seen, especially in the early fall when the air was so sharp that he could see a passing schooner under full sail five miles out in the shipping lanes. The time of year when the fruit and vegetables were fresh-picked, and there was a deer hanging out in every cellar. Ava Coombs, who had never served him white food, would set a generous table for him tonight, and he sighed to think of it.

Had he been alone, Henry would have chosen the box of stereoscope slides labeled PICTURESQUE POINTS OF AFRICA so he could study yet again the bare titties in the PRIMITIVE VILLAGE DANCERS scenes. But he was in Gladys's parlor with his Uncle Walter, who was reading the *Ellsworth American*; his mother was in the kitchen, and Ava and the doctor were beyond the bedroom door with Gladys, so he chose the slide marked SUCCESSFUL ANTELOPE ON SADDLE from the PICTURESQUE POINTS OF AMERICA box, and with his face in the laminated hood of the stereopticon examined the three-dimensional image of a mountain man with an antelope draped over his horse's back. The man's rifle was a Winchester lever-action .30-30. When he had first seen this same slide ten years before, he had promised himself that he would one day go west, wear fringed buckskins, ride a wild stallion, and scout for the cavalry. But now, Henry thought, when Uncle Sam needed every man he could get to save the world for democracy, he had to put aside his childish dreams and enlist. He replaced the mountain man with a slide showing a man leaping across a sixty-foot chasm in the Wisconsin Dells, and wondered where Virgil was.

As softly as a spirit, Ava shut the bedroom door behind

her and stood motionless in the dim parlor. Her brother Walter sensed her there and lowered his newspaper to learn from her face how Gladys was doing. On the other side of the parlor, Rachel stood in the kitchen doorway, her hands in a linen dish towel and her eyes on Ava.

"She's the same." Ava smoothed her apron. "Not even the slightest contraction since the doctor got here. Isn't that the way it is? Rachel, you leave those dishes alone."

Rachel wiped her brow with the back of her wrist. "They're done," she said. "I'm going to fix a supper for the doctor."

"I'll help you," Ava said. "He doesn't need me in there. Where's Virgil?"

"I don't know," Walter said. "He didn't come up from the cove with the doctor. He's in the barn, I guess, or down at the cove frigging with something in the shed."

Henry put the stereopticon back on its stand and cupped his face in his hands to see out the window.

"There's a light in his shed," Henry said. "And the lantern I hung on the wharf for them coming home is still there."

"Walter, you go find him," Ava said. "Tell him she's all right. There's no use in you sitting here, and Virgil could use some company, if that's what you could call you and your newspaper."

"Christ God." Walter stood up, folding his newspaper. "First you call me—"

"Watch your tongue, Walter Coombs," Ava said.

"Christ God," said Walter. "I can't finish hauling my traps because you have to have me here, then you tell me I'm of no use. I'll be—"

"Walter, please," said Ava. "Tell Virgil he can come home. She's not suffering now; she's sleeping."

"Let's go, Henry," said Walter. "It's breezing up some. We ought to check on the boats, too. I knew I should've finished hauling that string."

"You should go home soon, though, Henry," Rachel said. "It's nearly nine and you need your rest. There's a pitcher of sweet cider in the icebox."

While they put on their boots in the mudroom, Walter thought that he would like to get some rest himself, but he knew that he was too afraid for Gladys to sleep. He stood on the stoop with Henry at his side and waited for his eyes to adjust to the dark. The wind, no longer a breeze, was gusting from the northwest, sighing through the oak trees on the ledge, uplifting their leaves in the thin moonlight.

"When the wind runs down the meadow like that at this time of night, it means it's backing to the north," Walter said. He hiked up his trousers and pushed his hat down snug. "We'll get a blow tonight; you wait and see if we don't."

Beyond the orange glow of light in the shed window, and the lone lantern on the wharf, the sea was breaking on the south shore of the cove, and their boats swayed slowly on their moorings. Walking down through the meadow with Henry following, Walter thought that tonight he would have something a little stronger than sweet cider—perhaps a sup of rum would help him to sleep.

Henry returned the lantern that he had hung on the wharf to the toolshed, and in the darkness felt his way with his feet along the path through the ledges to the house.

Inside, he lit the big vase lamp and set it on the table in the front window for his mother's way home. She hated the wind, especially the northeasters that threw limbs and sheets of rain against the house and drove the sea into the cove to pound against the cliff. When he told her that he loved storms, she said he was just saying it to be contrary, but he really did. Maggie Bowen loved storms, too. He remembered one night when he was little, when she had read him the part in a Dickens book about a girl who runs out onto a rotten wharf in the middle of a hurricane and dances in the wind and waves. Maggie had told him that she had done the same thing on her father's wharf in the big storm that fall; his mother had made a noise of disapproval, which had made him admire Maggie even more. Henry wondered if they had storms in France, and thought that they must, though they were probably different somehow.

He cut a thick slice of bread, heaped it with rhubarb jam, and sat at the kitchen table, glad to be out of the cramped and smoke-filled fish shack and away from his uncles. In half an hour Virgil had not said a word, just leaned on a stool painting a buoy like there was nothing on his mind but a damned yellow spindle. Walter drank one toddy, then another, but tonight the rum did not loosen his tongue. He did not tease Virgil; nor did he make the usual crude jokes about Tessie Wedge's hefty ledges. Instead Walter worried about his mooring line, which was frayed at the chain, and said twice how odd it was to be getting shedders this late in the season. It galled Henry that neither of them mentioned Gladys, that they weren't worried about her in the least.

That was bad enough, but when he asked them if they thought that German submarines might sink American troopships when they crossed the Atlantic, neither of them even bothered to answer, as if the war was no concern of theirs. It drove Henry out the door.

He climbed the stairs in his stocking feet and shut the door of his little room behind him. He lit the desk lamp and opened the window to better hear the wind in the trees and listen to the sea making up outside. If it turned out to be too rough to haul in the morning, he would dig the new hole for the outhouse and get Walter to help him to move it. When that was done, there would only be the chicken coop roof to shingle, and he would be finished with the things he had promised his mother he would do before he left for school.

Five more days.

She had said she wanted to see him off at the mail boat again this year, but he had told her he wanted to sail up to Stonington in the peapod, to have it there so he could sail back on the weekend to haul his traps, start taking them in. When she had agreed, with so little of the usual "discussion," he had felt certain that she did not suspect anything.

He would tell her that he wanted to haul his southern strings of traps on the way to Stonington, and he would if Virgil or Walter was out on the water to see him. He would sail around the southern end of the island, and when he was out of sight he would set sail to cross the mouth of the bay. He would be in Rockland before dark. He would sell the lobsters and the peapod, and in Rockland he would find out where the nearest recruiting station was and how to get there. If he could not sell the peapod, he would sink her in the harbor. Friggit. He would have thirty-two dollars—he would leave the fifty in an envelope for her—in case he could not sell it. It would not be until the next day, Sunday, when he did not show up for supper at the boardinghouse in Stonington, that anyone would miss him. On Monday, when he did not show for school, they would send word down to the island that he was absent. By then he would have a two-day head start from Rockland. If anyone followed him to bring him back—it would be Virgil who would go, for his mother's sake—he would see that the peapod was not in Stonington harbor, and would not know where to begin to look. Even if he left her a note begging her not to, Rachel might send Virgil to find him and rat him out to the army about his age.

He turned down the wick and lay back on the bed, wondering if he would hear her footsteps on the road in such a wind. He thought that he would stay awake until she came home, to find out about Gladys and let Mother talk some to ease her worries, but he fell asleep.

Dr. Harry Banks, napping with his chin rested on two soft folds of flesh, dreamed that someone's child was lost in the night forest, and calling out piteously for help. Its cry came from far off to his left, then suddenly he heard it close by, to his right. There was a ship's lantern on the stone wall; it was unlit, and as he groped for it in the dark he realized he that did not have any matches. Someone poked his shoulder with a pointed stick, and he awoke to see Ava standing over him.

"Rachel's put out a supper for you," Ava said. "You must be some hungry. I put a clean hand towel by the washbasin. You go eat. I'll sit with her now."

In the kitchen doorway Dr. Banks paused to rise to the surface from his sleep, and nearly gasped at the sight of his supper. Around the place setting at the head of the table she'd set out a galaxy of side dishes, all in easy reach: mashed potatoes, green beans, biscuits, iced cucumbers in vinegar, a sliced tomato sprinkled with parsley, a little boat of brown gravy, deviled eggs, and a nice tall bottle of beer.

"I'm frying you up a venison steak," Rachel said. "Walter got an early deer, so it's fresh. I hope you like it fried with peppers and onions."

"That would be just fine, Rachel, thank you," he said. "I'll just go out back, then wash up. You're very kind."

As he leaned over the basin and splashed cold water over his own face, Dr. Banks thought that he would like to watch Rachel doing the same, and softly toweling her face and smooth neck.

At the table he tucked a corner of his napkin into his collar, pinched two more corners to spread it wide, smoothed it daintily over his wide vest, and smiled at the sight before him.

"You're the one that's kind," Rachel said. "To come all the way down here again."

His mouth full, Dr. Banks waved his hand and shook his head, while she poured him a glass of beer. Her forearms were freckled and sunburned.

"I want to quiz you about Gladys," Rachel said. "But I'll wait till you finish."

"It's all right," the doctor said. "She's—"

"No, really, I was rude. You eat first," Rachel said. "I need to finish drying."

She turned her back to him and adjusted the reflector on the lamp bracket to spread the light across the countertop.

When he had heaped his plate with portions from the surrounding dishes and begun to eat in earnest, Dr. Banks listened to the wind in the trees and the distant breaking surf outside, and felt with pleasure the warm embrace of silence inside the house. In the yellow lamplight, Rachel, her back to him, dried and set plates on the cabinet shelf without a sound. He thought for a moment that he could hear her humming beneath her breath, and thought that a man could do far worse than to live in a simple house like this one on a cold remote rock seven miles at sea.

He made a crater in his second helping of mashed potatoes, and as he filled it with gravy he heard the pitiful cries of the children in his dream riding on the night wind.

"What was that?" he asked.

Rachel did not turn around. "Only the sheep on Burnt Island. You can hear them bleating when the wind's like this."

"Ah." The doctor speared a cucumber slice.

The table cleared of all but a half-finished slice of rhubarb pie, his second, and a cup of tea, Dr. Banks removed his napkin, folded it, and sat back with a sigh and a heartfelt thanks to Rachel, who stood across the table.

"You were hungry," she said.

"It's not often that I'm offered such a repast on a house

call," he said. "It's usually a slab of salted cod and potatoes baked in milk and butter. You and Ava spoil me."

Rachel smiled slightly and stood waiting, her hands in her apron.

"Yes, Gladys," said the doctor. "She's as weak as she was the first and second times, dangerously weak. Anemia doesn't go away, you know. Her pulse is seventy-two, for pity's sake." He put his fingers to his lips to suppress a little burp. "But this time, this time the baby is healthy; plenty of movement and a strong little heartbeat."

"Might you have to do a caesarian?" Rachel asked.

"I hope not. But I will if I have to," he said. "I've done my share, but I don't like them. In this case I worry about bleeding, and septicemia, though there is no fever yet, nor chills."

"Blood poisoning?" Rachel asked.

"Very like," he said. "And especially dangerous for someone as weak as Gladys is. But I am hopeful this time, more so than in the past."

"What can I do?"

"You can go home," Dr. Banks said, building himself to his feet. "You need your rest. Sleep if you can. I'll send Virgil for you when the contractions begin, if he ever comes in from the shed."

"He will soon," she said. "We've made up a bed for you upstairs, if you'd like to lie down."

"No thank you. I've had my eye on that wide wicker chair in the parlor window," he said, thinking that if he lay down now, after such a prodigious feed, it would take more than a pointed stick to rouse him. "I'll be quite comfortable."

"I hate to leave," Rachel said. "But you're right, I should." Beneath the folds of her apron, her agitated fingers pinched and picked at one another. When she saw that Dr. Banks had noticed her unruly hands, she let the apron drop, smoothed it, and, calm now, untied it behind.

"Then I'll say good night, Doctor," she said.

"You can trust me, Rachel."

"I know."

Dr. Banks wanted to offer to walk Rachel home, but he knew that she would decline, saying that she would be fine, as she certainly would, even on an angry night like this one. There is a beauty in these island women, he thought as she turned away—a composure, a gentle strength, a secret source of compassion—that attracts and confounds a man at once. He took his cup of tea and went to relieve Ava at the bedside.

Rachel caught the screen before the wind could bang it against the house and awaken Henry. Inside, she turned down the big green vase lamp and carried it back to the parlor table, comforted to think that Henry had put it in the window for her. At the foot of the staircase she saw the thin light from under his door; she called his name just loud enough to be heard if he was awake and was glad that he did not answer. When the kitchen was tidy and ready for breakfast, she washed and, with a generous dollop of Bag Balm, soothed her tortured hands.

Henry was asleep fully clothed on top of his bed. She shut the window to stop the insistent wind and covered him carefully with a quilt. She put out his lamp, kissed him lightly on the forehead, and touched the shock of sandy hair that was so much like his father's. Sitting on her own bed in her shift, Rachel brushed out her hair. Tonight she would like to be comforted. She slipped the two big down pillows—wedding gifts from the Wedge family—into the soft flannel sleeve she had sewn to hold them, and buttoned it at the top. On her side beneath the covers, she put one arm over the pillows and curled her legs up to them, waiting for the warmth to come as it had from John's back when they had slept this way, nestled like spoons.

Amos sat on the step of the fish shack waiting for the moon to show through the scudding clouds so he could better see how the sea was building up against the outer ledge of Head Harbor. He was tired, so tired that he could fall asleep there, sitting up out of doors with the wind in his face, but he would not go back into the house until he saw Maggie's lamp in the turret room window, and the kitchen dark. Since Maggie had moved in—it hadn't even been a week—she and Clytie had been like a pair of crabs in a trap, circling each other sideways, their claws open and ready, watching each other for a weak moment. Clytie was the larger of the two, and meaner; the house was her territory, and she let Maggie know it. "We keep that chair in the corner because that's where Father kept it." Snap. "Leah doesn't want to be read to; she wants to go to sleep." Snap. And with her war claw: "I guess you're just not used to having a man around, are you?" Snap. But Maggie did not snap back; she slipped aside out of Clytie's reach, careful not to get cornered. Maggie would not lock claws with her sister, because she knew that she would be crushed; instead she put Clytie off guard with a pleasantry, or confused her with a kindness. It would be amusing to watch, Amos thought, if he wasn't trapped in the house with them.

He, too, avoided Clytie's claws; it had become a habit of being for him over the past five years, especially the last three since her father Charles had died and left them alone in the house. When Charles told them that the house would be theirs, and he made Clytie promise with Amos as witness that the door would always stay open for Maggie, Amos had thought that Clytie finally had what she wanted. He had thought that when he agreed to live in her father's house, rather than in the cove among his family, he had paid her in full for "what he did to her" (he had thought that they had done it together, his first mistake) that night they took a tumble in the Turner graveyard. But he soon realized that she would never be satisfied until she wore him down with meanness, or drove him out of the house, and away from Leah, for good. Recently, when he was tired, he thought she might succeed—the tools in the shed were "Father's tools," Leah was "her little girl"—and he would move back to the cove where he could live peacefully, but his fondness for the child, and something else he did not understand, pride perhaps, gave him the strength to suffer Clytie's sharp claws.

But tonight it was not claws that kept him out of the house; it was something unfamiliar and troubling.

Clytie and Maggie had been getting up from supper—it had been a short, silent meal—and Amos had been sharing his pudding with Leah, who sat in his lap. He remembered that he had chuckled first, then had said in a joking way, with maybe a little bit of brag . . . What were his exact words? "Henry talked about going off to join the army again. I told him he wouldn't dare to. Didn't he puff up like an old blowfish and say the hell he wouldn't?" Clytie hadn't heard him, or acted as though she hadn't. Maggie had stood stock-still, plate in hand, and stared at him for a long second. Then she had asked, "Was that wise?" and his stomach had collapsed, the same way it had done in school when he had been made to sit in the sandbox behind her desk for some reason and she had looked over her shoulder at him. If Henry did run off to enlist, it would be Amos's fault for saying he wouldn't dare to, his fault that the boy didn't finish school, his fault that Rachel was bereft again. He pulled his visor down to shield his eyes from the salty spray and thought that even if it was not his fault, he would believe that it was, and Maggie knew that, too. He would stay outside till midnight to avoid her eyes, if he had to.

In the parlor chair by the window, Clytie slept over her knitting. Across the room Maggie sat with the Sears catalog open in her lap, figuring three percent of $7.50 in the margin with a stubby pencil. Maggie cleared her throat, and Clytie blinked awake.

"I'm going to order a writing desk," Maggie said. "If I include cash in full with the order, I'll save twenty-five cents. We can put it there by the east window; it's three feet long and two wide and will fit quite nicely. Mother always wanted one."

Clytie looked toward the window, then took up her knitting again. "Mother never bought one because Father said it would clutter up the parlor. Where will the chair go?"

"Mother didn't buy one because she didn't have the money," Maggie said, and paused. "I do."

"I thought you was going to find a place of your own to live somewhere closer to the schoolhouse," Clytie said.

"Were," Maggie corrected. "I still hope to. I'll take the desk with me when I go."

A gust of wind struck under the eaves like a blow from a giant shoulder, then whistled through the window frames in passing, drawing through the ceiling vent over the sisters' heads a thin, sibilant cry from Leah's bedroom. Clytie cocked her head and waited.

"Mommy?" A little louder this time.

"What's the matter?" Clytie had no patience with little girls who were supposed to be sleeping; she never had.

"I'm scared," Leah's voice said. "There's a big bug."

"A bug?" Clytie snapped. "Well, kill it."

"I can't. I'm scared of it," Leah whimpered. "It's looking at me, Mommy."

"Oh for God's sake," Clytie said.

"I'll go, Clytie." Maggie stood up and stretched.

"Suit yourself. She made me drop a stitch."

Maggie held her lamp aloft in Leah's room and found the outline of a little girl beneath the quilt. She sat down and put her hand on what was a bottom, not a shoulder, and laughed.

"You come out of there, Leah; you'll smother," she said. "What bug? I don't see any bug."

"It's on the screen," Leah said from beneath the covers. "It waved at me."

A luminous gray-green moth, the size of a girl's splayed hand, clung to the window screen, one wing rising and falling lightly, disturbed by the wind. On each of his four gossamer wings was a transparent circle made bright by glaring rings of blue and gold.

"It's a luna moth, dear, and a very big and beautiful one," Maggie said. "Come out and look at him; you don't see them often."

"No."

With one mighty pull, Maggie swept the covers off Leah, who rose quickly to her knees clutching her doll and pillow, goggle-eyed with fear. Maggie sat by her on the bed and wrapped her around with a protective arm.

"It's a special moth," Maggie said quietly. "You almost never see them. Those aren't his real eyes on his wings; they're only designs that look like eyes that God gave him so birds would be afraid of him. See? It's good luck, for girls especially, to see a luna moth."

"Why?" Leah asked.

"I don't know," Maggie said. "It just is. Your grandmother said so."

"Make him go away."

Maggie sighed. She flicked the screen with her forefinger, and the moth tumbled into the wind and disappeared.

"There," she said. "Now will you go to sleep?" She pushed Leah gently down and pulled the quilt up to her chin.

"I will if you stay with me," Leah said.

"I'll sit right here until you fall asleep and even after. But only if you shut your eyes."

Leah did, and Maggie turned down the wick to the smallest flame possible. She had a sudden dreadful feeling that she had just done something wrong, something hurtful, and she felt deeply sorry for it.

Chapter 4
From Whence Cometh My Help

"She's a mite stiff, but Miss Tessie looks out for others, her own kind especially."

Cyrus Weed, September 3, 1917

The Reverend Nathaniel Sharpesdale stopped at the boot scraper and, with careful attention, cleaned every last mote of dirt from each shoe before he began the granite steps to Miss Tessie Wedge's ornate front porch. He stood for a moment before the prodigious door of oak and frosted glass, girded up his loins, then reached for the knocker. The prim, prune-faced little maid opened the door and wished him a solemn good morning.

"Miss Wedge will be down shortly," the maid intoned. "She will receive you in the parlor. Cyrus is bringing the surrey around. You're early."

On the parlor threshold the reverend handed her his hat as he had done countless times. He noticed that even the maid was wearing a black armband, and he was not surprised, as Gladys was—had been—a Wedge.

Miss Tessie's darkened parlor was as chilly and silent as a mausoleum; the only light was that which crept in beneath the skirts of the ponderous velvet drapes, the only life two hanging ferns. The reverend dropped his worn prayer book on the organ stool—every inch of tabletop and shelf space was crowded with displays of expensive Asian bric-a-brac—and settled into the gentleman's chair, his accustomed seat next to the rigid, armless lady's chair from which Miss Tessie held forth at church committee meetings. Even the overbearing, unamused Queen Victoria herself would be comfortable in this parlor, he thought.

On an easel before the fireplace Miss Tessie's father, the formidable Captain Ulysses Wedge, looked out from his gilt-framed portrait, his empty eyes masters of all that they beheld. Behind him and above the mantel, the carved-scroll nameplate of his schooner, *Accumulator,* reminded the guest of the source of the captain's, and now Miss Tessie's, wealth and social weight. When the Reverend Sharpesdale had first arrived on Barter Island, fresh from seminary, years before, Captain Wedge had been the first deacon and chief benefactor of the island's only church. Having started out as an emaciated cabin boy, Ulysses Wedge had clawed his way to a captaincy aboard a coastal trader, where he had accumulated enough money in six years to build his own schooner. Somewhere along the way to becoming the wealthiest man on Barter Island, Captain Wedge had assumed a cheerless and disapproving Episcopalian air, and with it had presided over the Reverend Sharpesdale's little Congregationalist church until he died and his crosier passed on to his favorite daughter Tessie, an entrenched spinster and the church's treasurer.

"Good morning, Nathaniel." Tessie Wedge, in mourning bonnet and veil and her finest funeral weeds, stood in the doorway, silhouetted by the light behind her. "I hope I haven't kept you waiting; you *were* early."

"Good morning, Miss Tessie," the reverend said as he rose. "I was a little early; I hope you weren't inconvenienced. It's given me time to gather my thoughts. Shall we go?"

"Yes," said Miss Tessie. "Cyrus is waiting. Come along."

On the front porch Miss Tessie paused to inspect her fine Michigan surrey, and her man Cyrus, who stood beside it proudly. The deep green sides and fenders of the surrey shone softly in the morning sunlight, but the carriage's splendor was tempered, appropriately, by the ebony ribbon bows that Cyrus had fixed to the headlamps and the hames of the dappled team. Miss Tessie gave Cyrus a curt nod of approval, and the man touched his hat brim with a knuckle in reply.

"Such a fine autumn day," said the reverend. "For such a sad occasion."

"It is not a fine day, Nathaniel." Miss Tessie adjusted her veil to shield her cheek from the sunlight, and started slowly down the stone stairs. "It is a sad and dark and dreary day. And I am bereft."

She took Cyrus's proffered hand; when she was seated, the surrey listed to starboard until the reverend climbed in next to her and righted it with his weight.

"Time will console you, Miss Tessie," he said solemnly. "Let time and prayer be your comfort. There *is* balm in Gilead."

"Drive slowly, Cyrus. Very slowly." Miss Tessie wanted to relish their somber and dignified passage through the town, and she did not want to get to the graveyard until all the other mourners were in place, waiting for her and the reverend to arrive in a stately manner.

As they passed through the town, the reverend smiled wanly and nodded in reply to those who raised a hand in greeting. Miss Tessie did not acknowledge the doorway gestures, but rode resolutely with her eyes on her driver's neck. As the team climbed the long hill outside the town, they passed the boardinghouse and the knoll where the Wedge family cemetery lay trimmed and enclosed by a freshly painted white picket fence amid a field of swaying timothy.

"At least we keep ours tended." Miss Tessie did not look around. "Which is more than I can say for some people on this island."

"Yours is the most beautiful family plot on the island," said the reverend, who meant it. "I love the way it sits above the sea."

"Tell me, then," said Miss Tessie. "Explain to me why the Coombses would not allow us to bury Gladys here, among her own. No, they would have her down in that dreary unkempt plot in that cove, dark and damp between those ledges."

"Ava said that Gladys asked to be buried in the cove," the reverend offered. "She wanted to be with her two lost children, and with Virgil."

"Ava *said*." Miss Tessie waved her hand to dismiss a thought. "All right. I'll accept that. Now explain to me why Virgil kept at her like that—one miscarriage after another and her getting weaker with each—why he kept . . . Why, not one of the people in that cove, not one of the women, told him to stop, or told her, for God's sake."

"Gladys wanted children," the reverend said. "Surely you knew that. She wanted to be fruitful and multiply, as the Lord bids us."

"Multiply?" Miss Tessie asked. "Surely you mean subtract, in this case. That poor child. It's an abomination."

Abomination, the reverend thought, was without a doubt Miss Tessie's favorite word.

"Where in the name of all that is holy have you been, brother?" Ava, trimmed in crape from her collar to her hems, accosted Walter as he came through the kitchen door.

"I been to Stonington," Walter said. "Don't bark."

"To Stonington?" Ava said in disbelief. "My God, it's gone past nine-thirty and you haven't closed up the casket yet. What if you didn't make it back in time; what if the wind let off? Whatever did you go to Stonington for?"

Their kitchen table was overladen with baskets of food, pies and puddings, the overflow of offerings that Virgil's kitchen could not hold. Walter followed his nose to a basket of fried chicken and biscuits, lifted the linen towel that covered it, and chose a juicy thigh. Why would anyone eat white meat, he wondered, when he could have a . . .

"Walter!" Ava barked.

"What?"

"Why'd you go to Stonington?" she demanded. "Put that down."

Walter took a bite. "Virgil said yesterday that he so wished he had gotten Gladys the atomizer he promised he'd buy her last time he was up there. He said he wished he had it so he could put it in her coffin. He was some remorseful."

Walter took another bite, wiped his hand on his pant leg, and drew a little box, wrapped and tied with string, from his coat pocket.

"So I went and got it," he said. "I took the *Gladdy C.* in case the breeze let off."

"Well I'll be damned," said Ava.

"You've been damned since you was six," her brother said.

"Shut up, Walter Coombs."

"Where is everybody, anyway?" he wanted to know. He chose a biscuit and looked out the kitchen window. "I didn't see anybody around when I came up from the shore. I saw Amos's wagon."

"Clytie and Maggie and Leah are sitting up with Gladys," Ava said. "I sent Virgil and Henry to get hammer and nails to close her coffin up, not knowing where you were. Rachel is to home yet; she has the baby. They couldn't find the oakum and caulking maul."

"That's because they're on the cellar stairs where I left them," Walter said. "I'd like to have a piece of that pound cake."

"You wait," Ava said. "People are going to be arriving soon. Look." She nodded toward the window. "Here comes Virgil now; he must have been in the barn. Just look at him, Walter; it's not only grief. He's all skittish, like he's afraid of something."

"He is," Walter said. "Well, not afraid, but nervous, you could say. He has been since we struck solid ledge not five feet down when we were digging Gladys's grave last night.

If that wasn't bad enough, water started seeping into it."

"Oh my," Ava said. "But what's to be done?"

"Well, nothing." Walter pocketed a pair of biscuits. "He's afraid, see, that her grave will fill up with water and freeze this winter and push her up out of the ground. He wanted to dig another hole, but we didn't have time. Imagine it. He can't get the idea out of his head, her rising from the dead like that."

"I don't want to think about it," said Ava.

"No. Who does," Walter said. "I tried joking him about it. I said, *Hell, we ought to put her in right away—she's got solid ledge and running water; what more could she ask for?* I guess he didn't think that was very funny."

"I wonder why," Ava said.

"Dunno," Walter said. "Here's Virgil. I'll get the caulking, and you ought to get the women going; Virgil will want to be alone with her when we close it up, you know."

Unlike the Wedge family plot, the Coombs family cemetery did not oversee the bay and island approaches beyond from a bright and prominent hilltop; it lay between two broad blue granite ledges, down among the ferns in a narrow swale that tended toward the cove below. Like the houses for the living that crowded around it in the little cove, the Coombs graveyard was protected from the ravaging fearful winds of the open sea by ledges and ancient red oaks. In late morning, especially in the waning months of the year, the sun, riding lower in the southeast, spread across the reflecting sea to warm the houses and shine upon the white marble obelisk that marked the grave of Experience Coombs, mother and matriarch of the first Coombs family to settle in the cove. Beside her, but casting no shadow, was the leaning headstone of her husband, Captain Stillman Coombs, its carved anchor half obscured by a rusty splotch of lichen. In the rows around Experience and Stillman, their children and grandchildren lay beneath stones of various sizes and shapes, many of them beneath miniature markers and infant slabs of polished granite, beside two of which lay Gladys's open grave.

Shoulder to shoulder in their own dark rank, the six members of the Barter Island chapter of the Penobscot Bay Rebekahs formed up in the edge of the shade on the west side of the little graveyard, each as solemn and veiled as their president, Miss Tessie Wedge. Another cluster of mourners, with several children among them, gathered quietly at the south end with the sun at their backs, and watched as the Reverend Sharpesdale scurried to assume his place at graveside. Quietly at first, then with more force when he saw the funeral procession approaching, the reverend read the prayer of consecration.

Down the old path, recently cleared and widened, the four Coombs men carried Gladys's oak coffin, followed by the women and little Leah. Ava carried a spray of purple loosestrife and heather, and beside her, pale and drawn, Rachel carried Gladys's child cradled in a blanket of soft blue.

As they entered the clearing, Henry, who shouldered the narrow end of the coffin with Amos, whispered, "What's he saying?"

"He's blessing her grave probably," Amos whispered.

"The hole we dug," said Henry.

"Which is why he's blessing it," said Amos. "Watch your feet here."

The men set her coffin down gently beside the grave and stepped back while Ava and Maggie removed the pall, replacing it with flowers. Virgil, alone among family and friends, folded his arms across his chest, hugging himself, and looked up into the trees for help.

The Reverend Sharpesdale waited piously while a latecomer, a young woman with a child on her hip and another in tow, made her way past the ranks of Rebekahs to Miss Tessie's side, where she subdued her frightened children. The only sounds in the cove were a hush of breeze in the leaves and, high above, the insistent chirping of an osprey. When Ava looked over the coffin and headstones, she was not surprised to find that Miss Tessie's gaze rested on Rachel and the infant in her arms. Nor was she surprised when Miss Tessie quickly transformed her covetous and angry expression to one of pity and sorrow when she saw that Ava was looking at her.

"O God," the reverend prayed, "whose mercies cannot be numbered: Accept our prayers on behalf of thy servant Gladys, and grant her an entrance into the land of light and joy."

Ava looked at Miss Tessie and her fellow arbiters of island rectitude. *Amen.*

Walter rested a hand on Virgil's shoulder.

While the reverend read through the service, Henry, who stood with Amos behind his uncles, tugged impatiently at his shirt collar. Amos's fedora, which had fit him perfectly the last time he wore it, now sat atop his red head, a size too small, begging to be knocked off by a whisk of Henry's hand.

At a signal from the reverend, the men lifted the coffin onto the planks and lowering straps over the open grave. In her final struggle Gladys had worn so thin, lost so much blood, that it seemed the coffin must weigh more than the lifeless servant inside.

"Thou compassest my path and my lying down,
And are acquainted with all my ways
For there is not a word on my tongue,
But lo, O Lord, thou knowest it altogether."

Ava caught Miss Tessie's eye: *There's not a word on* your *tongue that the Lord and every woman on Barter Island knowest it altogether.*

Miss Tessie nodded to Ava in response, turning to smile beatifically at her niece's children at her side, as though it was they that comforted her, and not the threadbare appearance of Ava's simple brown serge dress; Miss Tessie's own, of course, was one of three mourning dresses purchased in the Matron's Department at Filene's. *Some of us shop in Boston with summer people.*

The reverend nodded to the Coombs family, and the men took up their positions at the sides of the grave; the women, Rachel foremost with the nameless baby in her arms, stood at the foot of Gladys's coffin. As the men pulled away the planks and slowly lowered Gladys toward the watery ledge at the bottom of her grave, the reverend read Gladys's favorite psalm as Virgil had requested.

"I will lift up mine eyes unto the hills,
From whence cometh my help.
My help cometh from the Lord
Which made heaven and earth.

He will not suffer thy foot to be moved:
He that keepeth thee will not slumber."

The reverend stooped for a handful of soil and dropped it onto the coffin; Virgil did the same, then the other family members did so, all save little Leah, who could not be coaxed toward the open maw.

With one hand raised, and head bowed, the Reverend Sharpesdale blessed the gathering and sent them on their way. Walter offered Ava his arm, and together they led the family toward the other mourners, leaving Virgil bent down on one knee at the head of Gladys's grave, and at Gladys's feet Rachel stood motionless, her tears dropping from her cheeks onto the sleeping child's soft blanket. Tears for Gladys, tears for Virgil, tears for the child, tears for her own lost husband, her own empty bed, tears for all those who mourn.

Half hidden by the woodshed, Amos stood as far apart as he dared from the cluster of townspeople who milled quietly around his family to express their sympathy. He would rather be scolded by Ava for being antisocial than risk having someone he hardly knew hold his hand and gaze mournfully in his face. When he saw Miss Tessie leading her niece and two little ones toward the gathering, her eye on Ava, he stepped even farther back to hide in the shade.

Miss Tessie and her niece, and two of Miss Tessie's attendant wraiths, waited patiently until most of the crowd had dispersed, then slid forward to console Ava and Walter. Tessie took both of Ava's hands in hers and looked deep into her face, reminding her that she, too, had lost a family member, her dearest and most beautiful niece. Neither spoke.

Until Maggie stepped up, put her hand over Miss Tessie's, and said, "I'm so sorry for you, Miss Tessie. I know that you and Gladys loved each other so."

Miss Tessie thanked Maggie and thought that she might have cried right there, had the woman not been wearing a navy blue foulard dress, had her hair not been sheared off like schoolboy's, and had she not been wearing a hat one would wear on a streetcar. Miss Tessie stood aside with an eye on Rachel and Virgil at the grave while her other niece, children in hand, exchanged condolences with Ava.

"I wish there was something I could do to help, Ava," said Dottie, the niece. Dottie was a husky young woman with plump cheeks, a feeble smile, and a newborn of her own at home. She hoisted her sniveling daughter onto her hip and wiped her nose with a hankie.

"We'll manage, Dottie," Ava said. "Thank you, though."

Rachel still stood at the foot of the grave, rocking the baby, who had begun to fuss, in her arms. Bent over in prayer, his hat in his hand, Virgil was unaware of Rachel and the child, and the men who stood at a polite distance with shovels.

"She's waiting for Virgil," Ava said. "To give him the baby."

"Yes," Miss Tessie said. *She's been waiting for Virgil for five years, since John died, with a baby on her mind.*

"I should go back to the house," Ava said. "Maggie will want help with the food. I hope you'll join us."

Miss Tessie looked at Dottie, who merely gawked.

"Thank you, we shall," said Miss Tessie. "But wait. We think—Dottie, the reverend, and I—that it would be best for the child if he could be nursed, and be among other children. Dottie's breasts are so engorged with milk that she is leaking; you blush, Dottie, but it's true. We would be happy to take the child with us; it would be no strain for Dottie, and—"

"Oh, no, thank you," Ava said quickly. "You're very generous, both of you, but the boy will stay with his father, and as I told Dottie, we will manage quite well." *I'm not surprised. Not one bit. I should laugh out loud. I should.*

As if he had heard Ava, or was aroused by the sound of a woman calling her child in the meadow beyond, Virgil rose, brushed his knee, and received his bundled son from Rachel.

"Come to the house, ladies," Ava said. "Come watch the reverend wolf down the raspberry muffins you sent over this morning. The sight will cheer us all up."

Ava smiled.

Miss Tessie lifted her chin. *Abomination.*

Virgil took the wooded path back to the house, his boy in his arms, and Rachel followed them. When they were out of sight, Amos spit into his palms and rubbed them together.

"Feel that breeze?" he asked Henry. "The tide must've turned. Let's get this covered over."

Henry pushed his spade into the mound with his foot and dropped a shovelful of wet soil into the grave; it struck the coffin lid with a sullen thump.

"Spread it," said Amos. "I can't stand that sound. Spread the dirt out, like this."

When the last wagon had passed on the cove road and

the grave was nearly filled in, Amos, in his shirtsleeves now, leaned on his spade and watched while Henry marched knee-deep in the grave to tamp down the earth.

"I wonder where Virgil put that atomizer," Henry said.

"Next to her arm," Amos said. "Walter said he tucked it in next to her arm."

"I hope he unwrapped it first," Henry said wiping his brow on his sleeve.

"Well of course he did. What do you think?"

September 9, 1917
Tuesday night
Dear Ruth,

It's nine o'clock and I am the only mouse still stirring in the house. I've just finished tomorrow's lesson plans and wanted to send you a short note to tell you that our poor Gladys died giving birth in the wee hours of Friday morning. (You might remember Gladys from the photograph on my bureau: She is the beauty in the bow of the rowing boat.) On Monday, the Reverend Sharpesdale presided over a short service at her graveside in Coombs Cove. Her child, the boy she had wanted so badly, survived and will be raised with the help of Rachel and Aunt Ava, who is in the "opposite house." I think that the death of an island resident, especially one so young and hopeful, is more deeply felt because we are so few and so closely bound together by our isolation.

I am so busy with school and settling in that I have little time to miss you and the "big city," though I do think of you at least once a day, and hope that you are busy, too, with school and work and fending off the fellows. I hope you are enjoying having our rooms to yourself; my old turret room here is the smallest as it always was, but it is my own and the view is majestical.

You know, during the service I thought about how badly Gladys wanted a child (she'd had two miscarriages and nearly died herself during each, but she was still willing to risk her life for a baby) and I was struck by what a cruel irony it was that a girl like me, who did what I did last spring, should be standing at Gladys's graveside, alive and in good health.

I'm off to bed. Sleep well, my dear.

Love, Maggie

Chapter 5
The Burnt Island Gull

"He's going to call himself John Clair—without an e—
so that every time they call his name, he'll think of me."
Claire Schuyler, September 21, 1917

Rachel set her picnic basket on the smooth granite shoulder that rose above the schoolyard, sat down next to it, and arranged her skirts to cover her ankles. Earlier that morning, bent over her desk in the steam and stench of the cannery, she had felt that she was so tired, so emptied by grief and Henry's departure, that she could not go on, that she wanted nothing more than to curl up in a blanket in a quiet corner somewhere and lose herself in lonely sleep. But now, spread out beneath the sky on her bright perch, she breathed deep the sharp sea breeze, and began to allow herself to be restored, however slowly.

The Barter Island schoolhouse, freshly painted in white with green trim, sat on a slope that rose above the tangled alder swamp at the bottom of the town hill. Through the tall window nearest her, Rachel saw Maggie (Miss Bowen, if you please) leaning over a boy at his desk, with one hand behind her back, the other pointing to the page of what must be the child's cursive lesson; and Rachel remembered Miss Griesly leaning over her in much the same way, telling her to close her *As*, while she counted the slow minutes left until the lunch hour. If you put lilies of the valley in your inkwell, you could watch the ink rise in the stems, then spread through the veins of the little white flowers in tiny tendrils of bright blue.

Rachel thought that Maggie, Miss Bowen, would be a far kinder teacher than old Miss Griesly had been; she hoped that Maggie would enjoy teaching on the island, and with her natural patience and competence she was bound to quickly prove indispensable, even to the most critical member of the school board. Should the board ever find out why Maggie had left the school in Bangor after her first year to come down to the island to teach, there would be hell to pay, Rachel thought, but they would never know, not if she could help it.

By the front of the schoolhouse, on the roadside edge of the alder swamp, a fawn struggled through the clinging branches and emerged onto the road, blinking in the sunlight and dancing for balance. It saw Rachel, snuffed once, and skittered across the roadbed, *clickety-click*, to disappear in the brush on the far side. Rachel waited for the fawn's mother, who would be close behind, and watched as she pushed her way through the alders, crossed the road and plunged into the brush to follow her little one. Once she and Sylvia Turner had braved the alder swamp to try to find Hannah Barter's grave and see if it was true that the alders had grown so thick and entangled around it that Hannah's spirit could not come and go. Hannah Barter had been the first person to die on the island, and her husband Peletiah had buried her near the spot where they had first stepped ashore. Rachel remembered vividly, even now, their frightful struggle through the alders—the limbs tugging at their hair, scratching their cheeks, tearing the fringes of their dresses—and she remembered as vividly the choking nightmares she had suffered from it for years afterward. She remembered Sylvia crying quietly when they finally found Hannah's headstone flat on its back, overwhelmed by thick branches; she remembered scraping away the moss and debris with a twig and finding an eyeless angel, the HEAVE of HEAVEN, and the year of Hannah's birth, 1757. When Sylvia had come back to the island to visit a few years ago, bringing her husband and three boys all in knickers like Henry was, Rachel had reminisced about their adventure—Sylvia's tears, and the scolding they had gotten from Miss Griesly when they emerged from the alders all tattered and torn—and Sylvia had laughed at her, saying she remembered no such thing, and had chided Rachel for her wild imagination, her outlandish memory.

Inside the schoolhouse chairs scraped, shoes scuffed and pummeled the floor, a babble of voices rose and fell, and the students, the big boys first, the smaller ones behind them, burst out of the side door and spilled into the schoolyard. When the two oldest boys, both Hutchinsons, saw Rachel (Henry's Coombs's mother!), they stuffed their hands in their trouser pockets and strode manfully across the schoolyard toward the road, taking no notice of the three younger boys who galloped past them to beat them home for lunch. The students who lived some distance from school, who would stay for lunch, dispersed in clusters with their dinner pails—the boys sitting along the old stone wall, the girls gathered on the front steps in the sun. With little Leah clinging to her skirt, Maggie stood in the doorway, closed her eyes, and massaged the bridge of her nose with thumb and forefinger. When she opened her eyes to see Rachel and her picnic basket, Maggie smiled and took Leah's hand in hers.

"Isn't this a treat, Leah?" They stood at the foot of the boulder and watched while Rachel arranged muffins and apples and plates on a linen towel. "Your Aunt Rachel used to bring me picnic lunches like this when I was a schoolgirl; we sat on this very ledge. Look, she's brought custards."

Rachel laughed. "And now little Maggie is the schoolteacher, the 'stern preceptor.' It must be some strange, Maggie, to be teaching here. Is it so different from teaching in Bangor? Is it strange?"

"Yes to both," Maggie said. "But I like it. The children don't know what to make of me yet, but we'll get used to one another soon enough. Leah, wouldn't you like to take a muffin and an apple and go sit with the other girls?"

Leah shook her head no, and Maggie, with a shrug, lifted her onto the boulder next to the basket and climbed up to sit with her and Rachel.

"How is the baby?" Maggie asked.

"He's fine," said Rachel. "Virgil named him John." Rachel swallowed hard against the lump that rose in her throat.

"I hoped he would," Maggie said, and added quickly, "You and Ava must be so busy, with the baby, an extra house, and Virgil to care for; Walter, too."

Rachel buttered a muffin and handed it to Leah on a little napkin. "It's Ava who does most of it. I help with supper when I come home, and with the baby, John, in the evenings, but she tends to him all day and keeps both houses. Since Henry left we've all been eating supper at Ava's, but I think that starting tonight I will eat at home. I need to get used to Henry being away all over again."

Maggie polished an apple—a nice round Jonathan—on her skirt. "Ava is a saint," she said. "She is a pillar."

"A pillar perhaps," Rachel said, "but not a saint. She . . . You don't want the boys playing down on the shore, do you?"

Maggie looked up to see Cecil Barter slinking away from the other boys toward the path to the shore, with the gangly Fuddy MacFarland, a year younger and a head taller, following him.

"I most certainly do not." Maggie stood up, and with her little fingers in the corners of her mouth, whistled so shrilly that every child, bird, and fawn within earshot snapped its head around and froze in fear, except Cecil Barter, who merely slowed and looked over his shoulder with an annoyed expression. Cecil's mother was on the school board and had been loud in her opposition to hiring Maggie.

"Cecil, Fuddy, come back to the yard this minute," Maggie shouted.

Fuddy scampered back to the grinning boys at the stone wall; Cecil turned, put his hands in his pockets, and strolled back.

"I'm going to have trouble with that boy," Maggie said.

"I hate him," said Leah, her first words at the picnic.

"No you don't, dear," Rachel said.

"You'll have as much or more trouble with his parents, Maggie; they have poisoned the boy with slanderous stories about Bowens and Coombses alike. Those Barters have been looking down their noses at us since the first lobster trap got pushed overboard down here. I don't know why; I don't suppose that anyone knows anymore. You must remember the ill feeling at least; it's been bitter ever since I can remember. John never spoke to any of them. Virgil still doesn't."

"I guess that's one of the things I didn't want to remember about this island while I was away," Maggie said. "When I first left here I was glad to be shut of the malicious talk, all the petty suspicion; I suppose that over the years on the mainland I let myself remember the good things about this place, and forgot the bickering, the spite. Or perhaps I . . . but never mind."

Maggie stroked Leah's hair and watched the noon mail boat as she turned into the thorofare, a sloop under full sail crossing her wake.

"Amos is worried about Virgil," Maggie said. "Last night at supper he said that he and Walter have been keeping an eye on him out on the water, when they can. Amos is worried that Virgil isn't paying attention to what he's doing."

"I'm, we're, worried about him, too," Rachel said. "He's sore distracted, the poor man. I didn't like him fishing alone after Henry left last year, and this year . . . What's this?"

Rachel leaned on one hand and turned toward the road to watch Cyrus Weed approach, driving Miss Tessie's dogcart, slapping black Tink's haunches with the reins to keep her at a brisk walk. Cyrus pulled up beside the boulder and tipped his hat to the ladies.

"Hullo, Rachel, Miss Bowen," he said. "The fellahs at the factory said I'd find you up here, Rachel. Hold still, Tink."

"Hello, Cyrus," Rachel said. "What is it?" She and Maggie exchanged a curious glance.

"Well, I drove Miss Tessie down to the landing, she's gone off-island for the afternoon, and the mail boat captain, he gave me this letter for you. He said it's not officially a letter to go through the post office because there's no stamp on it, so I could deliver it. He said the girl that gave it to him in Stonington this morning thought you would want to get it right quick."

Cyrus handed the envelope to Maggie, who passed it to Rachel.

"What girl?"

"Haven't the foggiest," Cyrus smiled. "Though he did mention she was some pretty."

"Open it!" Leah said.

Rachel opened it and read. The girls on the schoolhouse steps, who had fallen silent when Cyrus arrived, sensed a drama and leaned forward to hear. Rachel read the page a second time, then sat down on the edge of the boulder, leaned forward on her knees, her eyes closed, her head bobbing slightly as though she was falling asleep.

"Rachel, what is it?" Maggie asked. Cyrus turned away, embarrassed to have been smiling.

"Who's it from?"

Rachel sat up, her shoulders pulled back but eyes still closed. "The little Dutch girl," she said, and handed the letter to Maggie.

Dear Mrs. Coombs,

I feel you would want to know that Henry was not in school yesterday. The teacher marked him absent. I inquired at his rooming house and he has not been there, either. His peapod is not in the harbor, and no one has seen him, not even Stevie Robbins. I hope he is still at home, and in good health, maybe he's staying down there to haul his traps a few extra days. But I fear otherwise; I fear he has gone off to join the army. I would very much like to know about him, if you don't mind.

I am sorry about Gladys Coombs.

Yours truly,

Claire Schuyler

"Damn him," Maggie whispered, meaning Amos. *She's a competent young thing, the little Dutch girl.*

"Oh, Maggie!" Rachel choked back a sob; her eyes were wide with fear. "Something happened to him on the way up the bay. That damned old peapod." Her shoulders trembled. "And it was a Saturday, too, like John." Rachel saw Henry clinging to the foundering peapod, saw John's drowned face.

Maggie wrapped her arms around Rachel and whispered "No, no," patting her back softly and giving the girls on the steps a look that made them turn away. Leah began to cry.

"No, no, Rachel," Maggie said. "He sailed up to Castine or somewhere on the mainland, and he's gone off to enlist."

"He would have told me; he would have at least left a note." Rachel pulled away from Maggie and stared at emptiness.

"Did you look for one?" Maggie asked. "If he had told

you he was going, you would have tried to stop him. Did you look under his pillow, in his bureau, places like that?"

"Why no," said Rachel. "I didn't think to."

"Hush, Leah," Maggie said, holding her head against her skirts. "Hush. Henry is safe."

Rachel gathered the four corners of the towel, hefted the whole picnic, and dropped it into the basket.

"What are you going to do?" Maggie asked.

"Why, I'm going home to look for it," Rachel said. "Cyrus will carry me over to the cove, won't you Cyrus?"

"Certainly."

"You'll stop on your way back, won't you?" Maggie asked. "I'll want to know, too."

Rachel promised that she would and climbed aboard the cart, high on the seat with Cyrus. Maggie took Leah's hand and walked across the schoolyard, thinking that Henry had not told his mother where he was going and had not left a note where it would be seen because he'd wanted to get a head start, lest she or someone else try to follow and bring him back. She did not dare to think about the alternative, and what it would do to Rachel to have her son drowned, too.

On the steps at the side door of the school Maggie clapped her hands and called to the children to pack up and line up. As always, Fuddy was first in line. Maggie rested a hand atop his head and watched while the others fell in behind him.

"That's some whistle you got, Miss Bowen," Fuddy said. "How'd you do that?'

"I'll teach you," Maggie said.

In the next week or so Rachel and Maggie set a pattern that would last longer than either of them ever imagined. Rachel left the cannery at four o'clock, met Maggie and Leah at the school, and together they walked to the cove. If Amos was done fishing and cleaning up, they would find him waiting for them, the wagon hitched up and ready to carry Maggie and Leah home to Head Harbor. If they got to the cove early, having ridden home on the back of a passing wagon, or the men were late in returning, Maggie and Leah went with Rachel up the cove road to visit Ava and the baby. On the second Friday of the school year they walked home in a rare September fog, one so thick that it condensed on the leaves and dripped damp shadows of the trees onto the road. Rachel walked apart in silence, her hands gnawing on each other inside the pouch pocket of her smock. When they got to the cove, they found the men still aboard their boats, the *Gladdy C.* on her mooring and the *Grampus* rafted up beside her.

Virgil, in khaki shirt, oilskin cuffs, and gabardine vest, tied off his second crate of lobsters, half full, and slid it across the gunwales to Amos, who stacked it with the others on the afterdeck of the *Grampus.* Walter stood up from scrubbing to watch the women, with Leah scampering to catch up, as they passed the waterfront on their way to see Ava and the baby.

"If only she knew for sure," Walter said.

Virgil nodded sadly in agreement and laid his apron out on the transom for scrubbing.

"Who?" Amos asked.

"Rachel, for Christ's sake," Walter snapped. "If only Henry would write to her; he said he would in the note. If only he'd write and tell her where he is, she'd at least know he's safe and not drowned somewhere out in the bay."

"He doesn't want her to know where he is, not yet," Virgil explained for the hundredth time. "He's afraid she'll come after him, or send one of us to find him and tell the government that he's only sixteen and a half and bring him home, put him back in school."

"He doesn't have to say where he's at," Walter said. "He only has to tell her he's okay. If he could see what he's putting her through, damn him, if he had to watch her in the dooryard with that faraway look, if he could see her living on sweet tea and maybe a little toast, then he'd sure as hell write to her."

"He didn't think she'd be worried about him drowning," Amos said. "He just didn't think about that part."

"Didn't think of it, hell," said Walter. He wrung out his gloves and slapped them against his thigh. "He didn't think she would imagine him drowned, when that's what happened to his father? The hell. He's buying time, and she's the one who's making the payments. Unless . . ."

"Yes," said Virgil quietly. "Unless."

Walter looked up at the trees that were beginning to stir in the slight breeze, then out at the parting fog.

"We're going to take these lobsters over to sell," he said. "Then we're going to stop off at Burnt Island on the way back."

"The witch?" Amos felt his knees weaken. "You mean go ashore there?" *We?*

"Yes," Walter said. "We're going to see Huldah and see can she help us, tell us something."

"Christ, Walter," said Amos, alarmed. "Nobody's seen her in months. What if we find her dead?"

"Then we'll bury her. I believe she could tell us something even if she was dead. You don't remember it, but years ago when Leon went missing—caught in that sudden ice squall while he was hunting on the mountain—they went to Huldah and she said they'd find him asleep at the top of the stairs. They went right to the stepped ledges in the notch below the Black Dinah, and sure enough they found him there on the top ledge, curled up like a baby, frozen stiff. Take in that line, Amos."

"That was a coincidence," Virgil said. "You don't believe in that hoodoo stuff, too, do you Amos?"

"No, I don't think so," said Amos, coiling a line. "But maybe she can tell us something." *And maybe, oh please God, maybe Walter will let me wait in the boat while he goes to see her.*

"Give us a push, Virgil," Walter said. "We'll be back by dark."

Virgil smiled and shook his head slowly.

"Jesus wept," he said, and sluiced his apron with seawater.

Burnt Island had had nearly a hundred years to recover from the fire that gave it its name, but most of its forty-some acres were still open meadows and rocky outcroppings where several Barter Island families kept their sheep. When Grandfather Cain bought the island in 1826, he built his house on level ground facing south toward Barter Island across a deep thorofare not a hundred yards wide. Around the house he planted cedars to block the wind, and an acre of fruit trees. By 1842 Grandfather Cain had sired six sons and, at last, his wife's dream come true, a little girl. In 1862 the sound of the drums beating for volunteers on far-off Deer Isle reached Burnt Island, and three of Grandfather Cain's sons, contrary to his wishes, went off to join the Deer Isle Brigade of the Sixteenth Maine and march south to put down the rebellion. Only one returned, and that one swore, with his hand on the Bible and the other upraised, that his brothers had not been killed, but had gone west to Missouri, an oath that Grandfather Cain never believed. By 1870 the three remaining Cain sons had all gone off to seek their fortunes in the coasting trade, leaving Huldah, a thirty-year-old spinstress who'd never left Burnt Island, alone with her failing parents.

For years Huldah tended to the orchards, the sheep, the kitchen garden, and her ancient infirm parents, keeping them alive, some said, far beyond their years with goat's milk, herbal remedies, and secret potions that she coaxed from the dark crannies of her island. During the fierce winter of '85 both her parents had died in their sleep—her father in December, her mother a month later—and Huldah laid them out frozen stiff in the toolshed until April, when the ground thawed. As the years passed, Walter and the other east-side fishermen who sailed regularly past the Cain house watched from their decks as the orchard, the weathered house, and the front meadow were choked, then gradually overwhelmed and hidden by a dark forest of spruce. In fair weather they sometimes glimpsed Huldah in her white cap through the open front door of the house, or spied her moving among the boulders in the meadows beyond. She wasn't alone, some said: Oh, she might be the only *person* on Burnt Island, but the place was crowded with the spirits of her brothers and parents, who gathered around her in the house at dusk. Occasionally someone reported having seen a strange boat tied up at her old wharf, but no one on Barter Island had talked to Huldah for years; the only indication of her mere existence was the thin strand of smoke that rose from her chimney to be assumed by the fog, or to be plucked away by a stiff breeze.

Riding a tidal rip and a soft wind aft, Walter sailed through the narrow thorofare and swung in to the rotting wharf in the lee of the ledge below Huldah's house. From the bow, Amos dropped a line over the nearest worm-eaten piling; when he pulled the line snug, the piling broke beneath the waterline, bringing with it a beam and shreds of dry-rotted planking that disintegrated when they struck the bow of the *Grampus*. Amos fell back and away from the debris, letting go the line.

"Christ God," Walter laughed. With an oar he found the bottom and held the boat steady. "I've got a purchase," he told Amos. "Gaff that other piling and see will it hold up."

Amos pushed and pulled a second piling with the gaff. "This one will hold," he said.

"Still, I don't trust it, with the tide running the way it is," Walter said. "I'll take another line ashore, and you wait here lest she break free." He watched Amos scan the shore for signs of Huldah. "Unless you want to go."

"No, you go ahead." Amos brushed the ancient dust from his sleeves and shoulders. "I'll tend to the boat."

Walter pulled up his boots, slipped over the bow, and waded ashore with a second line that he secured to a protruding root. He climbed the bank and disappeared behind a leaning fish shack with a birch tree growing through a hole in its roof. If he had looked back, he would have seen Amos stationed at the washboard with the gaff, ready to repel boarders.

Walter emerged from the thicket of spruce into a broad clearing, in the center of which sat the old house in the soft afternoon sunlight. The cedar shakes on the exposed sides of the house had weathered to a lifeless gray and grown mangy green beards of lichen; the roof was so grown over with plant life that Huldah might have grazed sheep on it, if she had thought that it would bear up under their weight. The little dooryard was swept clean—a twig broom leaned against the well cover—and arrayed on two sides by bright profusions of zinnias and marigolds, barely contained by borders of scallop shells. In the center of the picture tiny Huldah stood in the open door, framed by the whitewashed lintel, a saucepan in her hand. She wore a dress of russet-colored homespun that she seemed to have shrunk inside of; beneath a cap of startling white, her little face was as dark and wrinkled as an old chestnut. She watched Walter with eyes that grew bluer and brighter as he approached.

"Good afternoon, Miss Huldah." Walter removed his hat.

"Not miss," she said. "Just Huldah. And you are Walter Coombs." Her voice was far larger than she was, and was as ripe and full as a psalmodist's.

"I'm sorry to—" Walter began.

"Never mind the wharf," said Huldah. "It's been wanting to collapse for years now. How about these raspberries?" She held out the pan for Walter to see, then pulled it back quickly, and studied his face.

"You're not here about Gladys," she said. "No. It's somebody else, somebody lost. Who?"

"It's Henry, my nephew, Rachel's boy," Walter said. "He's run off and we want to find him."

"Well, come in, then." Huldah pointed to the doorway with the saucepan.

Inside, Walter kept his head down to avoid bumping into the bundles of drying wildflowers and herbs that dangled from the beams. Huldah offered him her father's armchair at the head of the wide plank table; he sat with his fedora in his lap and watched her as she cleared the center of the table with her little forearm—pushing bundles of papers to one side, and dozens of little labeled paper sacks to the other. In the clearing she set a teacup, its delicate pink design worn to only a suggestion of a pattern. She selected one of the bags, opened it, and sprinkled a pinch of leaves into the cup.

"You're scared of me," she said. "There's some that are. You think I'm a witch. Normally I drink this tea; it's chamomile and quite good. I'm not a witch, though I don't mind people thinking I am. I have a way of seeing things others don't, is all, and often I'm not very good at that."

"No, I'm not scared," Walter said. "I'm worried about Henry, or about his mother, I should say. If we could find out where he is, she wouldn't worry so."

"He's tall," Huldah said. "He's your brother John's boy."

Walter nodded uncertainly.

Her chair was a rocker piled with thick embroidered

cushions to raise her up to table height. She sat forward, put another pinch of leaves in the cup, and gave it a thoughtful shake.

"I'll want you to look away while I do this," Huldah said. "And don't you dare shut your eyes. I don't want to see what you're thinking; I want to see what the leaves have to show me. I warn you, though, that the last two times I did this I saw nothing, unless you count that ewe last spring. Turn away."

She leaned over the cup, disturbed the leaves, and peered into it.

In the *Grampus* Amos slacked both lines, cleated them, and sat down with the gaff resting across his thighs. An old gull landed atop the piling, shuddered his wings, and stared straight at Amos as though he had come to confront him. Amos, who hated gulls, stared straight back. The bird's black pupils were dilated so wide that they nearly eclipsed his eyeballs, and for a brief second Amos thought he saw himself reflected, tiny and shy, on their surface.

"Gorr," the gull said.

"Same to you," Amos said. He would not blink.

The gull opened his mouth, showed Amos his snaky red tongue, and said, "Go."

"Christ," said Amos. "*You* go, you son of a bitch." He stood up and brandished the gaff, to show that he was ready to swing it.

The gull sat still for a moment, gave Amos a bored look, then lifted off to turn into the wind.

Huldah arose from the teacup, sighed, and sat back in her rocker. She blinked once and smiled triumphantly, delighted to have seen something so clear so soon, and grateful once again for her gift.

"I'm done," she said eventually.

Walter turned to her. "Where is he?"

"I don't know," Huldah said, and crossed her arms over her chest, still smiling.

"What do you mean," Walter said, flustered. "You look like you just won you a prize. Did you see where he sailed to? What direction, maybe? Did you see where—"

"If you'd stop talking, I could tell you what I saw." Huldah raised a forefinger between their faces. "Set still," she said. Walter obeyed.

"I saw Rachel and her husband in a field between a road and the water's edge. And what they're doing is watching Henry walk home through tall grass. Henry is wet—soaked through to the bone—and his arms are outstretched, like this." She held her arms out before her, waving them slightly.

"Well then." Walter sat back, his hands holding the arms of the chair. "Well, that's good I guess. I mean you saw him coming home. But how could Rachel be with her husband? John's dead."

"I don't know," Huldah said.

"Was Henry wearing a uniform?"

"I don't know that, either," she said. "I'm lucky to have seen what I did, and so clear."

"Yes," Walter said. "At least I can tell Rachel that you saw him walking home; that will be a comfort for her."

"When you do tell her," Huldah said, her smile gone, "when you do tell her, don't mention that it wasn't a field of timothy I saw him walking through, it was eelgrass."

"Under water, you mean?"

"I only saw that it was eelgrass, though I don't know where else you'd find eelgrass."

"Goddamn," Walter said. He flattened his hands on the edge of the table and pushed himself to his feet. "I've got to think about this."

"Yes, you ought to," Huldah said, standing. "I'd think on it, too, if I thought it would do any good."

"I guess I owe you a thank-you," Walter said. "What can I give you for doing this?"

"You can't give me anything."

"I want to use you right," Walter said.

"Well then you can do something for me." Huldah nodded her head.

"You just name it," Walter said.

"You can take half of these raspberries to Ava. Half will be just enough for a nice pie."

As Walter walked up the road to his house, he was startled by a flash of bright red that whipped past him and disappeared in the oaks behind the barn. Under the clothesline, her back to him, Ava folded a little flannel bedsheet and smoothed it on top of the others in the laundry basket. She felt the diapers on the line to be sure they were dry, and took the clothespins out of her mouth when she noticed her brother.

"I just saw that scarlet tanager," Walter said.

"I saw him this morning, too," said Ava. "Where'd Amos go?"

Walter smiled. "He saw the wagon was gone so he cut

through the woods to see if he could head them off on the road. You should've heard him swear."

"He won't catch up to her; she's been gone twenty minutes," Ava said. "Anyway, he's better off walking. Maggie's on the mean side of ugly right now. She was grumpy enough when she got here, then Virgil told her you'd gone over to Burnt Island. She waited half an hour before she marched Leah to the wagon, muttering under her breath about tea leaves and oracles. It was comical. Even Rachel laughed. What's that?"

She nodded at the little woven basket that Walter held.

"It's berries for you from Huldah," he said. "For a pie."

He handed her the basket and she lifted the layer of sphagnum to see.

"They're beauties," Ava said. "How is the old girl? I haven't seen her in ten years, but I bet she looks the same. Did she go into a trance for you?"

"I don't know, she wouldn't let me watch her; I guess she did," Walter said. "She stared at them leaves and said she saw Rachel and her husband watching Henry walking home. Henry was all wet."

"That's all?" Ava said. "Not when, or where? What husband? John? That's all she said? Nothing more?"

"No, nothing more. Cross my heart," Walter drew an X in the middle of his chest. Ava knew he was lying. "She didn't know what husband; I asked her that."

"Well then, it was a waste of time, wasn't it?" Ava set the basket down in the grass and reached for a diaper.

"At least it's something hopeful for Rachel," he said.

"I suppose," Ava said. "I wouldn't tell her the part

about the husband, though."

"No, I won't," he said. "I'll put these berries on the table. I'm going down to the shack; you call me for supper?"

Ava did not answer. Walter stood on the stoop and watched the swallows as they flashed and dipped and skittered over the meadow, feeding on the insects that rose from the grass. *If Henry is under water like Huldah said,* he thought, *then he is watching the same kind of thing, only for him it is the big fish that are diving and swooping down on the little ones in a free-form feeding dance and for him there is no chirping, and no air. Only Christly cold darkness.*

Chapter 6
When the Little Man Is Outside

"He doesn't think I've noticed, but Walter's been sitting up in the kitchen half the night these past two weeks. Worried about Henry, though he won't say so."

Ava Coombs, October 12, 1917

Oct. 24, 1917

Dear Ruth,

If my script seems improved, it is because I have a new writing desk, which arrived by freight today, and is as sturdy as it is handsome. It sits in the east window of the parlor (which is dark tonight and will soon be frosted), and it is oak, it has an inkwell and five drawers, two furrows for pens and pencils, and I have a new green blotter for it, and Clytie hates it, which is the icing on the cake.

Remember last year when you deduced that I was seeing far more of poor Richard than I was admitting, and in your little triumph you said that you would make a "zinger" of a detective if you had the chance? Well, here's your chance, dear one.

It's been well over a month since Rachel's Henry ran off to join the army, and still she has had no word from him, other than the note he left behind that I told you about, saying only that he had gone to enlist and he would write her when he could. Though she denies it for our sake, Rachel is sick with worry; she thinks that something terrible must have happened to him on his way to enlist, either on the water or on land. She has lost weight; her eyes are sunken and surrounded by dark circles, and she wears cotton gloves to keep her hands from tearing at one another. Her despair has infected everyone in the cove, Walter especially, why I do not know. Rachel wrote to U.S. Army headquarters in Washington, D.C., to inquire about Henry, but she has had no answer. I don't suppose that she will.

Will you go to the Bangor recruiting office on South Street and there employ all your charms and wit to find out where a boy would go to enlist if he were from this part of the coast, what happens to him once he signs up, and where he might be a month or so later? Amos says that Henry was determined to join the army, rather than the navy, which would make more sense (his choice had something to do with bayonets, which is beyond me, unless it has something to do with Joshua Chamberlain and the Twentieth Maine at Gettysburg, though I suspect it is not so high-minded and has more to do with mysterious male aggression), but you might inquire about both just in case. I should have written sooner to ask you to do this, but I've thought every day that a letter from Henry would come. I thank you ahead of time, and Rachel will be deeply grateful; we all will.

I wish I could have gone with you to hear Mrs. Stevens speak on voters' rights. I'm not surprised that Adam went with you, but I was surprised to hear that there were eight men in the audience. Was Richard among them? You didn't say. Down here on the island the suffrage issue is never discussed. Never. If I were to mention suffrage, or reform, or God forbid birth control, I'd certainly be labeled a Bolshevik (if that word were known down here) and tarred and feathered. I do miss the larger world, but for now the *Ellsworth American* is news enough.

Amos has fallen asleep on the settee: he doesn't so much snore as he snuffles. Little Leah is curled up warm beneath his arm, her head in his lap. I'll wake them on my way up, and I will close reminding you of my gratitude for this errand (I hope you make goo-goo eyes at the soldier behind the desk) and of my love for you.

Maggie

P.S.: My desk wants a little vase, and in it, one geranium.

Virgil swung the *Gladdy C.* around his buoy—red, with a yellow spindle—gaffed it, and hauled in the trap, coiling the line around the buoy at his feet. It was a cold, overcast day, unusually dull and bone damp for October, however late in the month. The hurricane that had veered offshore earlier that week had turned into a cruel northeaster that had cost him seven pairs of traps, Walter eight—more than ten percent of all their gear in the water. And unlike the fall storms that Virgil had seen in the past, this one did not wash the sky and water clean but left behind it a murky, menacing sea and a low, somber sky. On the island the wind tore away the bright red maple leaves and left only the browns of the oaks and yellows of the birches along the shore and scattered among the spruce on the mountain. Virgil wondered if the mainland had gotten hit as hard as they had. He doubted it. He rubbed his chin on his shoulder and smelled through his sweater the powder and sour milk left on his blue shirt by baby John that morning.

He told himself as he dragged the trap onto the washboard that Gladys was done suffering, and he wished for the hundredth time that he could be sure that she had known that it was a boy, an alive one this time, before she died. Ava believed that Gladys knew, and Virgil wished he had Ava's faith. He threw a snapper overboard, removed two keepers from the trap, then wrapped his hand around the claws of an old stone crab and raised it over his head to smash it against the trap to sweeten it with its juices, but then he remembered that he was bringing in his traps and dropped the old fellow overboard and watched him skim backward into the darkness below. When he tried to imagine Gladys still alive holding the baby or feeding him, he pictured Rachel holding Henry when Henry was a baby, or was it Rachel holding baby John that he saw? He suspected that it was Rachel with his boy that he dreamed of, and he felt both guilty and heartened at once. He stuffed the buoy and line inside the trap and lifted it, heavy from its long summer soak, onto the top of a pyramid on his transom.

To the south he could see the *Grampus* taking in Walter's string of pairs in the Turnip Yard, the deep, bowl-shaped area of sea protected by Boom Beach and the Eastern Ear of Barter Island and the low, bare nesting islands to the east. Of all the Coombs waters on the east side of Barter Island, the Turnip Yard was the richest in lobsters and, in the baffling currents on the rocky bottom, the hardest on traps. Walter had insisted this year on leaving the string of pairs close in to Boom Beach during the months of fall storms instead of moving them out into deeper water in September, and it was that decision that had cost him eight of the ten pairs in the string. When Virgil had teased Walter—who was always such a safe man—about risking his gear, Walter had not answered with a cheerful insult as he was wont to do, but had muttered into his stew and looked away. Virgil thought that Walter's and Amos's fears about Henry were unnatural, unreasonable. If anyone should be worried, aside from Rachel of course, it should be him, Virgil, who was so close to Henry, who fished with him. He thought for a time that Huldah had told them something that had scared them, something that they were keeping to themselves, but Amos swore that she hadn't, and Virgil believed him. He watched as the *Grampus,* her stern loaded down with traps and her bowsprit pointing up to the mountain, turned toward him and home and ran before a southerly breeze. Virgil thought he could handle four more traps of his own, and be in the cove with Walter to unload and eat a dinner on the wharf before they went back out for an afternoon load.

Ava's little weather house hung on the mudroom wall between the coatrack and the outside door. Made of tin, and painted in detail that included the tatting patterns on the curtains, the house had two doors. When the weather was fair, the girl came out of her door; when stormy weather was coming or was upon them, the man came out of his door. In the last week of October the man was outside all day, every day, and the thermometer on the wall next to him seemed to have settled on thirty-five degrees as its permanent reading. It seemed as if the rain would never let up: When it was not pouring, coming in off the sea in steady sheets, it was drizzling, and dripping from the eaves and trees and brims of oilskin caps. When the fog settled in it was so thick that it condensed on the screens and wrinkled books in the parlor, while outside it continued to rain. And when the fog stayed for the night it made the darkness so profound that a lantern was useless out of doors, so Walter had to follow the path from the wharf to the house by feeling his way with his feet, wishing with every step that the little son of a bitch would go back inside his weather house.

They had finished taking in their traps on Tuesday, and by the next day had sorted them and stacked them on the wharf and the shore between the two fish shacks. Though they were done fishing for the season, Amos still came to the cove in the morning, where he and Maggie and Leah, dry beneath a canvas, picked up Rachel and took her to town in the wagon. When Amos returned to the cove, he drove past Ava, who stood in her kitchen window with baby John in her arms tapping on the window and waving in a futile attempt to get the baby to do the same or at least look. Past her house he crossed the bog on the old tote road, and in the spruce forest north of the cove, he could hear two axes at work, one cutting a trunk, the other pinging as it sheared off limbs. He tied his mare to the tailgate of Walter's wagon and took up his own ax—both blades glistening from the attention he had paid them with the stone that morning—and pushed his way into the thicket to join the others.

The rain fell steady and light as it had all night long, but when a breeze overhead disturbed the needles in the spruce tops, the men below were doused by a heavy shower. Soon after Amos joined Walter and Virgil, he began to perspire; he shed his oilskin coat to hang it on the limb next to theirs. They worked in familiar silence, wet, but warm in flannel shirts and wool caps. Walter felled two trees the thickness of a man's thigh to replace the runners on the *Grampus*'s cradle; he limbed them, stripped off their bark, and moved on to find more of the same to be cut into sections and carved for buoys during the winter. Virgil cut the full lower branches of the younger trees, and Amos limbed and tied the branches into bundles and hauled them out to the wagons to be used for banking the houses in the cove and his own in Head Harbor. The almanac called for a mild winter, but Walter called for uncommonly heavy snowfalls and wicked cold, saying that it might be a mild winter on the mainland but the almanac didn't know jack shit about offshore weather—it never had.

When they came in at noon for their dinner, Ava met them in the mudroom with dry shirts. She turned her back while they stripped to the waist, then collected their wet things and spread them on the collapsible clothes bar she had set up by the kitchen stove. Virgil took the corner chair to be in reach of baby John's cradle. He dangled his pocket watch by the chain and flicked it to set it spinning just out of the baby's reach, making foolish noises and laughing under his breath as the baby swatted the air. Ava set the table with wide bowls of chowder sweet with fresh scallions, and corn bread and tea. While Walter and Virgil ate in silence, Ava sat with her tea beside Amos. The steam that rose from the chowder pot on the stove, and from the wool shoulders of the shirts on the rack beside it, lent a warm, ripe texture to the air in the kitchen and had turned Amos's cheeks bright pink. Ava inquired about how Clytie and Maggie were getting along in the same house—"Just fine I guess"; about Clytie's health and the effect of Dr. Chaise's Nerve and Brain Pills—"She's been sleeping good enough"; about Miss Tessie's visit that Sunday, which Ava allowed she had heard was a strained one—"Heck, I don't know; I was in the shop." Until Walter, returning from the stove with a second bowl of chowder, said, "Christ, Ava, why don't you let him eat."

While they waited for the tide to come in—it would be over eleven feet at three o'clock—Virgil and Amos lugged the thick poles that Walter had cut from the woods to the shore. Walter rigged the block and tackle for the *Gladdy C.*'s cradle while the tide rose slowly beneath it. The afternoon breeze that came in with the tide dispersed the fog and drove it in wisps among the spruce trees. Low clouds rolled in off the sea, bringing an occasional short shower. When the tide was nearly full, Virgil and Walter went aboard the *Gladdy C.* and, with Amos in attendance alongside in the skiff, paddled the boat onto the cradle, where they secured her, to be hauled over rollers up onto the bank at low tide in the late morning.

Virgil helped them turn the *Grampus*'s cradle onto its side so they could replace the runners; he handed Amos the auger and asked him if he would tighten down the *Gladdy C.*'s lines once more when the tide began to go. Hands in his pockets, and happy to be by himself, Virgil strolled through the drenched meadow to fetch a pair of tin snips and an open can of kerosene from the toolshed. They had piled the wagon so high with bundles of spruce boughs that Virgil had to take care to lead the mare with the wagon behind out the bumpy tote road before he climbed aboard when they reached the smoother cove road. Walter had said that there were enough boughs in that load to bank a whole house, but Virgil knew he would want twice as much brush to bank Rachel's house and do a good job of it. He parked the wagon in her dooryard, pulled on a pair of leather gloves black and sticky with pitch, and began to unload the wagon, untying each bundle and draping the length of cod line over the wagon seat. He started on the north side of the house, the side she would see first when she came home that evening. He cut each bow in two, making one pile for the thicker, sparser trunk end of the limb, another for the bushier, lighter end piece. Virgil was pleased, but not surprised, to find that Rachel had already raked the oak leaves away from the granite foundation and sill to prevent rotting. With the stouter limbs he devised a knee-high skirt along the north side of the house, adjusting one branch here, replacing another there, to create a frame onto which he could weave the lighter and fuller second layer. After a patient hour he stood back to look, and was satisfied that this spruce bank would gather and support any blanket of snow, and hold the warmth in Rachel's house all winter long. Henry, if he were here, would say he was being too fussy; John, if he could see it, would be satisfied, and Rachel, Virgil thought, would be grateful.

He cleaned the resin from the snips and set the can of kerosene down on the front porch. Through the window in the thin gray light he could see into the kitchen, where she had hung a blouse, some hankies, and underthings on the drying bars over the stove. He thought to go in and stoke the stove, but he could not bring himself to enter her house unbidden.

On his way back to the barn with the empty wagon, Virgil met Amos coming down the cove road in his wagon, setting out to pick up Leah and the women in town. Virgil pulled over onto the grassy patch beneath the graveyard so that Amos could pass. Amos had drawn himself down so deep into his oilskin coat that Virgil thought he looked like a turtle with a southwester hat, and wondered if he had even seen him as he passed. Amos never looked up, and probably would not hear a thing with his shoulders hunched up against his ears like they were. Hatless, Virgil buttoned his own collar to avoid getting a cold drop from the trees down his neck, and walked into the graveyard to see Gladdy for a second. That morning he had spied some late New England asters at the edge of the meadow and had thought to take her some, but he had forgotten. Instead he stood before her new stone empty-handed, blowing on his wet fingers. It was not just her stone, but theirs: her side carved with her name and MOTHER below; his side empty, and between them in an arch at the top a pair of hands joined forever. The fingers on the carved hand that reached from her side of the stone were as thin as Gladdy's had been in life, and now, as cold as hers were.

Clytie had been to visit Carla Wilson, the stern Bible quoter, that afternoon, and at supper she mimicked Carla's adenoidal tone of contempt as she described the heathenish games she'd heard were to be played at the Halloween party in Town Hall. Maggie and Leah tinked their glasses with spoons to applaud the performance, and Clytie rolled her eyes and smiled in reply. After supper Amos filled two galvanized buckets from the rain barrel and put them on the stove to heat for Leah's bath. The last dish dried, Maggie went straightaway up to her room, her hand on Ruth's letter inside her skirt pocket. Amos thought for a minute that he might sit for a while in the parlor with Clytie and Leah, who were looking at Leah's school drawings, but he went out to the shop to work on Maggie's bookshelves instead.

On her way up the stairs, Maggie tried to remember Emily Dickinson's precept for reading a letter. *Poems* was among the first books packed, so it would be on the bottom of the trunk, and would take too long to exhume. Something about distance from the door, a holy solitude and rapture alone with the writer—even the mouse exorcised. She drew the curtains on the turret windows closed and settled in the chair by her bed to read. Ruth wrote on the stationery that Maggie had given her before she left; in bold blue ink, Ruth's script seemed to stride across the page. Maggie read through the long letter twice, then sat with her eyes closed listening to the rain on the roof and imagining Ruth at the table in their sitting room above the bank.

In nightgown and robe, her hair brushed and tied back with a pink ribbon, Maggie descended the dark and narrow staircase with the letter in her hand. Clytie sat at the kitchen table with the Sears catalog open to Children's and Misses' Ready Made Dresses. On the floor beside her, Leah sat in the washtub playing with her floating toys, her hair still dry.

"I got a letter from Ruth today," Maggie said.

"Yup," Clytie said. She stirred her glass of warm milk. Clytie had met their distant cousin Ruth only once, several years before when they had visited Maggie who was boarding with Ruth's family in Bangor. She did not remember what Ruth looked like, but she did remember how she'd felt when Maggie called Ruth "Sis."

"Ruth went to the recruiting office in Bangor to ask some questions for us, about Henry," Maggie said. "She said the officer she talked to had dimples if you can believe that."

Clytie nodded.

"He told her that every boy in Maine that signs up or gets drafted goes to a Camp Devens in Massachusetts west of Boston. Every boy in New Hampshire and Vermont and Massachusetts as well. He said there are nearly twenty thousand soldiers and as many laborers who are building a cantonment there—a small city for troops. He said they—"

"Maybe Henry already went overseas," Clytie snapped. "Maybe he joined the navy."

"They have to train them first, to shoot and march and things, you know that," Maggie said. "There's no need to be contrary."

Maggie set the letter on the table. With a bucket from the stove she warmed Leah's bathwater.

"You could be happy for Rachel's sake that now we know

where Henry is," Maggie said.

"I will be when we find out he's there for sure," Clytie said. "She should send Virgil down there to find him and bring him home. Give him a good licking."

"She should," Maggie said. "She should, but she would never ask him to leave the baby, never."

Leah heard a scuffing noise in the mudroom, but when she looked up from her floating duckies she didn't see anything beyond the darkened door.

"*She* ought to go," Clytie said. "Rachel ought to ride the train down there and go to that camp and bring him home. A hundred armed men wouldn't dare stand in *her* way, by gorry." Clytie smiled. "She could take Tessie Wedge with her—they'd surrender the fort and give them a calvary escort all the way back to Stonington."

"Perhaps Walter would go," Maggie said. "Or Amos."

"No, not Amos," Clytie said.

Maggie started to laugh then stopped herself abruptly, but not before Clytie took offense and raised her war claw.

"No, I guess you're right," Maggie said hastily. "Amos doesn't like strangers or strange places. I can't imagine him riding the train to a place that's crowded with tens of thousands of unfriendly strangers. He wouldn't have the temerity to—"

"All your big words," said Clytie with disdain.

"Amos is too sheepish," Maggie said. "He's too shy."

"That's not it," Clytie raised both claws. She slammed the catalog shut and stood up to get busy with Leah's bath. "He wouldn't want to leave us alone; he wouldn't want to leave his family."

From the bench in the dark back of the mudroom Amos saw Maggie wince at Clytie's banging around, then look away to gather her wits. He saw her face reflected in the south window and remembered another very different pair of eyes, those black and dilated, and his reflection in them. "Go."

She called him sheepish, goddamn her.

Chapter 7
The Encampment

"She said that for five mornings in a row she guessed which color shirt I'd be wearing that day. Five in a row. Two blue, three khaki."

Virgil Coombs, November 1, 1917

In straight-backed wooden chairs that leaned precariously against the clapboard wall of a storage shed, two of the Eaton brothers sat smoking in the sun. The Atlantic Avenue hardware building protected them from the cold northerly wind that blew from the mainland, and from their chairs they could watch the town pier and the Stonington harbor beyond. In flannel shirts and flannel caps with the earflaps tied on top, the Eaton brothers could have passed for twins if the stubble on one's chin was not white and his nose was not so swollen. They had just bestirred themselves to move their chairs another ten feet ahead of the approaching shade on the wall, and were relighting their pipes, when the seaward of the pair, who had noticed the arrival of the Barter Island mail boat, nudged the other and asked if that wasn't Amos Coombs coming up the gangplank.

"Wouldn't know him if I saw him," the nudged one said. "Not up close. Not on dry land."

At the top of the gangplank Amos saw the two Eatons and looked around for a way to avoid walking past them, but he could not see any alternative route. He shifted his father's canvas seabag to his left shoulder and set a steady pace, hoping to swim past them as though he did not notice them. He knew they were Eatons, but he did not know which ones; he hoped they would not recognize him.

"Well, if it isn't Amos Coombs," said the nudger. "What you doing Amos, running away from home?"

Amos said hello; he slowed down but did not stop. He thought there should be a deaf old dog curled up in the sun between the leaning Eatons.

"Perhaps Barter Island burned over and Amos here is the sole survivor," said the swollen-nosed one.

"You fellahs haven't seen Stevie Robbins, have you?" Amos asked.

"Why, sure we have," the nudger said.

Amos slowed almost to a halt and looked into their blank faces then, angered and embarrassed by the nudger's little trick, said, "All right. Do you know where Stevie is now?"

"He'd be up to his father's barn," Swollen Nose said. "The old one on the Wheatfield Road. You know the one I mean?"

Amos said he did and nodded in parting.

"What you got in the bag?"

"Kittens," Amos said. "Want one?"

Neither of the two Eatons replied, and Amos did not look back.

Nor did he look back over his shoulder to see Barter

Island when he gained the crest of the hill above Stonington. On his way through town he had managed to avoid conversing with anyone by averting his eyes and moving along quickly. On the road beyond the hilltop he passed the ball field, the schoolhouse, and a smattering of outlying houses, then slowed to an easier pace once he found himself alone. Old Bill Cottle, driving his cobbler's wagon—BOOTS AND SHOES REPAIRED—with his wide white beard, passed Amos on his way to the Stonington harbor where he kept the scow that carried him and his business to the outlying islands. Bill raised his hand in greeting to Amos, and Amos returned the gesture with a slight smile of recognition. Bill would make one more tour of the populated islands this season, Amos thought. What did it say on his scow? YANKEE NOTION. HOME ON THE OCEAN. Amos turned down the Wheatfield Road, walking westward with the warm morning sun on his back.

He had lied when he'd said he knew where Stevie's father's barn was. He had never seen it. But he knew where the Wheatfield Road was, and he had heard Walter describe the barn's steep tin roof when he told stories about Stevie's father, who had been a horse trader with an undeserved reputation for honesty. On the Wheatfield Road he saw the steep tin roof beyond an old and broken apple orchard on the south side of the road. And as he drew near, he saw Stevie leaning against the side of the open barn door with his hands in his overalls pockets, talking with a young man Amos did not recognize, who sat astride a saddled mule. Above the big barn door was painted STEVE'S GARAGE, and Amos imagined Stevie's flivver and various other automobiles parked inside in the stalls where his father's horses had once stood.

Slowly, so as not to catch Stevie's eye, Amos sidled off the road to stand beside a broad-trunked old apple tree, keeping the trunk between him and the stranger on the mule. If Stevie or the stranger happened to see him, he would say that he had just stopped to rest in the shade—no—he would say that he had stopped to shake down a couple of the last apples for his lunch. Those gnarly late ones were his favorites; weren't they everybody's? It was not long before the stranger tipped his hat in farewell to Stevie and rode by the orchard; as he passed, Amos moved around the tree to keep the trunk between them, but he thought that the stranger must have seen him because he held his crummy little cigar perpendicular between two forefingers and puffed on it like he was a whore sitting in a billiard parlor.

Amos set his seabag down in front of the barn next to the granite watering trough that looked somehow familiar, and called into the dark interior. He called Stevie's name, timidly at first, then louder as he moved closer to the doorway. Stevie emerged wiping his hands on a gray rag and said that he would be goddamned if it wasn't Amos Coombs. Stevie was wearing a railroad cap and a denim shirt beneath his overalls; he was tall and long-waisted, with a brace of white teeth that could crack open a hickory nut. He had been nurturing a mustache that he'd hoped would be manly, but it had grown out thin and wispy, the color of his freckles, and it made him look younger than his eighteen years, instead of older.

"Let me guess." Stevie stroked his chin. "You're off to

join up. No, you're too old to enlist."

"I'm not too old," Amos said. "I've got a wife and kid. I'm going to see if I can find Henry." Amos explained that Rachel and the others were worried that something had happened to Henry on his way to enlist, and they wanted news of him, news of any kind.

"Yesterday Maggie's friend wrote and said that the army sends all the New England boys to Camp Devens, that's west of Boston."

"Christ, I could of told you that," Stevie said. "Anybody around here could of told you that."

"Well, down on the island we didn't know it." Amos was annoyed. "Henry was the first from the island to go, the only one; how were we supposed to know?" He shook his head. "Never mind. I came by to see if you've heard anything from him, from Henry."

"No, I haven't," Stevie said. "Maybe Claire has. I saw her the other night at the Opera House and she didn't mention him, but she was with her Christly mother, and maybe she didn't want to mention Henry, you know. How are you going to get to this Camp Devens? Walk?"

"I don't know," Amos said. He had envisioned a train ride, stopping in all the coastal towns whose names he had always heard, towns he could study from the train window without having to get out and talk to people, but he wasn't sure he had enough money, and the thought of changing trains and train stations in Boston—something Maggie had mentioned—scared him half shitless.

"Why don't you grab that seabag of yours and put it in the flivver." Stevie indicated the vehicle inside the barn that

Amos could now see. "I'll get us a couple of cans of gas, and we'll want a tarp I suppose. I'll need to stop at the house and get some things; it won't take but a minute."

"Where are you planning on going?"

"Why, to Camp Devens of course," said Stevie. "Or at least to Orland to the nearest train depot, if she'll get us that far."

"Well, I'm a son of a bitch." Amos smiled like a circus clown.

"Tell me something I don't already know," Stevie said.

Stevie pulled back on the hand brake and parked next to Miss Hatch's old Model T in the wide yard behind the high school. Ellmore Bliss stood near the stairs to the side door with his legs spread wide apart and the tip of his jackknife blade balanced on an upturned hull. Hilton Little, his feet even farther apart, stood facing Ellmore and watched as he flipped the knife off his pinkie. When his knife did not stick in the ground, Ellmore swore foully, snapped it shut, and left Hilton with the game to see what Stevie Robbins was up to. The boys who were smoking behind a wall of lobster traps in the neighbor's yard looked to see who it was, but stayed out of sight to finish their smokes. Several of the older boys left the kickball game and strolled over to see Stevie and the flivver. Amos watched anxiously from the front seat as boys he had never seen before approached the auto.

"Where are the girls?" Stevie asked the first one. "It must be recess."

"They're inside doing their exercises."

Stevie climbed out and packed a cigarette on his thumbnail. "How much longer is your recess?" he asked one of the boys.

"Maybe ten minutes," said a boy with oversized eyeballs and buck teeth.

"Come on, Amos." Stevie put his cigarette behind his ear, the stick match in his mouth. "Let's see if Claire will come out."

"She can't," said another boy. The center of the square of gauze taped to the boy's neck had hardened into a reddish yellow crust that made Amos turn his head. "She's the one leading them, Claire is," the boy explained.

"We'll go in then, and we can see them all in their bloomers," Stevie said. "When they wear their exercise blouses you can see their titties better."

"We can't go *in* there." Amos stopped at the wide double door at the top of the stairs.

Stevie cupped his hands around his face against the small window in the door. If Amos had dared to do the same at the other window, he would have seen a dozen teenage girls in rows of four facing Claire Schuyler, who wore a blouse and bloomers, and her yellow hair braided in pigtails. Like the girls facing her, she held an exercise bar over her head; with her arms straight, she lowered the bar to her thighs and back over her head, marking each repetition with a chirp from the whistle she held between her teeth. Stevie tried to get Claire's attention by waving in the window; when that failed, he knocked on the door, his face still in the window. Amos backed away to the edge of the steps. Claire glanced at the door, saw Stevie's face, and turned back to her class as though she had not seen him.

"She'll be out in a minute," Stevie told Amos.

It may have been ten minutes. To Amos it was an hour or more; to Stevie it was two cigarettes, the second of which he flicked off into the schoolyard half finished when Claire, who hated a smoker, finally pushed open the double doors and stepped outside. She stood with her back to the sun on the cold morning steps, and Amos watched as the steam that rose from her open collar spread into a halo around her fair head. She wiped her brow with the back of her hand, said hello to Stevie, tilted her head, blinked, and said, "Amos?"

"Yup," Amos said. "Hello Claire. I haven't seen you in a long time, since you were—"

"I saw you in July," she said. "At the contra dance down on Barter Island . . . but what is it, Stevie? Is something the matter? It's not about Henry is it? It's not—"

She clapped one hand over her mouth to stop the words and with the other clutched the whistle on the lanyard that hung in a narrow V between her breasts; and with that pose, whether she meant to or not, Claire nearly melted Amos.

"No, no," Stevie said. He reached out as though to put his hand on her shoulder, but he did not touch her. "I mean, yes, it's about Henry, but no, it's not bad news. It is news we're looking for. Amos wants to find him or find out where he is so his mother and the rest, but Rachel especially, can stop worrying that he drowned or got murdered by bandits before he ever made it to shore or to the army. You know they must be worried, if they sent Amos to the mainland."

"I came on my own," Amos said.

"We thought maybe you've gotten a letter from Henry," Stevie said. "That you could tell us where he is or that he's arrived safely somewheres." Stevie said that she could save them a wild goose chase, but he did not say that he hoped that she would not.

Claire let fall the hand that hid her mouth, but still clutched the whistle with the other. "Oh," she said.

When she looked into his eyes, Amos thought he saw uncertainty in hers, then—just before he averted his own—firm resolve, the same determined blue he so often saw in Maggie's eyes.

"No, I'm sorry, Amos," Claire said. "He hasn't written to me. When I saw your face in the door, Stevie, I thought maybe that you had come to tell me that he had written to his mother. I only know from word sent up from Rachel a month ago that he's gone to enlist if he can; I don't even know where; I'm sorry."

"We're pretty sure we know where he went," Amos said. "At least we know where the others went. That's in Massachusetts, so—"

"Aw shit," Stevie said. "Here comes the Cruel Mule. I don't want no part of her. Let's go, Amos."

Through the confusion of children who were moving desks back into place in the schoolroom behind Claire strode Miss Elthea Parridge, the iron-hearted principal of the Deer Island Consolidated High School, and down the steps scampered Stevie Robbins, the perpetual truant, followed closely by the fleet-footed Amos Coombs, who reached the shelter of the flivver ahead of its driver and sat in the passenger's seat while Stevie cranked her. When the engine had caught and Stevie had climbed in, the buck-toothed, goggle-eyed boy and his friend with the leaking boil stepped out from behind Miss Parridge's Model T.

"Where are you off to, Stevie Robbins?" the big-eyed boy wanted to know.

"Massachusetts," said Stevie.

"Massachusetts, my ass," said the boy with the scabby patch. "That thing won't make it to the Eggemoggin Ferry."

"You let us worry about that," said Amos.

"You'd best get your sorry ass back in that schoolhouse or old Parridge will have it in a sling," Stevie said.

"We're not afraid of her," Goggle Eyes said.

"Well, you ought to be—she eats a bucket of rusty nails and a dead baby for breakfast every morning," said Stevie, and pulled out of the yard and onto the Deer Isle road. Amos looked back in hopes of seeing Claire once more, but the big doors were closed. With clenched fists and raised forearms, Stevie wrestled the steering wheel to keep the flivver on the rough road. When they passed a farmer who sat squat like a toad on the seat of a plodding wagon carrying a load of pumpkins and yellow squash, Amos waved merrily to the man, waving farewell to the mumbling lobstermen, the stinking tidal flats, the disapproving wives, the tidal pace, and the numberless road apples of Hancock County, Maine, and hello to the frightful crowded mainland, which he imagined in sepia as he had seen it in the photos in the stereopticon.

"If we don't bust a gasket, or throw a tie rod, or overheat or lose a wheel or bog down, we can make Blue Hill before nightfall," said Stevie. "We can get a supper and a breakfast at Arnold's store in Deer Isle, and maybe find a jug of something to ward off the cold. When was the last time you were in Deer Isle?"

"I don't know," said Amos. "I was there once when I was a boy with Walter, but I don't know when that was. I've never been to Blue Hill; I've seen it from the water, but I've never been ashore there. I'd like to go to that soda fountain they talk about."

The front right wheel struck a hump in the road, sending Amos's side of the flivver airborne and his stomach into his throat before the machine came back down onto the road with a hard metallic crash that flattened his buttocks.

"Well, then this will be an adventure for you, I guess," said Stevie.

"Christ Jesus," Amos said. "You can slow her down some if you want."

Stevie pulled back on the throttle, popped into neutral, and, braking gently, coasted down the winding hill toward the stone bridge at the haul-over, under which rushed the coming tide. Amos eased his grip on the door.

"I think Claire was lying," he said. "But I can't think why she would, unless it was to—"

"Of course she was lying," Stevie said. "It's better to tell a lie than to break a promise, isn't it?"

"I suppose," said Amos.

When Stevie ground into gear on the bridge and accelerated to take the hill on the far side, the noise of his machine startled a great blue heron in the tidal pool. Amos watched the heron flapping with slow steady pulls, rising slowly as he flew the circumference of the wide pool once, then twice around, until he reached treetop level and gained enough altitude to fly away to the north.

On her way home from the school board meeting, Rachel stopped at the top of the town hill and plucked a handful of new-growth bayberry leaves. She rolled them in her fingers to release the little juice that was left and sniffed them to be rid of the lingering scent of camphor from Miss Tessie's parlor. Camphor and Cecilia Barter's White Heliotrope perfume. In the distance the lowering sun was yet a full hand above the Camden Hills. Virgil said he had read in the paper that the government was going to pass a law that would make everyone change their clocks an hour ahead in the spring and an hour back in the fall to save daylight. Walter had said he wasn't going to do any such thing because people changing their pocket watches wouldn't make any difference to what the sun did. Rachel pulled her shawl back over her shoulders and slowed her pace to cool off from the climb up the hill.

On the section of the road home that ran through a cedar swamp, the wide wrinkling leaves of the skunk cabbage growing in the dark water reminded her of how Henry used to like to shoot holes in those big leaves with his slingshot, how he and little Isabel, both of them perhaps four years old, had once played naked in the creek, and how Henry hated to be teased about that when he got older. Rachel felt her hands start to rise from their separate pockets, and to stop them before they got to each other she thought about the dessert she would take to Saturday supper that night. Pandowdy perhaps, and watch Walter wolf it down, holding his soup spoon in his fist to irritate Ava.

Rachel heard Ava singing, and when she reached the flat part of the cove road she saw Ava ahead of her, pushing the new Sears hood-topped baby carriage that she called a pram and singing Little John to sleep for his afternoon nap. Rachel hurried past her own house to catch up and walk beside Ava as she left the shade of the mountain and turned into the sunlit cove.

"I think he's in the Land of Nod," Ava said softly. In one of the fish shacks one of the men was driving trap nails, two blows each, the second louder—a slow, steady, *tunk–tunk* sound that resounded in the cove—an ominous drumbeat.

Ava asked how the meeting had been, and Rachel said, as softly, that they had talked about the Thanksgiving festival, about who would help with the costumes, who would cook which dish, whether it should be held in the afternoon or the evening on the day before Thanksgiving.

"Alice thinks that more men than just the reverend should be in costume, since it is the feast of the fathers," Rachel said. "But Lucille squashed that one by asking whose husband would dress up like a Pilgrim anyway, not mentioning because she didn't need to that the only reason the reverend was doing it was because he is afraid of Miss Tessie."

"What did they say about Maggie?" Ava asked. "Have they started complaining about her yet? It's been nearly two months."

"Cecilia Barter said that her Cecil says that they haven't done one of the moral lessons from the *Eclectic Reader* yet,"

Rachel said, then added, in Cecilia's tone of insincere disbelief: "Not one a week like last year, not even one all year."

"They won't get mean about Maggie with you there," Ava said.

"Perhaps not, at least not to my face," Rachel said. "As I was leaving I heard Miss Tessie whispering to someone that after all, she had heard that Miss Bowen had not left her last teaching job on her own volition, now had she? You know that voice she uses."

"Don't I."

"Well hello!" Walter emerged from the barn with a spokeshave in hand, surprised to see them.

"Shh." Ava put a finger to her lips.

"How was your meeting?" Walter did not lower his voice. "Any good gossip? Any news from the mainland?"

"Hattie Greenlaw had a letter from her Maurice." Rachel looked to be sure that the baby was sleeping; as she did, Virgil's distant hammering resumed.

"He's at Camp Devens," she went on. "He hasn't seen Henry. He says that there must be twenty thousand men or more there, all spread all over the place in buildings and tents. Some of them have to live in little pup tents while they wait for them to build barracks and they are wet and cold all the time. I hope Henry is in the barracks."

"I bet he is," Walter said. "He's been there a while. It's not like he's a new guy." Walter thought he would be happy to hear that Henry was living in a miserable pup tent, if he could just hear that he was there and safe, and he thought Rachel probably felt the same way.

"How about that Amos," he said.

"Clytie's not too happy with him right now," Ava said. "Maggie says she's not sure she believes he went. I think she's tickled."

"Let's see if he stays off-island overnight," Walter said. "If he does I'm a son of a bitch."

"Watch your tongue, Walter Coombs," Ava said. "Watch your tongue."

North of Blue Hill, the town, and north of the Blue Hill itself, which was not blue in the setting sun but a luminous gray-green, the road had been improved. The ruts had been graded smooth, the boggy wallows and marsh edges filled with gravel, and the roadbed widened to bear the traffic that ran heavier every summer from Bucksport, Route One, and the railroad down to Blue Hill and the coastal towns beyond.

Amos said they ought to start looking for a place where they could set up for the night. "There's not much daylight left; we don't want to be running in the dark, do we?"

Amos had six years on Stevie, but here riding in Stevie's dilapidated overheated machine over foreign soil, passing strange houses in which lamps were being lit by strangers who watched them suspiciously from their windows, Amos felt that he was the younger and dependent one. To tempt Stevie, he added: "And I wouldn't half mind a sup of that rum we paid so dearly for."

Bone tired and seriously sore, Stevie slowed alongside a stone wall that separated a hay field from the road, and then turned in to the rutted farm road on his left. The private road was two dirt lines with a grassy hump between running west across the field and ending on a rise, beyond which they could see the top of the roof of a farmhouse. Stevie turned off the farm lane, bounced across the stubbled field, and hove to alongside a stone wall.

Amos, deeply grateful for the silence and a chance to pee, stepped over the stone wall and unbuttoned in the evening shadow of a stand of elderly sugar maples. A plump young rabbit, his ears on the alert, watched Amos for a moment then broke for cover, disappearing beneath the stone fence. Emerging, Amos found Stevie buttoning up behind the flivver.

"Do you mean to stay here?" Amos asked.

Stevie stretched, rubbed his neck. "Sure. There's a creek just across the road. I'll cut us some poles and stakes and rig up the tarp against the frost. There's a canvas bucket in the back; why don't you get us some water and maybe get a fire going."

"What about the guy who owns this field, or this sugarbush?" Amos asked. "Suppose he comes along and sees us? Suppose he wants to know what we're doing. Suppose he runs us off?"

Stevie stared at Amos for a long second, then reached inside the tow sack for the rum bottle.

"This isn't Barter Island, Amos. Jesus," he said. "This is the mainland. People up here aren't scared of strangers. They don't expect to know everybody they see, or expect to know what everybody within five miles of them is up to. They don't want to, either."

"Well," Amos said.

"If the man who owns this field comes by, we'll offer him

a drink," Stevie said. "Relax, old dog. I'll find the cups and that lemon and sugar; you fetch us some water. And fill that thing right up. This radiator's thirsty, too."

Stevie cut a couple of ironwood poles and, with a pocketful of cod line, rigged up a low awning that spread out from the CAPACITY: 5 GALS side of the flivver. Amos borrowed flat stones from the wall to encircle the fire and knelt on the largest of them, blowing softly into a small tepee fire while feeding it kindling. When he had it going, he filled the coffeepot with water and stood with his back to the flames, his palms splayed across his buttocks, and watched the evening star increase in the western sky. Not a peep from Clytie, not even a whiff of her.

"This isn't half bad," Amos said.

"It'll be half better when that water warms up and I can mix us a toddy," Stevie said.

They opened cans of beans and brown bread, leaving the tops attached to be used for handles, and set them on stones at the edge of the fire.

"Jesus, that Claire Schuyler is some good looking," Stevie said. He unwrapped a slab of ham and dropped it into the pan. "I would so love to mess around with her. Imagine a tumble with a girl that pretty."

Amos shook his head no to the cigarette that Stevie offered. He saw Maggie climbing the evening stairs in her robe—her hair loose and brushed, the lamp she carried silhouetting her slim waist and hips through the gown.

"She wouldn't let you," said Amos.

"No," Stevie said mournfully. "I guess she's Henry's girl."

"She wouldn't let you even if she wasn't Henry's girl,"

Amos said. "Claire has taste; she also has certain standards of hygiene."

"Go to hell," said Stevie. "You don't remember what it's like to be horny as a corn-fed moose. You're a married man. You get it when you want it."

Which is never, thought Amos.

He stuck his finger into the coffeepot and drew it back smartly. "Water's ready," he said.

Stevie poured into Amos's outstretched cup.

"That's good," Amos said.

"Isn't it?" Stevie did not stop, but kept pouring until Amos's cup was half full of rum, then added sugar and hot water, and squeezed in a slice of lemon. They tipped cups, drank down a long pull, and sighed simultaneously. Stevie lit a cigarette.

From a low branch in the maples at the edge of the firelight, a horned owl launched himself at the field below and struck a fleeing mouse. The owl lost his grip for a split second and had to land on top of the mouse, his wings outspread, to get a better hold with his talons.

"That guy almost lost his supper," Amos said.

"Christly owl," Stevie said. "In the army they've got special guys who all they do is cook for you. Even on a long march or when you're out in tents, they have whole kitchens they carry on wagons and trucks, fires lit all day and night long, and they cook hot food for you for every meal. All you can eat. Coffee cake. Beef stew. Corned beef hash. Crullers."

"How do you know that?" Amos took another long pull on his toddy and stirred a can of beans.

"Alvie Gross told me," said Stevie. "He came home on leave to bury his father. They call it mess."

"Doesn't make it sound very good." Amos tasted a spoonful of beans. "I like it fine right here."

Stevie poured another round.

When they had eaten, Amos paid the woods another visit, stopping this time on the starlit field side of the stone wall and peeing over it into the dark maples. He returned to sit cross-legged on the blanket, poured himself two fingers of rum, and watched Stevie mop up the grease in the pan with the last of the brown bread. He wondered where he would be tonight if he had set out alone—certainly not this far, and not this comfortable.

"So what made you do it, Amos?" Stevie asked. "What made you, of all people, leave the island and strike out for Massachusetts? For Camp Devens, where there must be twenty thousand people, and a hell of a lot of them, hundreds of them Negroes?"

"For Rachel mostly, you know that," said Amos. He had not imagined that there would be Negroes; he had never seen one in the flesh, though he imagined, from the stereopticon pictures he had seen of them working in fields down south, that they were friendly people, gentle. "Virgil has the baby, so he couldn't go. But for Walter, too."

"Walter?"

"We went to see Huldah, you know, the witch on Burnt Island, and she told Walter that she saw Henry walking home soaking wet, and that made Walter nervous," Amos said. "It scared him somehow for Henry's sake. I don't know why. He says he isn't worried, but I know he is; Ava says he is, too. I'll just make sure Henry's at this camp, then go on home."

"Alvie says they live in buildings called barracks," Stevie said. "Pour me another one of those. Big wide-open rooms with rows of beds down both sides." Stevie held his forearms and hands parallel as Alvie had done describing them to him. "Every guy has his own locker and bed: blankets, pillow, sheets, mattress, steel springs. They got heat from a coal furnace, electric lights, shower baths with dials on them so you can choose how hot or cold you want your water, a room for reading magazines and playing cards in. Jesus."

"Yeah," said Amos. "And all this with some big guys yelling at you all the time, telling you what you're doing wrong, which is everything you're doing, pushing you down, kicking you, cussing you. Don't forget that."

"Flush toilets, whole rows of them," said Stevie. "Everything cleaned and polished to a shine every day. Fifteen dollars a month, a slick uniform, and wine and women in Boston."

Amos imagined Henry sitting on a toilet with twenty strangers doing the same thing on either side of him, grunting and stinking. He knew he could never do that. He would have to find a way to sneak off into the woods to move his bowels, if ever he could.

They spread out their blankets beneath the low-slung tarp and lay in the dark, their hands behind their heads watching out at the stars—Stevie at the dipper, Amos at Orion.

"Do me a favor, would you?" Stevie asked.

"Sure."

"Tomorrow don't wear your trouser cuffs tucked into your boot socks," Stevie said.

"Why not," Amos asked. "It keeps your cuffs from wearing thin."

"It's hayseed, Amos."

"Oh."

Chapter 8
Half-Truths

"You'd be surprised. Most of them that come in here are pretty rugged boys—loggers and farmers and the like. Simple and rugged—the finest kind of soldier. Indestructible."

Staff Sergeant Arthur Lewis
Baker Company, Second Battalion, Nineteenth Infantry
Camp Devens, Massachusetts
17 November 1917

Virgil quartered a small pumpkin with his clasp knife and fed the sections to the grateful cow, who chewed with her eyes closed. He wondered how far Amos had gotten on the first day, and thought that if he had been lucky enough to catch a few wagon rides, he would be as far as Deer Isle and tonight would be curled up in his blanket in somebody's barn or haystack, more likely a haystack where he would not be noticed. Like Walter said: *How about that Amos!* He worried that if Amos ever did get as far as Camp Devens, and he thought now that he might—if he had the scruff to strike out alone for the mainland, he would have the scruff to go the whole way—he might embarrass Henry by showing up, his bumpkin uncle blushing and scratching his head. Virgil knew without a doubt that Henry was already doing himself proud, and consequently his family. He was a rugged boy. He could outrun, and outshoot, and outfight the best of them. He could throw hand grenades like he threw baseballs. He was quiet, sure, a tad shy, but he would not back down or cringe when the sergeant or captain yelled in his face; he would look the man in the eye and not back down. They would be making him a sergeant soon, and when they did, he wouldn't yell at his men, he would treat them with respect, and they would follow his example and follow him forward when he led them in the attack on the Christly Hun. And when Henry came home, a row of bright medals on his chest, they would stand on the sidewalk in Stonington, Walter and Ava and Rachel, and him holding Little John's hand, to watch Henry parade with the rest down Main Street behind the band from Deer Isle. "That's your cousin," he would tell Little John, and when Henry passed—not looking over at them because he couldn't, being a proper soldier—he and Rachel would not cheer with the others along the walk because if either of them tried to make a noise it would come out in a sob of pride and pure joy to see him marching home safe. Jesus wept.

Virgil lifted the lantern from the hook, turned down the wick, and left the drowsy old cow to chew alone in the dark. He stood beside the barn letting his eyes adjust to the lack of light. It was a windless night, the sea flat calm and the air so clear that he could see all the stars in Orion's belt. There was no sound from Ava's house, no crying from the baby, not even the slightest lapping sound of the water on the rocks in the cove; he thought that it must be half past seven, and he thought that tonight there was almost no risk involved at all.

He took the back path to the graveyard, and there rested the lantern on one of the little headstones next to Gladys, spreading a dim yellow light across her fresh mound. Should Ava or Walter come looking for him for some reason or another, he would hear them and say that he had come to visit Gladys, and had just then gone off into the trees to relieve himself. Beyond the thin lantern light and the edge of the graveyard, he lifted his feet and brought them down slowly toe-first with each step so as not to disturb the leaves and twigs, as he did when stalking a deer, so quiet in the trees that not even a wary rabbit would hear him, moving so slow that even an owl would think he was only a shadow. When he found his familiar spot among the low intertwined spruce limbs, where he could see but not be seen, he stood and waited, thinking how much safer his visits were now that Henry and Gladys were gone, how much more private, how much more intimate.

Tonight her parlor window was already steamed over by the buckets and kettles of water boiling on the kitchen range. Tonight the reflector on the wall lamp over the kitchen cabinets was turned toward the parlor and him, so that she was illuminated only dimly. She poured the kettles both at the same time into the water in the tub in the middle of the floor, raising a brief rainbow of steam, then emptied both steaming buckets into the tub. Lifting the hem of her white cotton nightshirt, she tested the water with her toes, then stirred it a little with her foot. She unpinned her hair and shook it free. As she crossed her arms at her hips to raise her shirt over her head, Virgil thought he could hear music, faint and sweet and distant—a girl's voice, sad and tremulous, and seductive, too, somehow. Her soft round breasts rose with her arms as she lifted her nightshirt, and fell slightly as she set it aside; turning a little away from him, she drew down her panties, revealing the dimples above her buttocks, then her small round bottom. When she bent to step out of her panties, Virgil could feel the tender weight of her pendant breasts in his cupped hands. Tonight he watched her in profile as she stepped into the tub and lowered herself onto her knees in the bath. With a long-handled saucepan she scooped and slowly poured warm water over her head and shoulders, back and breasts.

Lightly, with one knuckle so as not to startle her, he would tap on the kitchen door. She would know it was him and say yes, only loud enough to be heard. She would rise out of the water as he came into the kitchen, facing him shy but unashamed, one forearm across her breasts, a hand covering her crotch. She would watch his eyes as he watched her lower the arm to reveal her breasts, and then let the other hand fall to her side. She would not turn away and she would agree only with her eyes and a tiny smile on her lips, as she handed him the soap and took hold of his wrist, guiding his hand to her tummy, moving it in a slow, soapy caress of her breasts, then guiding him downward before she released him. As he bent to moisten the soap in the tub, she would spread her legs a little to allow him to soap one leg, then would open them farther as his hand slid up her thigh.

When she was done bathing, she rose in the tub, her back to his window now, and toweled her hair and body, at last drying one foot while it rested on the rim of the tub, stepping out on it, and drying the other the same way. When she wrapped the towel around her and secured it with a tuck beneath her armpit, she turned suddenly toward his window and stood motionless looking straight at him for an eternity, before she reached for a bucket to begin to empty the bathwater into the sink. Virgil took two steps backward, ducked under a spruce limb, and walked quickly back to the graveyard. He was careful not to look at Gladys's grave as he retrieved the lantern. On the path back to the barn he stopped to turn up the wick and listen to the cove, which was as quiet as though it had been holding still in the dark for a hundred years.

"Hey mister." A cream-faced boy with flared nostrils and a skullcap of waxed black hair poked Amos's shoulder. "Hey mister, how about closing that window there."

Amos was crammed into the window seat at the rear of the train car on the port side, his feet on his seabag, his knees pulled up, and his head rested against a folded flannel shirt that acted as a pillow and poor buffer against the rattling slatted wall behind him. He opened his eyes in response to the poke, and shut them again, thinking that if he closed his window he would surely suffocate in the smoke and stench of the crowded car.

"He's gonna freeze my ass," said another voice nearby in a sharp upcountry accent. "Here, I'll get it."

Amos sat up slightly and with his arm blocked the

upcountry kid, who tried to reach across him.

"I guess I'll leave it open," Amos said. "Top and bottom. I don't see how you can be cold in here. Trade your seat with one of those guys on the floor; they look warm enough."

"Asshole," said Flared Nostrils.

Amos turned his face toward the window and met his own reflection, which flickered in and out of existence as the light from the setting sun on the opposite side of the car danced through the passing trees. He thought that there must be at least a hundred boys packed into the car. More than half the population of Barter Island. A hundred overheated, overexcited farm-boy heroes off to the Big Adventure and enjoying their newfound first-time freedom aboard the train by fighting, drinking buttermilk, beer, and whiskey, playing cards, singing, smoking cigars, cigarettes, and cheroots, eating, vomiting, sleeping, farting, and squirming in impatient, slavering expectation of the train slowing and passing or maybe even stopping at another small-town platform crowded with girls with soda pops, sandwiches, and sweet red lips puckered up for the acrobatic boys dangling from the train windows. Not only was it nearly dark, Amos thought, but they still had yet to go through Saco and Kittery where they would surely pick up hundreds more and pack them in somehow, the train not even out of the state of Maine yet.

That morning in Bucksport—the passenger line did not stretch as far east as Orland, they'd learned—Stevie had surprised Amos by declaring that he would go with him to Camp Devens. The train ride would be a hoot, he said; he'd never been to Boston, and maybe he would get to see Henry, too. They left the flivver under a feeble roof built onto the side of a livery stable on the Bangor Road at the edge of town, with a promise of four bits to the stable boy for keeping an eye on it. Stevie took the distributor with him so the boy would not be led into temptation. When the train pulled into the Bucksport depot at the water's edge, two elderly couples—both of the men wearing long white beards, gold-braided Seventh Maine Cavalry Stetsons, and Union army overcoats—were helped aboard the first passenger car by the stationmaster and conductor.

"Christ," Stevie said. "You can't see the end of the cars around the bend, and they all look nearly empty. Let's find one for just us."

They had found an empty car and took two middle seats on the port side, the Atlantic side. Stevie sat with his back to the window, his legs stretched out on the seat, and watched the countryside and trees stream by, the warm morning sun on his shoulders. Amos sat upright in the seat behind Stevie, the sun spilling in his lap, his eyes stretched wide, his mouth open in unabashed wonder as they rattled past fields and shoreline, houses and little harbors, and schooners he had to squint to see as they approached Stockton Springs. As they built up speed on the stretch before Searsport, blurring the passing trees, Amos gripped the back of Stevie's seat and watched with a widening smile as Stevie stood laughing in the middle of the aisle, hands on his hips, and rode the swaying floor of the car as he would a deck on a heaving sea.

In the Searsport station they watched as half a dozen young men bid their bare-headed mothers good-bye and lingered to hug and kiss the several girls who had gathered to see them off. The girl nearest Amos, whose hair was the same bold chestnut as Maggie's, looked over her beau's shoulder straight at Amos, and he ducked back away from his window. Before the young men boarded the train two cars ahead, they raised their hands one by one in salute to their fathers who stood silent in the background among their carriages and wagons.

In the nineteen-mile run between Belfast and Camden, Amos tried his train legs, walking forward up the aisle at forty miles an hour, then aft at the same speed. He stood out on the platform between the cars and, holding the railing with both hands, stuck his head and shoulders out to take the full force of the wind and the feel and smell of salt water as they slid past Ducktrap and Lincolnville Beach. His hair stood straight up, his eyes watered, and when he opened his mouth and shouted noiselessly his cheeks billowed out like a balloon jib in a gale.

At the Rockland station, where Amos thought that Henry must have boarded the train months before, the platform was crowded with people of all kinds, come to see the boys off, this time dozens of boys. As Stevie and Amos watched, Stevie in the seat ahead, several boys climbed into their car and sat together in window seats to call out and wave good-bye. Amos wished that Stevie would move back one seat and sit with him, so no stranger could, but he did not say so. In the door of the station house three older men played martial airs on flute and fife and drum. A schoolgirl whose pigtails were tied with red, white, and blue ribbons, and a young woman Amos's age carrying a covered basket, stopped beneath their windows.

The younger one asked if they would like something to eat.

Stevie leaned out his window and said, Oh, they certainly would, thank you.

"You can't take food," Amos hissed. "We're not . . ."

The older one, perhaps the girl's big sister Amos thought—they both had the same pretty pointed nose—opened the lid of the basket and handed out two sandwiches wrapped in butcher's paper that the younger passed to Stevie, who hung out the window teetering on the ledge at his waist. They offered him apples and cupcakes, as well, and he passed the food to Amos.

"Don't I get a kiss, too?" Stevie asked her.

The older one pushed her from behind, but the girl held her ground.

"Not from me you don't," the girl said. "But I bet there's others here that will oblige you."

"Get your ass inside here," Amos said.

At Bath the cars forward of theirs had filled with boys and any number of sullen men in coveralls from the three o'clock shift at the shipyard; later, in a stop at Brunswick that lasted more than an hour, their car and several others filled. The families and traveling salesmen and other civilians who boarded for Boston avoided the cars filled with young crusaders, seeking safety in separate cars for their children and suitcases and sample kits. When the train finally pulled out of the Portland station in the waning afternoon Amos and Stevie retreated to the rear window seat. For perhaps an hour Amos managed to keep Stevie in the seat between him and the others, but Stevie—who had met everyone within reach and learned what each of them used to do for a living, how many cigarettes he had left, how many sisters he had, and of what age, and what he planned to do with the fucking Kaiser when he got his hands on him—got busy with another boy building a card table in the aisle with suitcases, and left Amos in the seat with the boy with flared nostrils who made a peace offering to Amos with a tongue sandwich that smelled like a decomposing rat.

Amos thanked the boy and declined with a wave of his hand. The boy slid over next to Stevie, who was dealing cards to four red-faced farmers, to watch the game over Stevie's shoulder. While Stevie arranged his hand the boy bit into his sandwich and chewed appreciatively.

"Every day in the army is just like Sunday on the farm," said the boy across the suitcase from Stevie. "That's what my cousin said. I'll go one spade."

"What's this game called?" asked another.

"He told you; it's called Eighty-eight."

"You wouldn't want to give me a bite of that sandwich, would you?" Stevie was holding his breath.

Flared Nostrils, his mouth packed full of bread and rancid tongue, handed Stevie the sandwich with a charitable look in his eyes. Stevie took it, opened the car door, and pitched it out.

Flared Nostrils stood up and, with some effort of jaw and throat, swallowed the mess in his mouth. "Goddamn you. I ought to break your fucking nose, you ungrateful bastard."

"Sit down, shit-for-brains," said the boy who had bid

one spade. "It's you that's ungrateful. That guy just saved your life. If that Christly sandwich hadn'tve killed you, one of us would've done it to keep you from poisoning the air in here."

"Fifteen dollars a month," said another red-faced player with a pale hat line across his forehead. "Fifteen dollars and free food and free clothes. Your only expenses is tobacco."

"And wine and women on the weekend," added One Spade.

Amos turned toward the window to breathe as much fresh air as he could. The tobacco smoke burned his eyes and nose. He wondered how Henry, who never smoked in his life, had stood it. He was probably used to it by now; he might even be smoking himself by now; the army makes you hard.

"Lookit here!" a young warrior at a starboard window shouted. "There we go over the Piscataqua River and there's Portsmouth on the far side. Say good-bye to the state of Maine, boys!"

He was answered by whoops and huzzahs, a clarion call to alert Lafayette, and a loud snarling prediction of what would happen to the Kaiser's genitals when the Maine boys got ahold of them. A pale, dimpled boy with a round face and bowl haircut managed to stand at the door in the stern of the car and render an awkward but well-meant salute to the southernmost border of the Pine Tree State as the train crossed into New Hampshire, headed for Boston and Brest.

"Here you go, Captain." A round-faced boy with moist blue eyes turned in the seat ahead and handed Amos a green bottle molded in the shape of an Oriental pooh-bah with a top hat, which Amos knew to be Poland Springs sloe gin. He took the bottle, wiped the mouth on his shirtsleeve, and swallowed half a cup before he passed it to Stevie. It had grown dark outside the car window, dark and shapeless except for an occasional spark of light through the trees. The coach lamps inside the car reflected his face in the window so clearly that he could see the three-day growth of red whiskers on his chin. Ava said he looked some scruffy, like a clam digger, when he went a day or two without shaving; Maggie said he ought to let it grow, he would look like a mountain man. Henry, he thought, had to shave every day with the rest of them; he had to shine his shoes and keep his hair cut short, keep his gun clean, his bayonet sharpened, his bed made just so. He had ridden the same train, only he had done it alone. Henry wouldn't have been shrunk up in the corner like Amos was, but he wouldn't be playing cards and trading punches with everybody around him like Stevie was either; he would be in between, making friends in a quiet sort of way, friends he still had where he lived—in a barracks or a tent full of men. That was fine for Henry; it was good. But Amos would rather be perched alone on the stoop of Clytie's father's toolshed with the wet night wind in his face, or sitting by the fire under the stars in a cold open field, he would.

Walter sat in the captain's chair next to the stove in the Barter Island general store contemplating his morning onion. Today's was a yellow Bermuda onion, his favorite; he peeled away the papery outer layers one at a time with care, pushing each into the grate where it flared and died quickly. On the other side of the stove his cousin Irville, who was two years younger but looked ten years older, half squatted, half sat on an upturned wooden crate tamping his pipe with a charred forefinger. Irville lived and fished on the western side of the island, which made him a distant cousin to Walter, nearly a foreigner, but Walter enjoyed his company by the stove in the store in the off season because Irville rarely spoke, and when he did, he did not expect a reply or even suppose that his companion was listening. Irville struck a match, mumbled something, and puffed up a cloud of smoke. Walter looked out the window at the boats moored in the thorofare to see if the wind had shifted any, then took a bite of the sweet onion, shutting his eyes to avoid tears and fully relish the taste.

At the counter watching Cecilia Barter cut a quarter pound of store cheese, Dottie Wedge stood with a baby on her hip who was engrossed in catching the drainage from his nose with his lower lip and swallowing it.

"I seen that Cecil's home from school again," Dottie said.

Cecilia, whose hair was prematurely gray and whose face wore a cheerful expression for someone so miserable, glanced out the window, where she saw her Cecil aiming his slingshot at something on the store wharf.

"Four days," said Cecilia. "He had the grippe. That fever and wicked cough that's been going around. I think he's over it today, but he begged me to let him stay to home this morning; he hates school so much this year, you know."

"For pity's sake, Irville." Dottie waved a hand before her face to disperse the cloud of pipe smoke that Irville was building. "You'll suffocate us here."

"Open the window, Jesus Christ," said Irville.

"He's not the only one," Dottie told Cecilia. "You know, I guess, what Aunt Tessie heard from her librarian friend in Bangor."

Cecilia shifted her eyes toward Walter to remind Dottie that one of *them* was within earshot. She wrapped the slice of cheese noisily, and Dottie dropped her voice.

Walter watched little Cecil Barter out the window. The boy was eight years old but so small and pale and pencil thin that he could not weigh more than fifty pounds and might get blown off his feet at any moment. Cecil was shooting at something on the empty wharf that Walter could not see. With stones from the pocket of his flannel shirt, he loaded his slingshot, took careful aim, and fired, moving a few steps closer to the wharf after each shot. Through his own chewing, and Irville's sucking and puffing and muttering, Walter listened to what he could of the conversation at the counter.

He heard: "suffragettes," and "behavior unbecoming."

Cecil's target, Walter decided, was the last piling on the far side of the wharf, or something on it or behind it that he could not see. The boy released another stone that glanced off the side of the piling, then took a few more eager steps forward; he licked his fingers and wetted the strand of hair that fell across his eyes to hold it in place.

Walter overheard "reform this or that" and what sounded like "hardwood hanger," and he felt Cecilia's wary eyes on him.

With one leg ahead of the other, Cecil bent his knees, pulled back his sling until it nearly touched his cheek, and waited, frozen stiff like a pale-faced little Indian hunting a rabbit with a bow and arrow.

"No model for children."

A split second after he released the stone, Cecil leapt into the air, raising his slingshot triumphantly, and Walter saw a tiny kitten, perhaps two weeks old, drop from its grip on the piling into the water and, with a little flurry that made barely a wave, disappear beneath the surface. Walter thought of Cecil's father, Tip, a poacher of deer and a hater of Coombses, and thought that the fruit didn't fall too far from the tree. At the end of the wharf, looking in the water for sign of his kill, Cecil waved gaily to the passing mail boat as it turned into the town landing.

"There's more to it than that, I'll bet," said Cecilia. She licked the tip of her stubby pencil to record Dottie's purchase.

"If there is," said Dottie, "Aunt Tessie will find it out. Well, now, lookit here." She nodded to the front window where Claire Schuyler was passing with a fearful look on her face and her shawl wrapped tight around her against the increasing wind.

"Who would that be?" Cecilia asked, straining to see.

"It's Claire Schuyler," Dottie said. She gave the child on her hip a bump to keep him awake. "I haven't seen her in years, not since I boarded with her family when I went to high school. I wonder what she's doing down here? She must be almost seventeen by now; she's grown quite pretty."

When they turned back from watching Claire pass, the women found Walter standing between them, as close as he could be without touching. He leaned forward across the counter and released an appreciative sigh in Cecilia's face.

"Whoo," he breathed. "That was one good onion."

Cecilia's nostrils dilated, then collapsed. She backed up against the canned food shelves.

Walter patted Dottie's leaking child on the head.

"They say you eat a onion every day, the grippe won't get you," he said on his way to the door.

Claire raised a fist to knock on the big front door of the Barter Island cannery and hesitated, frozen in midmotion by uncertainty. She knew that the cannery was closed, but she had seen from her seat on the mail boat that one of the upstairs office windows was opened slightly for fresh air and thought that she had seen someone inside. She prayed that Rachel was here at work and alone, and she prayed that she was not—that she could postpone the meeting with a walk around the island to Rachel's house in the cove. She knocked timidly, listened, heard nothing, then knocked again, louder, quite manfully. A woman's voice, distant and irritated, said something that Claire could not understand; she lifted the latch and let herself in, to stand on the wide, vacant work floor. The huge iron steam vats were tipped onto their sides, at rest over the cold brick furnaces beneath them; the vats had been scoured to a dull sheen, the furnaces swept clean. The carrying trays were stacked against the sliding doors at wharfside; the packing tables were scrubbed clean and covered with crates of empty cans. The only sign of life was the sound of the water lapping at the pilings beneath the worn floorboards. Claire stepped cautiously to the foot of the open staircase and said: "Mrs. Coombs?"

There was no answer, but a chair scraped across the floor above, and in a moment Rachel stood at the top of the stairs, squinting curiously in the half-light at the figure below.

"Who is it?" Rachel asked.

"It's Claire Schuyler, Mrs. Coombs." Claire's voice trembled; she pushed her shawl back off her head and looked up, her cheeks flushed with apprehension.

"Claire?" Rachel began. "Oh, the little Dutch girl, Lavinia's niece, who sent the note. I'm so sorry. I didn't know what it was, the knocking, I thought it was one of the boys who works here come back for something . . ." Rachel started down the stairs. "How can I help you? Is it some business or other, or is it—"

"I've come to see you," said Claire. "I mean if you have the time. I can come back later if you're busy. It's not about the cannery, it's about Amos and Stevie Robbins, I mean . . ."

The explanation that Claire had so carefully rehearsed, the conversation that she had imagined so many times and fit together so carefully, was scattered like so many puzzle pieces by the hint of fear and confusion in Rachel Coombs's voice, and the sound of the same in her own.

"Come up, please," said Rachel, extending a hand. "We can talk up here; I have two chairs."

As Claire ascended, a little brown paper bag in hand, Rachel moved her own armchair out from behind her desk and arranged the other chair to face it by the window, thinking that the girl should be in school today, and telling herself that Claire was anxious because she was visiting her beau's mother, and nothing more. She kept her hands apart by keeping them busy, taking Claire's shawl, adjusting her chair, shutting the window. She patted her hair and, doing so, found the blue pencil she had been looking for earlier.

"I brought you some fudge," Claire said, placing the bag on the desk. "My sister and I made it last night; it's goat's milk, with walnuts, I hope you like walnuts."

"I love them," said Rachel. "Thank you. Were you up late cooking? You look tired, you haven't had the grippe have you?" Rachel realized, too late, that the girl was on the edge of tears, barely containing a convulsive sob. "I mean you're just as pretty as always, you just—"

"No, not sick like that," said Claire. "But it is true that I haven't been sleeping, not since Friday. That's why I'm here. I should have come on the Saturday boat, or sent a letter, but I was scared; I don't know. I felt so bad, so guilty after they came and said you haven't heard anything from Henry, not at all, and then I told them I hadn't, either, because I promised him that, if they came looking for him. I've been so upset. I've been so cruel to you, Mrs. Coombs. I can't eat anything. I couldn't study for my arithmetic test. I slapped my sister. I've never done that before."

Claire's face was composed and she made no sound of crying, but the tears coursed down her cheeks and fell from her chin. Rachel reached across their knees with a hankie and patted Claire's face dry before she handed it to her.

"Slow down, dear girl, slow down," said Rachel. "Here, let me ask you. When did you get a letter from Henry? Was it from Camp Devens?"

"Yes," said Claire. "In Massachusetts. It came about

three weeks ago, maybe. No, yes. He had already been there a couple of weeks."

Rachel leaned back in her chair, shut her eyes, and allowed her head to come to rest against the wall. A thin smile dared to form at her mouth, and whispering *Sweet Jesus, oh Sweet Jesus* to herself she released the first of her host of fears with a soft sigh. Her immediate impulse was to get up and go straight to the cove to tell Virgil, and Walter and Ava, *Henry is there; he is safe.*

"Are you mad at me?" Claire asked. "Please don't be. It's just that I always thought that he wrote to you, too, that he must have. I know you wanted him to finish school, but I told myself you knew about Superintendent White's promise to any boy who enlisted, that he would get his diploma when he came back. I thought—"

Rachel laughed. "Mad? No, God no. I am so happy, so relieved. I am afraid that if I laugh more I will cry. You don't know how grateful I am to you for coming down here; we will all be so relieved," Rachel said. "Tell me more, please."

"I should have brought his letter," Claire lied. "It was very short. He said he was busy and doing well and passing muster, whatever that is; Sophia Greenlaw says it's good. He didn't say it in the letter, but he was worried that Virgil or Walter would come after him and find him and tell the army that he is too young; that's why I told Amos and Stevie I didn't know where he was. Do you think they will see him? Will they try to bring him home?"

"I don't know," Rachel said. She thought her smile must look a foolish grin to the girl, and she did not care. "Amos went off on his own. He told Henry he wouldn't dare to enlist and he thinks that's why Henry went. He won't try to bring him home, only to find him. Did Stevie go with him?"

"They went off in Stevie's flivver," Claire said, relieved. "Maybe as far as Bucksport. Amos looked kind of, well, kind of scared."

"Amos always looks scared, only he's not so much scared as he is shy," Rachel said. "Do you have an address for Henry?"

"No, I, it just said Camp Devens, Massachusetts, on the envelope," said Claire. "I wrote to him and that was three weeks ago and he hasn't written back and I'm worried that he's been hurt or he is sick. Sophia says a lot of the boys get sick because they are so crowded together everywhere all the time; one gets a fever and he coughs on the others and they all get it. There was meningitis."

"If he was harmed, or sick, they would have notified me," Rachel lied to allay Claire's fears. "It's a law, a federal law. If he gets real sick, they have to send him home. He'll write back soon, I'm sure; he's so sweet on you."

Claire blushed to her ears.

"Henry blushes the same way when they tease him about the little Dutch girl," said Rachel. "Only you're not so little, are you? And you are far prettier close up than I had imagined."

"Thank you," Claire said.

"And you are playing hooky," said Rachel. "Can I write you a note, a letter to someone to explain? Maggie Bowen will, if you want, I'm sure."

"No, thank you," Claire stood, and Rachel stood with her. "Father talked to Miss Parridge yesterday and she said

I could miss this morning if I was back by noon. I can be if I catch this boat. I hope you're not mad at me, Mrs. Coombs, or disappointed in me; I so hope it."

"I'm only disappointed that you don't have time to come with me over to the cove so you can see Virgil's and Walter's faces when I tell them the good news you've brought," Rachel said. "Will you promise to come back for a visit?"

"I promise." Claire held out her hand. Rachel took it and kissed her on the cheek.

"You are a rare and wonderful young woman, Claire," Rachel said.

"I'm not, though, Mrs. Coombs. I wish I was."

Chapter 9
Wars and Rumors

"It wasn't until I realized that he must have heard me call him sheepish that I understood, and then how I laughed!"

Maggie Bowen, November 23, 1917

Soon after departing Boston's North Station (they did not have to change stations as Maggie had predicted) at dawn, the train bound for Camp Devens to which Amos and Stevie and the hundreds of Maine volunteers had transferred was sidetracked outside Tewksbury to make way for an eastbound freight that took two hours to reach them and half an hour to pass. The morning was chill and damp; the smoke from the farmhouse chimneys across the fields out the car windows rose slowly, heavily, through the light sprinkle. When their train finally began to huff and grind forward to get back on the main track, Stevie and another boy clambered over the sleepers in the aisle shouting, "Wait goddamnit!" They made their way to the platform at the rear of the car, and while his companion held him by the belt, Stevie leaned down, his hand outstretched, shouting encouragement to the three boys who had detrained to forage for food and were now galloping alongside the cars with bulging burlap bags, cheered by dozens of heads that protruded from the starboard windows of the cars they passed. The foremost of the runners reached Stevie, threw his sack onto the platform, and pulled himself up on Stevie's proffered hand; the second, breathing through a gaping mouth, handed Stevie his bag and was helped aboard, to lie on the urine-fouled platform gasping for air. As the train gained speed, the third forager fell back and was pulled aboard the car behind theirs.

Sweating and still breathing heavily, the foragers waited for the aisle to be cleared of sleepers, then deposited their sacks on the floor in the middle of the car; with high ceremony they took turns displaying their plundered treasures one by one—a smoked ham, a side of bacon, loaves of bread, giant farm sausages, a bag of badly bruised pickled eggs, a bundle of cigars bound with a blue ribbon—to the oohs and aahs and applause of the hungry and hung-over campaigners.

"That was damned decent of you, Stevie," Amos said. "They wouldn'tve made it without you reaching like that."

"Decent, hell," Stevie said. "That tall one owes me six bits from cards. If he hadn't made it, I wouldn'tve got paid, and you wouldn't be looking forward to six bits' worth of breakfast right now."

"Ah," said Amos. "I sure as hell could eat. I need to stretch, Christ, I been balled up and buried under boys for it seems like days. At least we're moving again."

But their train never regained its speed. It rolled cautiously west, crept past the Lowell mills, and in open farmland continued its reluctant progress. In midafternoon, in a gentle steady rain, they were sidetracked again, brought to a slow, groaning halt for no apparent reason. To the south of the side track on which they sat, out the port windows, was a wide pond, more a marsh, by which lay a muddy crossroad with a sign pointing away to Pingryville. Out the starboard windows, where those boys who were still awake after the morning feast had gathered, was the road to Camp Devens, recently widened, graded, and routed north of the town of Ayer to the new cantonment. In an amazed silence, a quiet awe interrupted only by an occasional belch or hack from a cigar smoker, the men from Maine watched a flow of truck and wagon traffic the likes of which none of them, or probably anyone else anywhere in America, one proclaimed, had ever seen. Going west toward Camp Devens were outsized lumber wagons drawn by mule teams of six and eight, other wagons loaded with barrels of nails, trucks moving at a mule's pace laden with spools of black wire, open trucks crowded with laborers, wagonloads of windows and doors, all moving past the motionless troop train in what seemed an endless stream of conveyances of all kinds not ten feet apart, with no end in sight in either direction. From west to east, headed back toward Boston Harbor and the train terminals, crept an equally steady flow of empty wagons and trucks, among them empty food delivery trucks returning to the city to be resupplied.

"Somebody's making himself a shitload of money," said one of the sleepy spectators.

"And it's only just started."

"More than one person is," said another.

"It's a miracle of Yankee ingenuity," said a fellow whose

cigar smoke brought tears to his own eyes. “They started on bare ground in late July, and by the end of this month they’ll be able to accommodate twenty thousand troops. I read about it in the *Herald*.”

Those listening to the young smoker deduced that his *Herald* was the Portland newspaper, as his speech was infected with a slight Massachusetts accent.

“Nearly ten thousand laborers, if I remember correctly,” he said. “The vast majority from Boston, I’ll wager.”

“Look there, professor,” said a thin blond boy, pointing. “The truck behind that hay wagon. Those fellows are Negroes; I can see their black faces.”

“You sound as though you’ve never seen a dark-skinned person before,” sneered the Portland man.

“No, I haven’t,” the blond boy said. “What do you expect? There isn’t any where I come from; it’s the same with most of us here. Not only is that the first one I ever saw, but it’s a whole truckload of them for Christ’s sake.”

“And one of them’s driving,” said a boy in coveralls. “I never would’ve thought a nigger could drive a truck.”

“Shut up, farmer,” said another blond boy. “You make me sick. Shut the fuck up.”

The little green depot named AYER and the houses at the edge of town behind it were still and dimly lit, drawing shades and closing up at the end of the day. Five minutes down the line, the train pulled into a station so new that it had yet to be named, so brightly lit by electric bulbs that the boys who stared out of the car windows squinted as if they were staring into the morning sun. The station platform was crowded with men in overalls, many seated with their backs against the station house walls, many with their feet dangling from the platform, all with weary postures and each with a dinner pail in his lap or at his feet. Behind the station and to either side scores more of the day-shift laborers gathered around concession stands and wagons or sat on the ground in clusters eating, all waiting for the eastbound train, none looking up or over a shoulder at the train that had just arrived. An open motorcar with a soldier in the driver's seat and two in the rear idled at the end of an open space on which were painted parallel white lines. Every surface, every wall of the station, and every billboard and signpost in sight was covered with numbered lists in black letters, illuminated by floodlights and titled in bold, underlined red: POST DIRECTORY, VISITOR INSTRUCTIONS, GENERAL ORDERS, CIVILIAN OFFICES, UNIT HEADQUARTERS, CHAIN OF COMMAND, and FRIENDLY SUGGESTIONS.

Amos nudged Stevie and nodded toward an approaching file of soldiers rigid in campaign hats, puttees, and faded but crisp uniforms. The file marched onto the open space, stopped amid the white lines, turned in unison to face the train cars, then dispersed to greet the wide-eyed recruits. The leading soldier, who had looked directly at Amos's window when standing in line with the others, moved to the far side to stand alone, hands behind his back, feet apart at shoulder width, a thin, bemused smile on his face.

While the volunteers fumbled with their jackets, hats, suitcases, and bags, struggling to comply with the shouting sergeant who wanted them to "unass the train and fall the hell in on the lines," a mocking voice among the laborers at the beer concession wagon sang, "You're in the army now / You're not behind the plow / You'll never get rich digging a ditch—" until he was silenced abruptly. As the train car emptied, Stevie made his way through the detritus in the aisle back to the seat in front of Amos, and with him watched as the volunteers were lined up, straightened out, turned to the right—"I said *right!*"—and marched, one formation after the other, up the well lighted road past the large sign that heralded the MAIN GATE.

While the last of the groups was forming up and learning from a stocky sergeant with a shrill voice that they were nothing but a bunch of sorry-ass, rednecked, bug-titted, peckerwood sons of bitches, the brakeman signaled the engineer with a waving lantern to move ahead and make way for the eastbound, and Stevie tugged on Amos's shirtsleeve to lead him off the train and onto solid ground. With Amos close behind, he skirted a milling group of laborers and approached the soldier who stood alone at ease at the edge of the lined ground.

"Excuse me, sir," Stevie said.

"Don't call me sir." The soldier pointed at the chevrons on his sleeve. "I work for a living. You want sirs, you'll find them settin' in the back of that touring car over there."

"What do I call you, then?" Stevie wanted to know.

"You call me sergeant," the man said. "And you'd best take my free advice and catch up with the others or there's gonna be hell to pay when you get inside, hell from another sergeant."

"We're not volunteers, or draftees, either," said Stevie. "You're from Maine."

"I know it," the sergeant said. "You, too. Whereabouts?"

"Stonington, on Deer Island," Stevie said. "And you?"

"I'm from Jonesport," said the sergeant. "What can I do for you?"

"We've come to find my friend, his kin, a guy named Henry Coombs," Stevie explained. "Do you know him? Where we can find him?"

The sergeant laughed. "There's maybe twenty thousand men in there, all wearin' the same clothes, livin' in a thousand tents and barracks houses. I couldn't tell one from the other, and I wouldn't want to try."

"Well," Stevie said. "We'll have to go in and look for ourselves, I guess. We'll know him when we see him."

The sergeant laughed again. "You try and walk in there and you'll either get yourself shot or get clubbed over the head and locked up."

Amos gripped Stevie's elbow.

"How do we find him, then?" Stevie pried Amos's hand from his elbow to restore the flow of blood to his forearm.

"You wait till zero-six-hundred tomorrow and you present yourselves to the military policemen at the main gate and you apply for a visitor's pass, is what you do."

"Till when?"

"Six A.M.," said the sergeant. "And if you're wise, you'll find someplace far away from the guard mounts around the camp tonight, lest you get mistaken for the enemy and get a bayonet thrust up your ass by a nervous recruit."

Amos took hold of Stevie's elbow again, and this time the sergeant saw it. "Tell you what," he said. "There's an abandoned barn up that old sand road about half a mile. If

I was you, I'd get me some sandwiches from one of these criminals who call themselves concessionaires and maybe a jug, too, and spend the night in the loft up there. You can see the whole east side of the camp, and it's all lit up at night while they work on the new barracks. It's quite a scene. They got a steam shovel that's two stories tall."

"Thank you." Stevie removed Amos's hand again.

"Can he talk?" The sergeant nodded at Amos.

"I can talk," Amos said.

"You fellows look pretty rugged to me; why don't you enlist and find your friend that way? Where are you from?" he asked Amos.

"You never heard of it," Amos said. "Barter Island. It's a ways—"

"Now I have," the sergeant said. "You'd be surprised how much I've learned about the geography and customs of my native New England in the last few months. They come from everywhere—some not even from a place, but only from near a place. Christ, there was one that came through here last week that wore his trouser cuffs tucked into his boot socks."

"Goddamned hayseed." Amos shook his head.

"I know it," said the sergeant.

Wrapped in a blanket and buried to his shoulders in the dusty hay of the barn loft, Amos stretched his legs, relishing the room, and fell asleep to the cadence of Stevie's inexhaustible voice speculating about the glories of army life. When Amos awoke, he sneezed and sneezed; standing at the edge of the open loft in the half-light of early dawn he watched his arc of steaming pee as it cascaded to the ground below. It had been a cold and clear night; the scrub oak and pine on the slope below the barn glittered with frozen droplets of yesterday's rain. As Amos buttoned up, Stevie stepped up next to him and began his own arc, talking as if he, like the men at work on the barracks in the distance, had never stopped all night long.

"Hear that?" he said, still peeing. "That's reveille, to wake everybody up. Doesn't that sound some sweet?"

"We ought to get going," Amos said. "He said be there at six. We've got to shake our clothes out good. I'd hate like hell to have pieces of hay or, worse, seeds stuck to me when we see the guy about getting that pass. Though Henry might find it comical."

At the bottom of the hill below the barn, the sandy road converged with a graded dirt road that skirted the train depot and beyond the depot joined the road to the main gate. They crossed the road behind two officers on horseback and fell in a hundred feet to the rear of a group of soldiers walking toward the wide gate over which arched a sign that said CAMP DEVENS. One car passed them, then another; as each entered, the guards at the gate slapped to present arms, their rifles oiled and bayonets polished. The guards stopped the soldiers on foot ahead of Amos and Stevie and examined their passes before waving them through. To the right of the gate stood a small building that Amos thought looked like the island post office. A small American flag flew over the near door, marked VISITORS; a soldier wearing white gloves and white puttees sat smoking in a wooden chair before a second door, which read MILITARY POLICE.

Amos caught Stevie by the arm as he approached the visitors' door. "It's five minutes till," he said. "We ought to wake till six like he said."

"For Christ's sake," said Stevie.

The two guards at the gate stopped a coughing and shuddering Model T truck loaded so full with wooden crates that it rode on flattened springs. One guard stood with his Springfield at port arms before the steaming radiator to block the truck's entrance; the other accosted the driver, asking him what the hell he had aboard and why he was using the main gate, who the hell did he think he was. While the driver explained in a thick Irish accent that he was carrying scouring powder, God forbid, he also fiddled with the needle valve, trying to keep the truck from stalling, which it wanted badly to do.

"You got to use Gate Three for the quartermaster," the guard said. "Turn this heap around and go back down to the main road and take a right. You'll see it."

When the driver backed off the road onto the shoulder, the truck wheezed once, coughed, and died. Defaming the mother of God and under his breath the mother of the guard who'd turned him around, the driver dismounted and opened the bonnet to lean inside.

"Fuel line's clogged," Stevie told Amos as they mounted the steps to the visitors' door.

The soldier behind the wide desk inside the door wore his hair parted in the middle and liberally oiled, along with a pair of wire-rimmed spectacles that a banker might prefer. He looked up at Stevie, and Amos behind him, then back down at the paperwork in front of him as if he had seen no one.

Stevie approached the desk and cleared his throat. The soldier looked up and scratched the end of his pimply nose.

"We'd like to get a visitor's pass to go in and see a friend of ours, his relation," Stevie said as he motioned to Amos to step ahead to the desk. "I'm Steve Robbins, this is Amos Coombs, and the guy we want to see is Henry Coombs, if he used his real name. We should be able to find him without much problem, if we can just—"

The soldier hooked a thumb over his shoulder at the chart on the wall behind him. "Read the instructions, if you can," he said. "You're lucky it's a Tuesday, with visiting hours, but not until nineteen-hundred and not without a letter of introduction and his unit designation and building number so I can get word to him and he can meet you at the reception area."

"We don't have a letter and we don't know any of that other stuff," said Stevie, who hoped the man would be reasonable.

Outside, a hatless soldier volunteer cranked the Irishman's truck while he fussed with the throttle and needle valve. It caught and died, caught and died.

"Then I can't help you," said the soldier, who seemed relieved.

"Come on, pal," Stevie began.

"Don't call me pal."

"All right then." Stevie's voice rose a little. "How about this. How about just one of us, you can choose which one, goes in there and walks around without getting in anybody's way until he finds Henry, chats with him a second, then comes out and we go home. We want to know he's here, that's all."

"Jesus Christ, you don't understand do you?" The soldier rose behind the desk. "This is government property. This is a United States Army post. There is a war on. There are twenty-five thousand American fighting men in there. They are training with rifles, bayonets, grenades, mortars, and the like. You could be a spy. You can't just waltz in there and snoop around in every corner wherever you damned well please. The army shoots spies. You could be a saboteur."

"Well, you don't have to worry about that last part," Amos said. "We can't be saboteurs; we don't even know what one is."

"Holy shit!" cried the soldier. "What am I dealing with here? What the hell is that noise out there?" He strode to the window to look out at the groaning truck.

"His fuel line's clogged, probably in the sediment bulb," Stevie said. "I'll take care of it, if you'll let one of us—"

"You better get the hell out of here right now, both of you." The soldier's voice was as cold and flat as iron.

"Look," Amos pleaded. "It's because his mother is worried about him. If she knew he was here and safe and not drowned, she could rest. All we want—"

The soldier jabbed his finger toward Amos. "Fuck his mother," he said.

Amos reached out with his right hand, caught the soldier by his shirtfront, and in a quick sweeping movement lifted him two feet off the ground and slammed him against the INSTRUCTIONS FOR VISITORS wall with such force that his spectacles flew off and his boot toes struck the side of his desk.

"What the hell?" asked a deep voice in the office behind the soldier's desk. "Corporal Bibbs?"

An officer with two silver bars on each shoulder, a cigarette in one hand, and a fountain pen in the other appeared in the doorway and stared in disbelief at his corporal, who was held pinned and twitching against the wall by a large red-faced man whose name, the captain thought, must certainly be Barnacle Bill. He tried not to smile and asked Amos to please put the corporal down and explain himself.

Amos let the corporal down and brushed his shirtfront smooth; Stevie picked up his spectacles and handed them to him.

"This son of a bitch just assaulted me sir," the corporal said. "I'm calling the MPs."

Outside the window the truck choked and grunted and gasped as if it was being strangled, something that Captain Weller had often wanted to do to Corporal Bibbs.

"I can see what's happened," Captain Weller said quietly. "I want to know why, and I asked this man." He faced Amos, who took a step backward, then explained why they had come and why they had been denied access, as best he could.

"You just want to see him and say hello, so his mother doesn't worry?" the captain asked. "You came from Maine to do that? Did you tell the corporal that, no, wait, you did, and he said something about the boy's mother, am I right?"

Amos nodded yes.

"Well then." Captain Weller smiled and stubbed his cigarette in the corporal's ashtray. "Then we have two options here, as I see it. Since you don't know what unit or building he is in and you're not even sure of his name, we can shut the whole camp down for the day, line up every man jack in the place, and let you fellows walk down the line, find the boy, chat with him, and then be on your way." Captain Weller took a deep breath. "Or one of you can get inside by stepping across the street here and signing the enlistment papers. Once you're inside you would find him eventually and could telegram his mother that all is well."

Stevie and Amos just stared. The corporal lit a cigarette and glared at his captain.

"The first option, shutting the camp down, is of course not really an option at all, unless you can get President Wilson to agree to put the war on hold for a day," Captain Weller admitted. "That leaves . . ."

Stevie turned to Amos. "Will you take the flivver down to the island with you and keep it under cover when you're not using it?"

Amos nodded.

"Then I'm your man," Stevie said. "Amos here is married with a kid and he has to stay home. I've had enlisting on my mind anyway."

"Good on you," said the captain. "Corporal Bibbs will be honored to escort you over to S-One."

"One thing," said Stevie. "Let me fix that damned truck out there first, before that driver kills somebody or Corporal Bibbs here gets driven out of his mind. It'll only take a minute to get it going right."

"If you can get that truck going, and then sign the papers, I can guarantee you a job as a driver or a mechanic, or both, if you'd like that," Captain Weller said.

"I'd like that very much," said Stevie.

At the truck, while the corporal and captain watched

from the doorway, Stevie tapped the cranking soldier on the back and dismissed him; he beckoned to the driver to join him under the bonnet, and began to roll up his sleeves.

"Look for a baseball game, Stevie," Amos said. "You find a baseball game and you'll find Henry; he'll either be watching it or playing in it, pitching probably."

"Tell Rachel I'll let her know as soon as I find him," Stevie said.

Amos shook Stevie's hand, slung his seabag over his shoulder, nodded to the captain, and started down the road toward the train depot.

"Hand me that wrench," Stevie told the Irishman.

WESTERN UNION TELEGRAM
Ayer, Mass. November 21, 1917
Mrs. Amos Coombs, Barter Island, Maine
AT CAMP DEVENS STOP ARMY NOT COOPERATING STOP STEVIE ENLISTED STOP HE WILL FIND HENRY CONTACT RACHEL STOP I AM NO HELP HERE STOP COMING HOME END
Amos

WESTERN UNION TELEGRAM
Ayer, Mass. November 21, 1917
Miss Maggie Bowen, Barter Island, Maine
BAA BAA BAA END
Amos

In the anteroom of the Barter Island schoolhouse Rachel pushed the door shut with her bottom, shook the melting sleet from her shawl, and hung up her coat. The Clean Up

Committee for the School Board's Founding Fathers' Feast was meant to arrive at eight; though she was early, Rachel heard voices in quiet conversation in the main room and entered to find Tessie Wedge overseeing the Reverend Sharpesdale as he knelt to kindle the fire in the schoolhouse stove. Tessie wished Rachel good morning in an uncommonly pleasant voice, then tied her apron strings and, with hands on her hips for emphasis, surveyed the aftermath of the feast with a grand sigh.

The Reverend Sharpesdale shut the stove door and stood, brushing his hands together.

"Good morning Rachel," he said. "You must be frozen. Did you walk the whole way? That sleet—listen to it on the windows; it sounds like someone is throwing rice or shot pellets by the handful—is blowing almost horizontal. It's 'a tempestuous wind down from the land.' Come warm yourself; I've left the vent wide open."

"I'm surprised Virgil, or Amos, didn't carry you over in that flivver that Amos brought back," said Tessie.

Rachel laughed. "I feel much safer walking. With either of them driving that thing, I probably wouldn't have gotten here until noon."

"I do hope Amos will take care with that dreadful machine," the reverend said with a familiar glance at Tessie to show that he was speaking for her. "I hope he doesn't drive it through town, and if he does, he will show proper restraint. And we hope, too, that he will paint over the lewd slogans on the doors."

"I don't think he intends to drive it at all," Rachel said to Tessie. "He's afraid of it, afraid of it breaking down or of doing serious harm to it. He barely got it down here from Bucksport. They're building a lean-to off the barn for it as we speak."

"That machine is an abomination," Tessie said with some relish. "Gladys never would have permitted them to keep it in the cove."

"I hear it took him six days to get it to Stonington," the reverend said. "I'll bet he rested on the seventh."

Tessie said *Hah Hah* and the Reverend's face fell when he realized that he had not only made a lame joke, but also likened Amos Coombs to the Almighty.

"Look at this mess," said Tessie. "Dottie said she counted fifty-six people. Looking at this mess, you'd think most of them were children. Still, it was a grand success, and much of the credit goes to Miss Bowen. All that preparation and Clytie sick, too. Mercy."

They agreed that they would shake out the tablecloths before they bundled them for the laundress, and that they should sweep the room before they did anything further.

"I've asked Cyrus to mop the floor after we're done," Tessie said.

Rachel chafed her hands over the warming stove and shivered slightly.

"And he will carry you home when he takes us," Tessie added. "The surrey is closed in."

While Tessie and the reverend, who was in shirtsleeves now, wrestled with the tablecloths, Rachel lit the wall lamps against the dark, blowing cold and began to sweep up the debris, thinking that Miss Tessie was in a pleasant mood this morning, and seemed almost, well, cozy, with the reverend.

The removal of the tablecloths revealed that the seven long tables on which the Thanksgiving feast had groaned were wide planks spread across sawhorses, which the reverend observed were probably much like the table that the first feast was served on.

The door opened and Cecil Barter's pale head appeared. His lips were blue, and a drop of liquid hung from the tip of his nose. When he had surveyed the room, he pushed the door open to reveal his mother standing behind him removing her mittens. Mother and child smiled happily with their mouths; with their cold blue eyes, they scanned the three who greeted them for weaknesses, and the work in progress for the easiest tasks.

"You see, she's not here," said Cecilia. With her hand in the small of his back, she pushed Cecil into the room and up to the others to say good morning and shake hands. "He was worried that Miss Bowen would be here," she explained. "You know how he feels about her, how most of them do. I told him that her sister has the grippe that he had last week and that Miss Bowen would probably stay home with her, rather than come all this way in the sleet and rain, when others, like us, could do the cleaning up."

"She wanted to come," said Miss Tessie. "I insisted that she stay at home with Clytie and Leah."

Cecilia nudged her son toward the sandbox and watched as Rachel and the reverend carried one of the planks out the door.

"She's trying to win Leah away from her mother by spoiling her," Cecilia said. "At home and at school."

"Take the other end of this," Miss Tessie said.

They worked in pairs, one pair going out the door with a plank while the other came back in. Outside, they leaned the planks against the building on the lee side, and as they worked Cecilia talked, sometimes aloud, sometimes in a whisper, depending on how close Rachel was, and the reverend hummed Tessie's favorite: "Beulah Land."

Though she did not hear any of Tessie's replies, Rachel heard enough of Cecilia's comments to know that the subject was Maggie and that the matter was the same one Walter had reported overhearing in the store. The more Rachel overheard as the pairs passed each other—"Dottie thinks it must have been a man"; "The rules for teachers are strict but fair"; "Suspicious politics"—the more she thought that Cecilia meant her to hear, and the angrier she became, until she could feel hear earlobes burning.

"Nathaniel, please," Tessie said in the doorway. "If you must hum, make it something pleasant, something that's not apocalyptic."

"But it's your . . ." began the reverend, but stopped when he and Tessie realized that she had used his first name in front of others and used it in the same coy, teasing tone that she used when they were alone. Rachel turned aside and raised her eyebrows; Cecilia looked at the floor and kept marching.

The last plank removed, the four rested on the sawhorses before moving them. Simmering from exertion and indignation, Rachel waited until Cecilia finished fussing with her boy then counted to ten, crossed her arms over her chest, and said:

"I want you to know, Mrs. Barter, that in the past twenty minutes and the past few days I have heard enough of your innuendos, your vicious gossip, your sniveling suspicions, your whispered lies about my friend to demand that you either confront her with them in the open or shut the hell up, excuse me Reverend." Rachel's voice was hard, determined, cold; her hands rested peacefully in her apron pocket.

"Well," said Cecilia, puffing up and stealing a glance to Tessie.

"I don't know who your source is, I doubt you do, nor do I know why anyone would inquire about Maggie's behavior in Bangor." Rachel looked at Tessie. "But I do know that what you are spreading is hearsay, so much manure. I also know that Maggie Bowen was not dismissed from the Center Street School. She did not apply for a second year because she thought the principal a mean-spirited busybody—a loveless, cheerless, man-hating virago who cared not a whit for children. Maggie applied for this job because she missed the island, God knows why."

"Please," the reverend said, holding up his hands.

Cecilia's face was alive with anger, and alight with the joy of battle. "I do not deserve your contempt, Rachel Coombs," she said. "I have only the well-being of the island school in mind."

"You *do* deserve my contempt," Rachel said. "And you are lying—you have only the pleasure of hurting a beautiful and successful young woman in mind."

"That's enough, Rachel, please," said the reverend. "Let's put the matter to rest and finish our task here. Tessie?"

"Yes," Tessie said. "There's been enough talk, Cecilia. Enough whispering. It's in part my fault. I will go to see

Maggie and tell her what I've heard and hear her side of the story. There's no need to be unseemly, Rachel."

Rachel lifted a sawhorse and carried it out the door. The reverend followed her with another, and the schoolroom was silent except for the engine noise that Cecil made with flapping lips as he pushed a little wooden model motorcar around and around and around in the sand.

Tessie moved a desk against the north wall and stepped up onto the seat. She waited until Rachel had done the same at the far end of the wall, then together they unpinned the ends of a paper chain of orange and brown links, coiling both ends as they moved their desks toward the middle to gather the entire delicate chain. Rachel held her arm out, and Tessie, with care, slipped her coils onto it.

"Tell me about Little John," Tessie said. "I'll bet he's gained weight since I saw him last month. I really should visit more often."

"He has big fat pink cheeks, a tiny chin, and he's all over as chunky a baby boy as ever you've seen," Rachel said.

The reverend carried the sheaths of cornstalks outside into the alders, humming the appropriate hymn. Cecilia unpinned and rolled up the mural depicting the original feast. She noticed now, as she had not the night before, that one of the founding mothers looked a hell of a lot like old Huldah on Burnt Island; another wore her white hair short beneath her bonnet as Cecilia did, and like Cecilia she was unnaturally broad abeam. Cecilia hushed her flatulent son and strained to hear Rachel and Tessie across the room, but she could not.

"I suppose you get up to Gladys's house—I mean

Virgil's—quite often now that the cannery is closed," Tessie said. *Especially when Walter and Ava aren't around.*

"Not to Virgil's house, no," Rachel said. She kept her hands busy taking down and stacking student drawings of *Mayflowers*, pumpkins, and turkeys. "Very rarely. Ava keeps his house clean and most of the time the baby is at Ava's. She does some of Virgil's laundry, though he still does his own shirts. With the men building and handlining and skinning and salting codfish, Ava does just about everything else. I help her out sometimes in the afternoons or sit with Little John while he's napping." *He banked my house all around, and he did it with such care.*

"It's so nice that Virgil has you, and Ava, to help him out with the baby," Tessie said. "I know that when Gladys looks down upon her child, she is grateful to you." *And she* knows, *and you know she does.*

Rachel took down a life-sized Pilgrim's hat made of several pieces of black and gray construction paper cut and pasted together, complete with silver buckle. She held it before her and showed it to Tessie and the others.

"Now *that* is wicked clever," she said. "Can you guess whose initials are on the back? Just who might C. B. be?"

She gave the paper hat to Cecil, who sat on a desk next to the stove. He accepted it without looking at it, or at Rachel.

"That's very nice work, Cecil," the reverend said.

Cecil did not reply. He opened the door of the stove, slipped the hat in, and watched it curl, then burst into flames.

"Cecil!" his mother said.

"What?"

Sunday evening
November 31, 1917
Dear Ruth,

I am late answering your last letter (yes, please do send the two suffrage articles) because poor Clytie has been down with the grippe and I have been caring for the house and her. Four of my students were out sick this week, poor Leah one of them; I'm surprised there weren't more with all the sneezing and coughing. I tried to get them outside in the wholesome air more often, but doubt that it helped much. Leah brought it home and gave it to her mother, who is only now beginning to recover. Of the females in this house, I alone have escaped. As did Amos, and the Coombses in the cove, whom Walter says are too "ordinary" to be chosen by some germ. I plan to go to school tomorrow and leave Clytie at home; she is sitting up now, though still peaked, and Amos will be in and out, he says.

Yesterday Amos brought the flivver down and took me and Leah for a spin up the road to the farm and back. It's a noisy, smelly, uncomfortable machine, more a jury-rigged collection of parts held together by baling wire than an auto, but it goes fast and Amos is a regular Tartar behind the wheel. Leah was scared to death at first, riding in the kitchen chair bolted upright in the back, but by the time we got to the Needle's Eye she was squealing with delight. Amos says there has still been no word from Stevie Robbins, but as I think I told you, Rachel had a postcard from Henry who says he is fine and hopes to get home on furlough in a month or so. We all hope that he and Stevie will find one another soon in that vast cantonment, if they haven't already.

This afternoon Rachel came to look in on Clytie and bring us one of her famous custards. While Leah and Clytie napped, she sat me down at the kitchen table and told me that Cecilia Barter has been spreading a rumor around about me, and that she, Rachel, gave Cecilia a piece of her mind for it on Friday. It seems that a "librarian" friend of Tessie Wedge's in Bangor (Helen Hingham? I doubt that.) told Tessie that I was dismissed from Center Street School for "behavior unbecoming a schoolteacher." The "behavior" is unspecified of course, to the delight of the island biddies who are casting stones, and to the absolute outrage of Rachel and Ava, who would be happy to do battle with Cecilia and Tessie. It is all too much fun to be concerned about. I would love to hear some of the speculation, and how close to the truth any of them has come. I am not worried, nor should you be: Only Dr. Douglass knows (and you and Rachel) and I have complete faith in his discretion.

Ava blames Tessie for starting it. I am tempted to confess to one of the island ladies that I was moonlighting as a prostitute in Bangor and eventually had to give up schoolteaching because I just could not find the time between assignations to correct themes.

It's late and I am tired. The sea is making up outside the harbor, the wind is northerly and cold. Sleep well my dear.

Love, Maggie

Part Two

1918

"I had a little bird
And his name was Enza.
I opened the window
And in flew Enza."

Children's song, 1918

Chapter 10
Easter Morning

"I never appreciated how nice it was waking up to the sound of that hermit thrush in the woods behind the house, not until now."

Henry Coombs, aka Corporal John Clair
April 17, 1918

Walter had been right when he had predicted back in the fall that the winter offshore would be a severe one. On the first day of December, as though scheduled, the blowing November sleet and drizzle abated, the skies cleared, the stars sucked up the warmth from the island, and in the morning the Arctic Mist rose from the surface of the sea in vague tendrils into the bitterly cold air until the sun climbed high enough to burn it away. Those who had banked their houses with spruce boughs in hopes of an early and lasting snow cover for insulation got none before Christmas. The pond froze smooth and black as shiny coal, so thick that the skaters could build bonfires on the surface. Ava's well, which was tightly covered and deep, froze so thick on the surface that she had to bombard it with a sash weight on a clothesline to break through. Pumps froze. Apples packed in sawdust in the deepest granite cellars froze. When

Maggie banished Cecil Barter to the far corner of the schoolroom for terrorizing Vince Coleman, Cecil was far enough from the stove that the diaphanous drop on the end of his nose froze. Trees cracked and split at night, and even in the day trees in the shaded forest snapped like pistol reports. When the tide was in, the salt water froze in the shallows; when the tide receded, it left behind pale salty skirts of ice, inches thick and yards wide. On the ninth of December, Tessie Wedge came to the schoolhouse at the end of the day to tell Maggie that she had received that morning a letter from her librarian friend in Bangor corroborating all that Rachel had said about the principal of the Center Street School and Maggie's reasons for leaving. Tessie and Maggie sat in front of the long stove whose door glowed red, their knees nearly touching. Tessie told Maggie that she had been mistaken to mention what she had heard from her friend to certain people in the first place, and that she would do her best to stifle further talk, though Maggie must know that it would continue as long as people were petty and confined to their kitchens by the bitter cold.

A few days before Christmas, Rachel received a long letter from Henry that she read aloud in the kitchen to Ava, Walter, and Virgil. Henry said that he had temporarily changed his name to John Clair and explained why, to no one's surprise. He said that he would not be home for the holidays as he had hoped, but that he and two friends (one from Boston who had Heine Wagner's autograph) would be spending Christmas Eve and Day with a family in Ayer. He said that Claire had written him about Amos and Stevie's visit, and Stevie's enlistment; he added that he wished he had seen them, and that he had not seen or heard of Stevie yet. He closed tenderly, saying that he missed his mother and family and the cove and he hoped that none of those things would change, ever, at all—would be just the same when he came home as they were when he left.

"He can be sure of that," said Ava. "Things down here won't change, but he will."

"John for his father," Walter said. "And Clair for the little Dutch girl. That's kind of foolish."

"It is not," Ava said. "I think it's sweet, and so do you."

The hard, dry cold persisted into January, freezing the coves first, then the harbors, and finally the thorofares between Barter and Kimball's Islands, and Barter and Burnt Islands. Virgil and Walter worried that the frozen surface of the sea would drag their moorings out with it when it shifted; Amos worried that the frozen Burnt Island thorofare would tempt Huldah to walk across to Barter Island in the night for secret ceremonies and spells. The mail boat could not get in to the town landing, so she put in at Point Lookout until the middle of January when the sky was alive and dancing with the Northern Lights every night; by the third week, the seven miles of sea between Stonington and Barter Island had frozen, so for three days running Tessie's man Cyrus and two others pulled a sled across the sea ice to fetch the mail and bring it down to the island. One of the deliveries included a broadside from the War Department asking all citizens to observe "wheatless Mondays and Wednesdays, meatless Tuesdays, and porkless Thursdays and Saturdays." When Cecilia posted the message in the store, Walter observed that there was no reason for alarm because there was no call for fishless Fridays or fishless any days.

Behind schedule because of the deep cold, the January thaw did not come until the first week in February. The thaw raised the temperature fifty degrees in as many hours to make amends for being tardy. The little man in Ava's weather house swung outside and stayed there. The sea ice groaned all night long. Maggie's students began to sneeze and honk into their hankies. Irville's arthritis got so bad so quickly that he could not rise from the chair by the stove in the store and had to be carried home in it, cursing the four schoolboys who bore him. Clytie's tender feet and hips throbbed with pain, even though she kept her feet elevated all day long and at night slept on her back, snoring like a seal.

The wind backed around from the southwest to the southeast and carried with it incessant rain from the central Atlantic, rain steady and heavy with salt. The granite shores were gray, the sky was gray, the sea was gray, the trees were gray; out of doors that month on Barter Island seven miles out in the gray sea, the only color anyone in the cove beheld was the dull yellow gold of the kerosene lamp in Rachel's front window.

"Thirty-three degrees and raining," Walter said. "What could be more miserable than thirty-three and raining?"

To answer Walter, the wind shifted to the north, driving straight down on the island from the icy Atlantic provinces. From the north it brought cold, and every tree branch, boat deck, rooftop, road puddle, buoy bundle was covered with a thin layer of ice. The wind shifted to the northeast and brought more rain, then at dusk shifted back to the north to freeze the new layer, and then do the same to another, until every exposed surface on the island was slick with a good inch of clear ice. Limbs broke under the weight and fell in crystalline explosions on the road. The gutter on the back side of Sarah Boyer's cottage grew so heavy with ice that it collapsed and fell on her cat Curtis, killing him instantly. Tessie Wedge's dour maid fell on the way to the outhouse and broke her wrist. On the afternoon that Clytie all alone slipped on the porch and sat smack down on her ample bum and tailbone, the ice on the roads and walks was so dangerous that Maggie and Leah spent the night in town, and Amos used it as an excuse to stay with Virgil in the cove, leaving Clytie alone to cry herself to sleep, lying on her side on the davenport in the parlor.

Not until April did the cold and wet weather begin its retreat out to the open Atlantic. The little man withdrew into Ava's weather house, and though she did not quite emerge, the little girl appeared in the doorway in anticipation of spring. An ad in the corner of the *Deer Isle Messenger* invited young men of Deer Isle, Stonington, and environs to attend the first practices of the Quarrymen in Stonington and the Mariners in Deer Isle, weather permitting. Walter began negotiations with Dane Stevens for the use of Dane's ox to winch the boat cradles down to the water. With an old sail, Ava and Rachel rigged up a windbreak between the houses so Little John could play and nap in the sunshine. Without telling Clytie, who was not so much crabby now as she was sickly and sour, Maggie ordered a pretty white Easter dress for Leah from the Sears catalog—one with a fancy silk ribbon running through loops of lace to form a large bow in front. The Reverend Sharpesdale announced in church that the Barter Island Rebekahs would henceforth meet every Tuesday and Thursday evening at seven to assemble Easter packages and May baskets for the boys in uniform. Amos and Virgil rode the mail boat to Stonington to buy a barrel of tar for their buoy lines and a ham for Easter dinner, a trip that was as certain a sign of spring as were the fiddleheads and skunk cabbage leaves unfurling in the marsh.

On Easter Sunday morning Maggie and Leah picked up Rachel at the top of the cove road, and the three rode to church, their Easter dresses overflowing both sides of the wagon seat. Rachel predicted that the warm haze that softened the sunlight in the open stretches of road would surely burn off within the hour.

"I thought Clytie was going to come to church this year," Rachel said. "I thought she said she promised the reverend that she would."

"She has to stay home to cook the Easter dinner, the cake, and the ham." Leah sat motionless and upright between her aunts, afraid to move lest she disturb the sash on her new dress or dislodge the bonnet her mother had made for her and pinned just so to her hair before they left.

"I hoped she would come," Maggie said. "It would do her good to get out and get even a little exercise. She says her feet hurt her so badly that she couldn't walk into church without suffering. Her legs, too, which are still quite swollen, poor girl."

"This will be the first time I've seen you in church

down here for, what is it, six years. Did you go to church in Bangor?"

"I did on Easter," Maggie said. "I love Easter service. Clytie said last night that I'm a hypocrite to go to church only on Easter because I once said that I don't believe in the resurrection. We were chopping cabbage."

"I do," Rachel said.

"I don't buy the literal, physical resurrection that Paul insists on, and when I told Clytie that, told her that I believe in it as figurative or symbolic, she got mad," Maggie explained. "What could be more beautiful, more sacred, than the rebirth of the world in the spring, the sudden abundance of life after . . ."

Leah, who had heard the conversation the night before, sighed as her mother had done. "We shouldn't call it sauerkraut anymore," she said, echoing Clytie the night before. "Because that's German and we hate the Germans. We only eat it because it was Grandfather's favorite for Easter dinner. We probably shouldn't, but we love Grandfather more than we hate the Germans."

Maggie pointed to a carpet of purple trillium in the shade at the side of the road. "Do you see?" she asked Rachel.

Rachel nodded and shielded her eyes from the direct sunlight as the road curved around the northern end of the island and turned south toward town. On the western side of the island, the haze had either burned off or been dispersed by the southwesterly wind, and in the sun they could see south across the bay as far as Brimstone and Saddleback Ledge. Maggie squinted and relished the feel of warmth on her cheeks. When she had gone to Easter services while in Bangor—twice with Richard, who was an atheist—she was reminded of the smell of sauerkraut in the morning kitchen at home, and of vinegar from dyeing eggs the night before.

"I had a letter from Ruth Friday," Maggie said, slapping the mare's haunches with the reins. "She said that the Germans have broken through all along the Western Front and the French and British are retreating. One of our divisions, I don't remember which, has arrived in France, though. They'll stop them."

"Henry says his division won't be going over for months and months," Rachel said. "His general said that they will be so well trained, nothing will stop them. How many men are in a division? Henry's is called 'Onaway' because that's an Indian war cry."

"Twenty thousand, I think," Maggie said.

"Good God. And there are hundreds and hundreds of divisions on both sides. I can't imagine it."

"It's inconceivable," Maggie said. "It's insanity. So many millions of boys being—" She caught herself, and caught the brake handle at the same time, as the wagon began the steep descent of the town hill.

"We'll park in the meadow at the top of the hill so we won't have to climb the boardwalk up to the church," Maggie said. "That is if Hortense doesn't balk among the alders."

The mare did balk when Maggie turned her into the narrow little road over which the alders had grown, forming an arch of infant green, but a word and a slap kept her going through the unfamiliar copse toward the open meadow.

They crossed the broad hilltop meadow where the natives and rusticators played baseball on summer evenings, toward the white pointed spire of the church, and pulled up in the shade of the spruce trees between the meadow and the church where a dogcart, a small open carriage, and a saddled roan were tethered. As they dismounted, the church bell began to toll, and the organ began "Christ the Lord Is Risen Today."

"Perfect timing," Maggie said, taking Leah's hand. "They're going in. We won't have to stand around on the steps making awkward conversation. Come on, dear. I'm a little nervous, too, but it will be fun. Rachel comes every Sunday."

As they approached the brightly dressed women and their reluctant menfolk waiting to go through the front doors, Maggie plucked something from a tree as she passed. On the church stairs, at the rear of the crowd, Maggie and Leah let Rachel do the talking, and both happily accepted treacly compliments on Leah's new dress. As they took their seats in the next-to-last pew Cecilia Barter, several rows ahead, nudged Dottie to look around at who was here, and craned over the shoulder of the woman in front of her to whisper excitedly. Maggie pretended not to notice.

"Look," she whispered to Leah. She held her closed hand between them, then uncurled her fingers to reveal a tiny maple leaf in the center of her palm. "Look, it's a baby leaf. It's exactly the shape and pattern that it will be when it's grown up, like an infant's perfect little hand. It's a miracle."

Leah looked and looked, but Maggie could tell by the girl's lack of expression that she did not see.

Corporal Steve Robbins guided the polishing cloth in a soft ride over the surface of the general's car, slowing to buff back to a shine a smudge in the wax on a door or wipe clean a new layer of dust on a headlamp. He would have liked to start the engine and while it idled adjust the timing, which was a little off, but the noise might disturb the Easter service that the general was attending in the crowded YMCA Pavilion across the road. Though he bitched and moaned to the other drivers in the transportation company barracks about how often he had to "hurry up and wait," how many hours he had to spend spit-shining and waxing and polishing the car and his own boots and belt and buttons, how few weekend passes he got, Steve had to admit he liked being the sole driver, monitor, and mechanic of the finest vehicle in all of Camp Devens. He suffered pangs of guilt when he watched the infantry companies training with bayonets and on the rifle ranges, or drove past them on forced marches, but he liked his unique uniform of spit-shined cavalry boots and polished Sam Browne belt. He was exempt from KP and any kind of work detail, he barely had to blink to get parts and supplies when he needed them, there was only one officer among the thousand on the post whom he had to fear, and he was kind enough, but best of all, the absolutely sweetest part of his job, was the expression of jealous resentment on the faces of the Boston snobs as they walked past him and the car, maintaining a respectful distance. Steve loved to catch their eye and, with his own face puckered up in the prissiest possible way, tap the ash of his cigarette with his index finger.

The YMCA Pavilion at camp headquarters in which

Major General Hodges sat for the Easter service was a long, wide edifice with a low roof and open sides. Like its five brethren throughout Camp Devens, the headquarters pavilion served as a classroom for lessons in French and etiquette, a canteen where volunteer women from nearby towns served coffee and doughnuts and other culinary delights, a place for edifying lectures and adult education classes in the Chautauqua tradition, and until a proper chapel was completed, which would be soon, as a church. When the service ended, the enlisted men exited the building at the rear and sides while the officers, who had been in the front rows, stepped outside at the left front. Steve watched as General Hodges emerged and stood among his officers while Major Hawker, the general's grim aide, struck a match on his pant leg and held it cupped beneath the general's cigarette. Steve started the car and stood holding the door, praying, as the general and major approached, that the major would not be going with them. Major Hawker, who was not a New England man, disapproved of and resented the genial relationship the general enjoyed with his driver. A grisly ex-cavalryman, Hawker was a mustang, commissioned a lieutenant in the field and promoted since, and hence he felt it his God-given duty to make enlisted swine like Corporal Robbins squirm uncomfortably at every opportunity. This morning, however, the major stopped short of the car, saluted the general, and parted with a smart about-face.

"How was the service, sir?" Steve asked as General Hodges settled into the leather seat.

"Boring, Robbins," the general said. "Incredibly boring.

I believe the man must be a Methodist. Not a hint of joy in his voice; as a celebration, it was flat as a thin griddle cake. Damned shame."

"Where to, sir?" Steve held the clutch down and slipped her into gear.

"Let's go back to my quarters," the general said. "Mrs. Hodges is visiting with friends. We need to be up in the division area by one o'clock, but I have time for a light lunch with the newspaper on the veranda, and Cookie can fix you up with a sandwich and a nice cold beer, if you can stand his grouchy kitchen."

"Can do, sir," Steve said.

The Seventy-sixth (Onaway) Division was the first American regular army division formed of draftees and volunteers. Other infantry divisions such as the First, which was already in France and about to go up to the line, had filled their ranks with volunteers, intensified their training, and were beginning to deploy overseas that spring. The Seventy-sixth was designated a depot divison, which meant that when it arrived in France, having trained for eight months, its infantry brigades, machine-gun battalions, supply trains, artillery brigades, and other units would be broken up and would provide replacements for other divisions already engaged. Steve pestered the general when he dared to find out when the division would sail for France, but the general said he did not know, perhaps late summer, and Steve believed him. Whether General Hodges, who was camp commandant, and his staff (and driver) would sail with the Seventy-sixth was a question that Steve thought it best not to ask, yet. He so hoped it.

When he had eaten, Steve went for a short stroll down Victory Drive, one of the few paved roads on the post that ran in front of the long row of officers' quarters. Two crews of Negroes in civilian trucks were planting maple saplings in the barren front yards of the officers' houses; across the way a dozen recruits with little buckets and brushes were busy painting white the rocks that lined the gravel path into headquarters and circled the base of the flagpole. When he had first enlisted, Steve thought, he could at least see trees on the low hills in the distance, and in occasional little copses here and there on the post. But now the numberless three-story barracks arranged in ranks that stood shoulder to shoulder blocked the view of the hills, and the myriad other buildings that had sprung up all over the vast acreage had crowded out all vegetation. Nothing grew on the sandy ground; there was no room for shrubs or flowers; the only natural odors in the air were of horse manure and fresh-cut lumber, the only sounds the steady hum of the power plants, the distant staccato of hammering, the drone of trucks and motorcars, and the tramp of men marching in step.

"I told General Weigel that we'd be visiting this afternoon," General Hodges told Steve as he settled into his seat. "He said he might meet us at the main gate, or send a colonel as escort. I hope not. I don't feel like talking business. This is an outing I want to enjoy, and one that I know you will."

"What is it, sir?" Steve asked. He had learned a way of talking over his shoulder, turning his head only slightly so that the general could hear him in the open car without him having to raise his voice.

"You'll see, Robbins, you'll see." A tall bald man with a pleasant countenance, General Hodges was fond of little surprises for others and himself. He lay his arm across the back of the seat, adjusted his Sam Browne belt, and crossed his long legs to enjoy the drive up to division.

Low gray clouds had moved in from the west, obscuring the morning sun. This afternoon there were no units marching on the roads, no formations on either side or on any parade ground, no mules at work, no trucks to raise dust, only quiet groups of boys and men here and there, sitting or talking quietly, as if the whole busy military city had heard that He had risen, and paused to contemplate just what that meant for them.

Steve downshifted into second gear as he approached the gate and guardhouse at the entrance to the division area. The arch over the gate said FIRST SONS OF THE NATION, and on the side opposite the guardhouse was a mural depicting a life-sized Indian in breechclout and Mohawk haircut. The Indian was down on one knee, his tomahawk raised in one hand, the other shielding his eyes; in a bubble coming from his mouth was written, ONAWAY! BE ALERT! Steve crept through the gate to give the guards a chance to render a snappy present arms for the general and give the fellow inside the guardhouse time to crank up his telephone and alert division headquarters that a two-star had just entered the area.

"The northwest drill field, Robbins, the one behind the big power plant," the general said.

Passing the ranks of barracks, Steve noticed that smoke rose from every company kitchen and sitting around each were boys in various stages of uniform peeling potatoes and washing vegetables for the evening meal, but there were no other signs of life among the barracks. When he turned past the westernmost rank of buildings and into the open treeless plain, he found thousands of soldiers in a great milling mass around an area on the far field. A line of cars, many of them civilian, was parked along the near road. The attention of the crowd—he thought there must be twenty thousand or more—was turned away from the general's car as Steve eased it toward the mass.

General Hodges tapped him on the shoulder to stop. When he did, the general stood up in the back of the car to see over the heads of the crowd, causing a visible nervous distraction in every soldier and especially every officer who had seen him.

"Go around the crowd to the left," the general said, very pleased with himself. "There's a slight rise on the far side; you can drive us right up there where we can see."

On the back side of the crowd, in places thin, in others filling in with new arrivals, Steve drove slowly, allowing those who had not seen the car at first to move aside. He ascended the rise in the ground carefully, lest he get mired in loose sand, and when he was tapped again, pulled on the hand brake to have a look.

He should have known. When he turned around to face the general, he saw what he would have called a shit-eating grin, had it not been on the face of a man with two stars on each shoulder.

"The blue hats and shirts are the Hundred and Fifty-first Brigade, the white ones are the Hundred and Fifty-second," the general said, pointing at the teams in the center of the mass of spectators. "The infantry brigades formed up teams, with tryouts and all, for a series of games this summer. At the end, whenever and whyever that comes, they'll choose a division team from these two."

Steve could only shake his head and smile with pleasure.

"Shut this thing down," General Hodges said. "They've only just now started; this should be the top of the first."

"Are we going to stay a while, sir?"

"I've got five dollars on the Hundred and Fifty-second's team with General Weigel," the general said. "Damned right we're staying. Step out and have a smoke if you like."

Steve did, and the crowd erupted as the batter went down swinging.

"Robbins." The general puffed a cigar to life. "You want the good news first or the bad news?"

"Well sir, I guess I'll take the bad," Steve said.

"Remember when you interviewed for this job you told me you played third base for your home team in Stonington?" The general watched the game, avoiding Steve's eyes.

"Yes sir?"

"Well, both these teams have crackerjack third basemen and neither of them is looking for a backup man. That's the bad news."

"I can live with that, sir," Steve said, relieved, and meaning it quite sincerely.

"The good news is that one of the boys who will be

pitching for the Hundred and Fifty-second is a young corporal, a squad leader, who says he threw for your team, the Quarrymen if I remember right." General Hodges paused to relish the moment. "I don't remember the name of the fellow you were looking for when you enlisted, nor do I know this guy's name, but I know he throws what you called a 'wicked inshoot' and he's long and tall and full of himself."

Steve wanted to shake the general's hand. "Henry Coombs," was all he could say.

"I suppose so," the general said. "I hope so."

"Sir, do you mind if I go—"

"No need to, Robbins. No need to. I've arranged for him to be brought up here as soon as the game's over. Relax and enjoy yourself. If it is your friend, and he wins this game, there's a three-day pass in it for both of you."

"Goddamn, sir," Steve said, nodding appreciatively. "Goddamn."

Amos liked to say that the mare Hortense lacked horse sense, which he thought was some clever. It was true. Hortense was known to stop while pulling the wagon on the road home and fall asleep in her tracks; feed sacks made her sneeze and snuffle so violently that she couldn't use them, and nobody could make her back up using the reins. This last lack of horse sense was what Maggie fully intended to correct, though she had yet to manage it. At the bottom of the hill on the cove road, Rachel got off at her house, thanked Maggie and Leah both, wished them Happy Easter, and said that maybe next year they should all have Easter dinner together, *all* of the family. The smell of wood smoke and tar mingled with the pervasive odor of the tidal flats in the cove, which made Maggie think that the men would have finished tarring for the day by now, as Ava liked to have her Sunday dinner at two o'clock. Rather than drive all the way up past Ava's and turn Hortense around in the field, Maggie chose to turn her into the graveyard road and try yet again to teach her to back out.

The mare turned into the shaded graveyard, and Maggie stopped her shy of the stones. For the hundredth time since she had come home, she tried backing Hortense out, using different tugs on the reins, different noises with her tongue, a new command or two.

"You have to hold her bridle under her ear and say 'Back girl back' two times," Leah said.

"I know, I know," Maggie sighed. "If we can just get her to do it with the reins once, then she'll have learned."

She stood up, holding the reins as high as she could and tried all over again, but the mare simply stood there. Maggie had not seen Amos watching her futile attempts, nor did she see him as he approached the mare, shaking his head and grinning, until he was ten feet from Hortense's head, and stopped, astonished, as the mare began to back out. Maggie lowered the reins, smiling victoriously, and stood in the wagon bed as she eased the mare back out of the graveyard onto the cove road.

Leah applauded and cried, "Hooray Aunt Maggie!"

Amos said he would be a son of a bitch and climbed aboard in the road.

Maggie handed him the reins.

"What was it you said that made her step back?" Amos asked.

"I don't know what I was saying, perhaps it was the angle of the reins," Maggie said. "But I have to admit that it was probably that she saw you coming and put two and two together and backed up."

"You said 'chuck chuck chuck' like that," Leah said.

"Teamwork," Amos said. "Hortense figured that we were working together and we had her outnumbered. It took her a while to catch on, but she finally did."

"We'll try it again when we get home," Maggie said.

On the empty road down the east side of the island, Maggie took off her bonnet, unpinned her hair, and shook it out in the sunlight, turning her head one way then the other to let the southerly breeze catch her hair before she pinned it back up. Along the pond they passed the sloping meadow of hay-scented fern, arrayed at the feet of the ancient birch that leaned to the south. Amos gave Leah the reins and lifted her into his lap.

"Aunt Gladys has a Easter basket on her grave," Leah said. "With two blue eggs like robins' eggs. And lilies, too."

"I didn't notice," Maggie said, surprised that she hadn't.

"You were too busy with Hortense," said Amos. "I'm surprised you didn't see the lilies, though, pretty white ones that you would notice. The basket is from Rachel, the flowers from Virgil. Ava saw the two of them in the graveyard just after dawn."

"Mommy says Aunt Rachel and Virgil are sweet on each other," Leah said. "She says they'll get married when the time comes. What time?"

Maggie looked at Amos and smiled. "I think she means a year since Gladys's death, a time of mourning. But I don't know about that; I don't know that Virgil would ask her even if he wanted to, or that she—"

"He might if somebody dared him to," Amos offered. "But no . . ." And now it was he who smiled. "No, he'd be too sheepish."

Leah pulled the mare to a halt beside the house and slowly, carefully, and quite correctly dropped the reins in a clove hitch onto the brake handle.

"I want to keep my dress on for dinner," Leah said. "Can I Aunt Maggie? I won't spill on it. Promise."

"Of course you can," Maggie said.

When they opened the door to the kitchen, they were beset by a cloud of stench that was so strong that it drove them back into the mudroom. Maggie recovered first and headed for the source of the stink—the pot of boiled beets on the stove that had been left so long that the water had boiled off and the beets, really only a brown slime by now, were burning on the bottom. She hurried the pot out the back door and threw open the kitchen windows calling for Clytie, who did not answer.

Leah called out for her mother, as did Amos, and they heard a muffled response, then, more clearly:

"I'm down cellar!"

The trapdoor to the cellar stood open in the corner of the room. At the foot of the cellar ladder sat Clytie on the backless old wooden chair, her arms folded across her chest, a jar of blueberry jam in her apron lap, looking up at the faces that peered through the trapdoor.

"Mommy?"

"I can't get up this damned ladder," Clytie said. She was exasperated and embarrassed. "It hurts my feet too much. I got to the third rung once, but then I was afraid I would fall. The two-by-four is still across the bulkhead. Are the beets ruined?"

"I'll go open it," Maggie said, as Amos started down the ladder.

Around the south side of the house Maggie removed the two-by-four that held the bulkhead double doors shut, and she and Leah each lifted open one of the doors.

Clytie, in her house robe, stood at the bottom of the cellar stairs squinting in the sudden sunlight behind Maggie and Leah. Amos stood behind Clytie and with a hand helped her onto the first step. She teetered there for a second, until he caught her at the midriff with both hands from behind to steady her and help her up. As Clytie climbed, two footsteps for each stair, and Amos pushed, his hands lost in folds of cotton and flab, his shoulder against her back, Maggie saw shame and anger in her sister's face, and revulsion in Amos's. She offered Clytie her hand as she neared the top, but Clytie acted as though she did not see it, and Maggie backed away, stepping into the little patch of mallow.

She has risen, Maggie thought. She has risen, and there is neither exaltation nor the hope of salvation, not here.

"Are you all right, Mommy?" Leah asked when her mother stood in the yard.

"I'm fine dear, I just feel a little foolish is all," Clytie said. "You go put your bonnet away and change that dress and come help us get dinner."

"Aunt Maggie said I could leave it on, she—"

"That doesn't matter," Clytie said with a look to Maggie. "You go change. Put on your nice blue calico one. Go on."

WESTERN UNION TELEGRAM
Headquarters, Camp Devens, Mass. April 16, 1918
Amos Coombs, Barter Island, Maine
FOUND HIM BY JESUS STOP PLAYING BALL LIKE YOU SAID STOP GROWN 2 INCHES STOP CPL LIKE ME END
Steve

"He uses Steve and not Stevie," Virgil said. He knelt on the flat granite ledge and fed two more sticks of wood into the fire under the tarring trough. A fair southwesterly breeze fanned the flames and blew sparks into the rockweed at the water's edge. He draped his khaki shirt over a boulder and put on a denim work shirt. Virgil hated tarring lines.

"Maybe he's grown up too much to use a boy's name," said Amos.

Walter pulled on his overalls, the legs stiff with dried tar, and fastened the straps. He took the telegram from Amos and studied it, grinning.

"You've shown this to Rachel, I guess," Walter said. "What's *CPL* mean?"

"Sure I did," Amos said. "*CPL* is 'corporal' and that's one stripe before sergeant, which is pretty damned good. Both of them."

Amos took the telegram from Walter, folded it into the envelope, and put it into his back pocket.

"Do any of Henry's lines need tarring," Walter asked.

"We did all his last year," said Virgil.

"You going to fish his traps?"

"Well sure I am," Virgil said. "He'll need the extra money. He told Rachel he's going to buy a powerboat when he comes home, he's already saved so much."

"When he comes home," said Amos.

Chapter 11
Revelations

"I have never seen Miss Tessie so exhilarated, so pleased, so altruistic, as she was the day of John Ulysses' christening."
The Reverend Nathaniel Sharpesdale, August 23, 1918

On the ground floor of Building 358, the barracks home of Able Company, Second Battalion, 303rd Infantry, Henry sat straddling his footlocker, his elbows on his knees, his chin resting in his fists, his eyes perusing a recent copy of *Sporting Life*. Folded at such awkward angles for such a tall man, Henry appeared to be uncomfortable; in truth he was entirely comfortable physically, and he was serenely oblivious to the barracks chatter that beset him on all sides. It was a warm August evening, at the end of a long dry day. Two weeks of drought had turned an already arid Camp Devens into a dust bowl, so that every footstep raised a cloud and every passing truck a dust storm.

Private Strong from Dorset, Vermont, sat cross-legged on the wide floor facing Private Hoskins from Belchertown, Massachusetts, over a cribbage board. Private Strong was naked above the waist except for his suspenders; Private Hoskins wore a blue bandanna around his forehead. Private Sabin from Castine, Maine, lay in his skivvies on his stomach on his bunk watching the game in progress, his chin resting on his folded blanket.

"The last of the Three Hundred and First went out before dawn this morning." Private Hoskins was a man known to be a fount of information, nearly all of it erroneous.

"Seemed like they marched by all night," said Private Strong. "I fell asleep to the sound of them passing, woke up only once when some damned company went by singing the baby carriage version of 'Yellow Ribbon.'"

"I wouldn't mind a little bit of a breeze in here," said Private Sabin. "It's some hot."

"Who would?" asked Private First Class Wilharm from Liberty, New Hampshire. Wilharm sat on his foot-locker sewing a button on a cuff; he wiped his forehead with the sleeve.

"They've started moving the Three Hundred and Second out, and they're filling up their empty billets right behind them with new recruits," said Strong. "Another division, the Twelfth, the Plymouth Division they're calling it—all Massachusetts men."

"We could get a breeze in here if these screens weren't all fucking clotted up with dust," observed Sabin.

"Christ, by the time they get the new ones trained, we will have wiped the Germans' asses with the Kaiser's mus-tache," declared Hoskins.

"That's funny, that," said Sabin, not meaning it.

"They say after the Hundred and Fifty-first Brigade goes, then they're gonna ship the supply trains and signal and artillery battalions, before they do us." Strong peeked over his cards at Hoskins.

"The rest of us here, we've lost most of our accents," said Hoskins. "But not you, Sabin, you still talk funny."

"Fuck you. I don't talk funny." Sabin pushed up on his elbows.

Corporal Gardinier from Scituate, Massachusetts, appeared beside Henry in his stocking feet, toothbrush and tooth powder in hand, a towel over his shoulder.

"How can you say you don't talk funny, Sabin," the new arrival said, "when you say *fun-ay* instead of *funny?*"

Sabin sat up. "Corporal Clair, he still says *fun-ay.*"

Henry did not answer.

"I tell you," Sabin went on. "Remember that Brit that taught us bayonet? Well, he said my speech was closer to the king's English than any other of you assholes."

"We're shipping out of New York," Strong said. "Maybe we'll get a night in the big city. I'd go for that."

"Shit," said Hoskins, moving a peg. "You get off the train, you get pushed into some tunnel in Hoboken, and from that onto a troopship. You never see a friggin' thing."

"How the hell do you know that?"

"A guy told me," said Hoskins. He looked over Strong and past Henry at a tiny, frail, bespectacled orderly who had appeared in the doorway with a clipboard. The orderly removed his hat and swatted his leg, from which erupted a brown cloud of Devens dust.

"Don't dump your goddamned dirt in here, you little turd," Sabin said. "We got to clean this place."

The orderly paid Sabin no mind. He lifted the top page on his clipboard and read aloud:

"Sonner, Garrett, PFC, Six-One-One-Six-Three."

"You mean Sonner, Garrett, second base," Strong said. He did not turn around.

"Sonner's in Baker Company, the building next door," said Hoskins.

"I bet this guy left Babe, his Blue Ox, parked outside," said Sabin.

The orderly pointed to another name on his page and proclaimed:

"Clair, John, Corporal, One-Oh-Three-Eight-Nine."

No one moved, or answered.

"Clair, John, Corporal, One-Oh-Three-Eight-Nine," said the orderly, louder this time, almost shrill.

"No need to shout," said Henry. He sat upright, almost surprised. "I'm him. What is it you want?"

"Corporal Clair you are to report to Major Hawker in Building Twenty-two in the uniform of the day," the orderly said. "Immediately."

"Little asshole," said Hoskins.

"It's been a pleasure meeting you fellows," the orderly said. He slapped his other thigh with his hat, leaving another cloud of Devens dust in the doorway to drift inside and settle on the floor.

Henry's suspicion that his summons had something to do with baseball was confirmed when he stepped into the classroom in Building 22 and found all but two or three of the boys from the two brigade ball teams, including Sonner, the second baseman, who had somehow gotten there before him. They were gathered around a table at the head of the room where a sergeant was reading off names and handing out sheets of paper that proved to be orders and, when they were read, were causing a garbled mixture of surprise and anger from the group. Before Henry could read his, the room was called to attention and Major Hawker marched in with Captain Bosowitz, the manager of the 152nd Brigade team, to stand before them at the front of the room.

"At ease, gentlemen," Major Hawker said. He put his hat and swagger stick down on the table and pushed back his slick black hair. "Take seats."

"As you can see, you have been transferred from the Seventy-sixth Division to administrative hold here at Camp Devens." The major clasped his hands behind his back; his paunch strained the brass buttons on his tunic above his belt.

"Your orders tell you to report here, which you have done," he said.

"The man is fucking brilliant," someone whispered.

"I am here to congratulate you on being chosen to be the Camp Devens baseball team, the Chippewas. Since the division will be broken up when it gets to France, the decision was made to form a camp team to play against other camps here in the States. Captain Bosowitz and the sergeant here will fill you in on the details such as where your new billets will be and when you need to report in."

Stocky Simon Burd, Henry's catcher, stood up. "But sir, some of us want to stay with the division, with our buddies. We want to go overseas; we want to fight; we signed up to—"

"Sit down, Private!" Major Hawker's face turned turnip red and he bit the air with his teeth, shouting: "What the flopping hell is the first word on that paper you got in your hand? Let me tell you in case you can't read it: It is 'orders.' It does not say 'request'; it does not say 'suggestion'; it does not say 'invitation'—it says 'orders.' Do you understand that, you ungrateful whimpering sack of pigshit?"

Burd said nothing.

"Any other questions?" the major asked. He held his hat in one hand, tucked his swagger stick under his arm in the British fashion, and nodded to the sergeant, who called the room to attention as the major made his slow exit.

Captain Bosowitz, a thin-faced man with crooked yellow teeth, sat the men down and hushed them, saying, "Gentlemen please. Gentlemen please," until they had quieted.

The captain explained that he, too, had wanted to go to France with his unit and that he, too, was disappointed. While he exhorted them to make the best of the situation, to set their minds on being a winning team, remembering that playing ball for the troops was a boost for their morale, Henry rolled up his carbon copy page, unrolled it, and rolled it again, thinking that there must be some way out of this, some way to get to France with his squad.

"Think of the good stuff," the captain said. "We'll be traveling to places like Camp Dix in New Jersey, and Camp Meade near Washington and playing against the best ball players from each of those camps. There will be scouts from the big-league teams at all of your games. General Hodges even talked about arranging an exhibition game at Fenway Park for us, and free tickets to the World Series in Boston next month."

At the mention of General Hodges' name Henry almost

stood up; instead he waited impatiently until the captain had finished and dismissed the Chippewas.

Henry did not notice that the lights in the company streets were coming on as he walked past them on Democracy Drive, nor did he slow to listen to a pair of fiddlers behind the mule stables. Without thinking that Steve might be in his barracks, or out for the evening, Henry went straight to the motor pool and there found him with his feet up on the bench next to the general's car and the *Boston Globe* open before him under a green-shaded light. Steve lowered his paper.

"It didn't take you long," he said.

"What didn't?" Henry asked.

"Getting here, after getting that." Steve pointed at the rolled page in Henry's hand.

"You got to talk to him for me, Steve, please. Get him to let me stay with my squad, my company. I have to go with them. I have to." Henry sat on the tall stool at the bench, rolling and unrolling the page.

"I told him you'd ask me that, and he said to tell you that your orders stand and he hopes that you will pitch for Camp Devens with all your heart, no matter how you feel."

Steve pulled a bottle of rum from behind the tool cabinet and poured a coffee cup half full. "It's not the best rum there is," he said. "But it's not kerosene either. Here."

Henry knocked it back. Steve took the cup, filled it again, and drank it himself, filling it halfway once more afterward.

"You don't know, Steve," said Henry. "You don't know how bad I need to go. You got to ask him again, beg him, or let me."

"If it's pity you're looking for, you can get it from me, because I'm a friend." Steve took a drink. "But you won't get it from him. He isn't going, either. He's as pissed off and disappointed as you are, maybe more, because he's been serving all his life for a chance like this. All his life; and then he got passed over by a fucking dim-witted ass kisser. And what about his driver? Is his driver going to get to go to Paris? Hell no, he's staying here, too, at fucking Camp Dusty. Have another sup."

Henry took a deep drink and a deep breath. "There's got to be a way. I can go AWOL, use my real name or make up another one and sign up somewhere else, start over again."

"Yes, perhaps, but by the time you finished training all over again and got to France, if you even went, the war would be over," Steve said. "You got to accept it. Hell, you love baseball; you love it better than you love Claire; your real name isn't Henry or John, it's Number Sixteen. And you're damned good. You could get noticed, you—"

"That's it or that's half of it," Henry said. "How am I going to feel doing what I love to do, maybe getting noticed, when my friends are at the front in the trenches doing what we trained to do, getting their licks in? You don't know, Steve."

"You keep saying I don't know. Well maybe I don't," Steve said. "And maybe you haven't given one fucking thought to how I might feel. I could have been driving an ambulance at the front, driving supply trucks, driving anything over there, but what am I doing instead? I'm a fucking chauffeur, a valet, a footman for Christ's sake. I drive His Majesty's carriage. I polish the car and the boots, too, sometimes, of a forty-year-old man from Cape Fucking Cod. Me! I'm an American. I'm a Maine Yankee for Christ's sake."

"I'm going to find a way to get over there," said Henry.

"If you do, I'm going with you," said Steve. "Here, have some more of this."

Monday morning
August 11, 1918
Ruth Dear,

What an astonishing summer morning this is! If E. D. were here, she would extol nature's "majesty," and rightfully so. The sun is not yet risen high enough to show over the ledges and trees of the Eastern Ear, but it is dancing and sparkling on the open water outside the harbor all the way out to the Roaring Bull Ledges. There is a promise of autumn in the air, however discreet.

Amos just left to go to haul, and Clytie and Leah are still asleep. I'm at the kitchen table with a second cup of tea, a raspberry scone, and the crumbs and empty bowls of Amos's and my breakfasts. I meant to be reading Hawthorne, but he is far too dreary for such a morning as this, so I write to you. Have I told you how surprised I have been to find that Amos and I are becoming friends? I think he is as surprised as I am, though of course neither of us mentions such a thing. Every day he and I have half an hour or more together in this quiet morning kitchen and though it was a tad awkward at first, it has become a very pleasant time for both of us. We rarely speak, and when we do it is in whispers, so as not to wake the sleepers upstairs and not to have the "racket shame us so." We talk about Leah. We worry about Clytie.

He tells me where his traps are fishing, and where they are not, and when they will move them, and to where. He worries about sufficient money for the winter and I pooh-pooh his concerns; I complain about the meddlesome school committee (even in summer) and he pooh-poohs them.

But neither of us can whisk away the fears and concerns that the other has for Clytie. She is not getting any better, not at all. On his first visit, as I think I told you, Dr. Banks said her diabetes could very well be temporary, brought on by all that sugary food she was eating (and still does when I am not looking). But now we are not so hopeful that it will pass. She grows more sluggish by the day, and more irri-table. Four days ago she bumped into the corner of the bed frame, and the bruise on her hip is still huge and angry and painful. Because she has to urinate so often, she drinks more milk and water to compensate; during the day she sits in Grandmother's chamber potty chair, so she doesn't have to stand on her tingling weakened feet. Dr. Banks has treated her with obesity powder, several elixirs, and arnica for her bruises. Her internal discomfort is so serious (when she groans I can see it in Amos's face) that Dr. Banks suggested paregoric or laudanum, but we have decided not to use either yet. The poor girl blames me for her misery, reminding us all that she was well before I moved in, and she hates me because I am healthy and (as needs be) I am taking care of her house and family, and even her. I try not to feel guilty, but the guilt is there, however furtive. Poor Amos is so distraught about her, and takes her blame so readily, that this morning he was near tears in the kitchen and I discovered as I listened to him that my hand of its own accord had found his on the table and covered it; we both noticed it at the same time and blushed simultaneously. In spite of our troubles, our kitchen mornings are all very pleasant, all very sweet, and all very innocent.

I'm not surprised that you're surprised that I've been going to church all summer. Rachel and Leah and I. I go not for the sermons, but for the morning light, and the music, and the sweet sense of security in my soul that I have when nestled between Leah and Rachel on the pew. Ava won't go with us, because it is Tessie Wedge's church, or so she says. Remember I told you that Tessie confided in me that she and the reverend are a little more than neighbors and swore me to secrecy on the matter? I told Ava that Tessie had trusted me with something about herself, something that could cause her great grief here on the island were it known; Ava said Tessie's avowed confidence in me is a ploy, that she is trying to draw me into a trap, as one would to capture another's king on the checkerboard. When I asked her to explain, she said only that I should not trust Tessie; she said it twice. I wonder if Tessie and the reverend do more than exchange Valentines? I hope so, I really do.

I must close. My tea is cold and Leah, bless her heart, will sleep all morning if I let her.

Love always,
Maggie

P.S.: Did I say that my hand "covered" his? No more than a little girl's white communion glove would cover Paul Bunyan's great mitt.

P.P.S.: Our boys held them at Soissons (what a beautiful

word) and are on the counteroffensive, we hear. We pray for peace every day.

From the tunnel of alders that Hortense had to be coaxed through on Easter morning, they emerged into the high meadow beside the church in two wagons, the first carrying Virgil, Ava with Little John in her lap, and Rachel, the second carrying Walter, Maggie, and Leah, and both carrying baked goodies of all kinds and gallons of lemonade and iced tea. They had left the cove with time to spare so that they could drive slowly and avoid damaging the sweets for the christening party on the way, and now they arrived in the meadow as the churchgoers were chatting in clusters in the shade. The August sun was high in a cloudless southern sky, and a brisk westerly breeze tilted the leaves in the tall maples. When Ava saw Tessie Wedge at the edge of the group, she handed Little John to Rachel, who took him in her lap without seeming to notice. The sight of Virgil driving with Rachel and Little John by his side was all that Ava had to say to Tessie Wedge on this day.

From behind the rank of the stalwart Rebekahs in the shadow of the spruce trees Claire Schuyler and her little sister broke out and ran into the meadow to greet the wagons, Claire calling Rachel's and John's names, her sister barely keeping up in the tall grass. In a delighted confusion of greetings and compliments, Maggie, Leah, Rachel, and Little John alighted to embrace the Schuyler girls while Virgil looked on and Walter and Ava drove the wagons off to the near side of the field, where they parked them parallel to one another. Claire, in a new yellow dress with tiny white dots and trim, made over the baby and his pretty christening gown, and made much of Leah, who stared at the fair-haired Dutch girls in unabashed awe.

Rachel told Claire that she was some glad she could come.

"Uncle Penny brought us down," Claire said. "I have such good news, Mrs. Coombs. I mean to show you, too, but you probably know already; I have it here."

From the pocket in the folds of her skirt Claire withdrew an envelope addressed in pencil to her, and from it a photograph of Henry and Steve that Rachel studied tenderly. Before a mural depicting the Eiffel Tower and the skyline of Paris, Henry stood in uniform, one hand behind his back, the other resting on the back of the chair in which Steve sat upright, his legs crossed to show his high shining boots. The shape of Henry's slight smile and the cast of his eyes told Rachel that her boy was a little embarrassed to be posing thus, but that he was, in all, unafraid and comfortable in his new world.

"He *has* grown two inches," Rachel said. She handed the photo to Virgil, who held it for Maggie to see, as well.

"I didn't know whether he sent you one, too," Claire said. "But the news, did he tell you?"

"I haven't had a letter in almost a month," Rachel said. "And no, I hadn't seen the photo."

"Well, he isn't going to have to go to France," Claire blurted. "He's staying at Camp Devens!"

"Are you sure?" Virgil asked.

"Yes sir, I mean he says he isn't going to go with his division, with his friends, and he was right pissed—sorry—and he says he's going to try to find a way to get over there. Steve is staying, too, and he thinks the two of them together can find a way, but he doesn't know what or how—" Claire laughed abruptly and handed the letter to Rachel.

"I hope they fail," Rachel said.

"I do, too."

"We've got to go in," Virgil said. He took Little John from Maggie and nestled him onto his shoulder. "Maggie, would you run over to the wagons and tell Walter and Ava the news; we'll walk slow so you can catch up. Won't she be tickled?"

"Aren't we all?" said Rachel, taking Claire, and by extension her sister, by the hand. "Let's go inside and thank Him."

While Walter unhitched the horses and tethered them, Ava lowered the tailgates of the wagons and spread white linen tablecloths over both, pinning the edges with clothespins to keep them down in the breeze.

"You did a good job scrubbing down these wagon beds," she told Walter when he returned.

"Christ, that's the nicest thing you've said to me since I knocked Buddy Winston off your swing. When was that, second grade?" Walter removed his jacket and hung it over a wheel. "You're not going in?"

"If Tessie Wedge so much as touches that child, I will tear her church down on her head, board by board," Ava said.

"That's more like it, old girl," Walter said. "You'll have to let me get the wine out before you knock it down. Here, help me with this."

Together they moved the large stone crock of lemonade

to the edge of the tailgate, and while Ava stacked cups next to it Walter began to open tins of cookies, slipping a sample from each into the pockets of his trousers.

"I'd like to see her face when the reverend reads out John's name," Walter said. "She's going to shit her pants when she hears Ulysses for his middle name."

"Don't talk like that," Ava said, thinking how wonderful it would be if Tessie *did* shit her pants in church. "No, the best will be her face when Virgil tells her it wasn't Gladys's idea, but his, to give the boy old Captain Wedge's name. I just hope nothing of that old bastard gets carried down into that sweet boy."

"Gladys never got any of his meanness." Startled by a sudden noise in the woods behind him, Walter looked around to see an agitation of robins and grosbeaks among the berry bushes at the near edge of the field. "It was some clever of Virgil to think of doing that, saying he chose it for Gladys."

"Virgil might not say much; he might be peculiar when it comes to shirts; he might walk into more doors than most, but he is no fool," Ava said. "Look at this. These are the ones Clytie sent."

She removed the top of a shoe box and showed Walter its contents: eight plump cupcakes with white frosting and the initials J. C. in blue on each.

"Jesus Christ," said Walter, reaching for one.

Ava held the box out of his reach. "No, you fool. John Coombs."

The Reverend Sharpesdale was the first to emerge from the church, followed closely by the sound of the organ processional and Virgil, who carried an alert and wide-eyed John Ulysses Coombs in his arms. One by one and in pairs the senior parishioners stopped in the doorway to fuss over the baby and shake the reverend's hand. From the side door the children emerged cautiously, then broke into a run for the wagons when they got clear of the church; Maggie and Rachel and several others used the side door, too, with an eye on the children ahead of them. At the church door Tessie Wedge lingered, holding baby John's little hand between thumb and forefinger and talking ardently with Virgil and the reverend, a sight that made Ava think she'd liked Tessie Wedge better when she was contemptuous of Virgil and openly hostile to the rest of the Coombses.

Ava caught Leah and Claire's little sister by their hands, guided them to one of the snowy quilts she had spread out on the sweet-smelling grass, and sat them down on it.

"This is the place of honor," Ava explained. Leah was disgruntled; she crossed her arms. Claire's sister was curious, uncertain.

"This is where the baby is going to sit, and you two are going to be in charge of him," Ava said. "I will bring you lemonade and cookies, all you want whenever you ask, and you will show all these people how grown up you are by taking care of the baby."

On the ball field at the far end of the meadow a group of boys gathered around the Hutchinson brothers, who were choking up the bat to see who would choose first, and consequently who would get stuck with Fuddy and Skippy. In the lee of the women and the dainties, several men gathered to smoke around Irville, who squatted to light his pipe and mutter the Lord's name in vain. With a school of cheerless Rebekahs in her wake, Tessie Wedge approached the wagons, her self-satisfaction as ample and ripe as her melonous bosoms. Ava nearly gagged, but smiled instead.

"You should have come in, Ava," Tessie said. "If for nothing else than to see the flowers, Dottie's beautiful roses. And little John Ulysses! Why, he was so well behaved, not a peep; he knew just what was expected of him, such a little angel."

"We were busy out here setting up," Ava said. "Would you like some lemonade, Tessie? It's fresh and not too sweet." *Bitter the way you like it.*

Maggie put three of Clytie's monogrammed cupcakes on a doily napkin on a little tray and carried them to the quilt where the girls sat with the baby.

"Oh, how cute," said Cecilia Barter as Maggie passed with the tray. "Who made those?"

"Clytie did," said Maggie.

"Oh," Cecilia said. "Then she must be feeling better; I thought not because Amos didn't come with you."

"No, not better, I'm afraid," Maggie said. "We're quite worried. Doctor Banks is coming back Tuesday. We watch for hopeful signs."

"And pray of course," said Cecilia with a grim smile.

"Of course," Maggie said.

Oblivious to all but the tender shoots before her, a doe munched her way into the clearing until a waft of tobacco smoke alerted her; she looked up to see the picnickers, then quickly slipped back into the forest.

Sitting cross-legged on the quilt with a napkin in her lap, Leah ate the bottom of the cupcake first, saving the frosting for last. Claire's sister whispered something and Leah looked up to find Cecil Barter, pale and rigid, standing before her with a clump of daisies, roots and all, in one hand. Leah said nothing.

"They're for you," said Cecil, holding them forth.

"You're getting dirt on the quilt," Leah said.

Cecil withdrew the flowers.

"I don't want them," Leah said. "I don't want flowers from you."

Claire's sister whispered "Leah!"

Cecil stood staring, first at the daisies, then at Leah. He took a step backward. "Amos is fustin' Miss Bowen," he said. "Amos your father."

Leah looked down at her cupcake. Cecil turned and walked away past the wagons and the smokers until he reached the center of the meadow; there he sat down and began to thrash the ground slowly, methodically, with the bouquet of dirty daisies.

Virgil told the other Coombses that he needed to go into town to talk to Danny Mack about getting more laths and that he would just as soon walk home if Rachel didn't mind taking Little John. He stayed well after the last of the parishioners had left to help clean up and hitch the wagons, then walked down into town to the landing with Claire and her little sister. On the landing Virgil lingered talking to Claire's Uncle Penny, who was an Eaton not a Schuyler, until Claire told Penny that they should be going and kissed Virgil on the cheek when she said good-bye.

Alone on the wharf, Virgil sat on a trap and watched the boats in the thorofare swing slowly on their moorings. He thought that if he waited until five o'clock, the reverend would be home and about to have his supper.

When he finally began the hill to the parsonage, Virgil was surprised that he was not at all anxious, not now, not like he had been so many times in the past when he imagined this scene. The drive and walkway to the parsonage were covered with crushed clamshells and lined with smooth stones. Virgil thought he heard voices and even brief laughter inside as he stood at the door, and thought that he should come back another time. But then the house was quiet, except for some distant rustling and the bang of a door, and he smelled a boiled dinner, so he knocked.

The reverend opened the door soon after Virgil's second knock. Rosy-cheeked, his hair slightly disheveled, and obviously quite surprised, the reverend invited Virgil in with a generous sweep of his arm.

Once they were seated in the parlor, Virgil in a straight-backed chair, his hands folded in his lap, the reverend comfortable in his armchair, Virgil thought that the reverend looked more like the man they called "The Little Bishop" in the cove than the unraveled man who had met him at the door.

Virgil, who did not want anything to drink, and did not like insincere pleasantries, told the reverend he didn't want to delay his supper, and got right to the point.

"I want to ask Rachel to marry me," he said. The reverend did not seem surprised, and only nodded. "She's religious you know and she . . . What I want to know is how long I need to wait after Gladys's passing away before I can ask Rachel. Is there a rule for that? She would want to obey the rules."

The reverend enjoyed a superior smile. "No, not a rule. But it is customary to wait, or mourn, for a year. And that is coming up soon, isn't it?"

Something made a scratching or slithering noise behind the door to the back room.

"Mice," the reverend said quickly.

"We've got them, too," said Virgil. "I don't want her to think that people will judge her wrong if she accepts. And I want to make sure the Bible says it's okay for her to marry her brother-in-law in a situation like this."

"On the contrary," the reverend said with a glance to the door. "In Genesis the Lord tells Onan to go in unto his brother's widow and give her children."

"Onan? Wasn't he the guy that God killed for pulling his pud?" Virgil was surprised.

"I beg your pardon?"

"For beating his tom-tom, you know, for . . ."

"Oh." The reverend understood. "It was for coitus interruptus actually."

"Say what?"

"Spilling his seed on the ground," said the reverend, who did not want to bother to explain that Onan had not been punished for masturbating, or spilling his seed, but for disobeying God.

"Oh," said Virgil. "Anyway it's all right to ask her?"

"Yes, of course," said the reverend, standing as Virgil

did. "And if she accepts I will be delighted for both of you, and for Little John. The whole island will be delighted."

"*That* would be a surprise," Virgil said.

Did he hear a *Humph* beyond the bedroom door?

Chapter 12
Loomings

"... the 1918 triumph marks the fifth World's Series that the Red Sox have brought to the high brow domicile of the baked bean. Boston is the luckiest baseball spot on earth, for it has never lost a World's Series."

New York Times, late edition
Wednesday, September 11, 1918

The 1918 World Series between the Boston Red Sox and Chicago Cubs began on Thursday, September 5 in Comiskey Park on a soggy field, the baseball season having been shortened by the war effort. Babe Ruth, who already had a thirteen-inning World Series scoreless streak to his credit, started for Boston, facing Jim "Hippo" Vaughn of the Cubs. In the seventh inning a navy band played "The Star-Spangled Banner" for the sailors in attendance from the Great Lakes Naval Station and the patriotic audience, beginning a tradition that would continue through the 1918 series and beyond. Playing the series in a three-and-four format, the teams left Chicago on the Michigan Central Railroad with Boston enjoying a two-to-one advantage and looking forward to playing at home in Fenway Park.

At the fourth game, the first at Fenway, Corporals

Robbins and Clair were in the stands with the Chippewas and over a hundred other soldiers from Camp Devens who had managed to get special passes. They saw Ruth hit a triple over the right fielder's head and put Boston ahead by three games to one—one game shy of victory. In the next game Hippo Vaughn pitched a shutout against Boston's Sad Sam Jones, keeping Chicago alive in the series and providing an opportunity, thanks to General Hodges, for Steve and Henry to see another game.

On Wednesday morning Steve dropped Mrs. Hodges and the general at the officers' club for a luncheon, drove the car back to the motor pool for his replacement, and hurried on foot to the Camp Devens train depot to meet Henry and catch the ten forty-five to Boston. It was a warm September morning and promised to be a perfect day for a ball game—sunny, with a stiff breeze off the Atlantic. The pair of tickets that the general had given Steve—he patted his tunic pocket to make sure he had them as he hurried through the main gate—had been given to the general by an ambitious lieutenant colonel; the seats were in the middle of the third row above the Boston dugout on the first-base line, something Steve had yet to tell Henry.

At the same depot where he had arrived nearly a year before, Steve found Henry standing apart from a milling crowd of men and boys in brown who were smoking, jostling one another, coughing like hags, and babbling excitedly about baseball and another World Series title for the Red Sox. Steve tapped a cigarette on his thumbnail and lit it while Henry craned his neck down the westering tracks to see the train they could hear approaching. Behind him and Steve a long line of empty trucks and freight wagons, many of them marked HOSPITAL or MORGUE, stretched from the depot up the side road, waiting for the freight cars.

"What kind of seats did he give you?" he asked Steve.

"It's a surprise." Steve blew a screen of cigarette smoke toward the swelling crowd; he believed that smoke protected him from influenza germs, working like it did with honeybees. "But I'll tell you this much, Corporal Clair: You'll be able to count Babe Ruth's nose hairs from where we're sitting."

The engines passed Steve and Henry and the dozen or so others waiting near the closest wagons; then the passenger cars passed as well. When the train had shuddered to a stop, the brakemen pulled open the doors of the two freight cars, releasing for those New England boys standing nearby an overwhelming sweet nostalgic smell of fresh-cut pine that would have brought homesick tears to their eyes had it not been coming from stacked carloads of freshly made empty coffins.

While the depot crowd waited impatiently for twenty or more new doctors and nurses to detrain with their suitcases, a pair of staff sergeants appeared and conscripted Henry and Steve and the group next to them to unload the coffins from the train and into the wagons and trucks.

"You corporals. You, too." The curly black hair that grew out from underneath the collar of the shorter sergeant gave him a rare authority.

"Aw Sarge," Steve said. "We've got tickets to the ball game. This will be the last game of the series. We can't miss it."

"What the hell difference does that make?" the sergeant

wanted to know. "This train is going nowhere until those coffins are off-loaded and put aboard those wagons. So you might as well just pitch the hell in."

While the curly sergeant was talking to Steve and Henry, and the other was trying to stir the drivers of the first few trucks into some semblance of motion, the dozen or so other soldiers standing near the coffin cars melted into the larger crowd that was pushing aboard the passenger cars.

Henry assessed the situation.

"Jesus."

He shouldered his way through the boys crowded onto the stairs and platform of the nearest passenger car, then forced his way into the car through those crammed in the aisle, getting elbowed and cursed vigorously for his pains. The boy whose face was inches from Henry's broke into a fit of coughing. Henry whistled shrilly and shouted, "At ease!" in his best command voice. The car settled to a murmur, then silence.

"Listen up." Henry was loud, but he was not shouting; his voice filled the car, overcoming the rustling and hacking and wheezing.

"We need your help back there unloading two freight cars." He spoke slowly. "We'll need all of you to pitch in so we can get it done quick."

"I don't know who the hell you think you are," came a husky voice from the middle of the aisle.

"I think I'm a guy who doesn't want to miss even a minute of the final game of the World Series, with Babe Ruth pitching. They're not going to move this train until those coffins are loaded onto the trucks and gone. If you sit here, it will take two hours or more; if you unass this car and help us, we can be out of here in fifteen minutes and waiting in line at the beer concession stand in two hours. You choose."

With the two sergeants and another corporal, Henry and Steve organized the troops into grumbling details—one on the boxcars, one beneath the cars, and one at the trucks—so that they kept a steady flow of man-sized pine boxes, passing from train to trucks without the drivers having to alight. On each truck or wagon bed they stacked the coffins in tiers of six—headfirst, feetfirst, headfirst in each row. When a vehicle was loaded, Hairy Sergeant spanked one of the horses or slapped the hood, and off it went.

"Jay-sus," said an Irishman, wiping his face on his sleeve. "There must be a thousand of them."

"My hands are getting sticky," said another. "There's hundreds at least."

"Old Man Grippe," a hospital orderly said. "If they have it bad, in just a couple of hours they start getting these big brown blotches on their cheeks, then it spreads all over their faces so you can't tell a white man from a colored man."

"It knocks them into a cocked hat." Another orderly sat atop a wagon seat, his face covered with a surgical mask. "They take the boots and socks off the ones waiting on stretchers outside, and if the guy's feet are black, they leave him there to go straight to the morgue. It's how they weed them out. There's only so many beds, you know. They die in a few hours. They suffocate."

A truck in the receiving line stalled. Steve went to investigate, taking with him a team of four to push if need be.

"Yesterday they moved a signal company out of their barracks to make an extra morgue," said a blond boy. "A guy I know saw it. He said they're lined up in double lines on both sides of the floor, up and down stairs, all laid out dead in uniform and in ranks, like for a parade only they're on their backs. He said it makes you some uneasy to walk through there. If I was going to get it, I would've been sick already."

"So far neither team has won by more than one run," said a boy sliding a coffin in place. "The Red Sox can't hit the Cubs."

"It's a plague, I say. You know that fish we eat? It's poisoned with flu germs let loose by German submarines in the ocean outside Boston. How many sailors at the Commonwealth Pier have died from it? More than sixteen just yesterday, that's how many."

The stalled truck, revived by Steve, rolled into position to be loaded, with instructions to idle high. The first of the two freight cars was empty and the second close to it when they ran out of wagons and trucks and began to stack the coffins at railside in neat tiers like lobster traps. In twos and threes the men whom Henry had recruited trickled back to the passenger cars.

When they were done, Henry and Steve joined the overflow from the forward cars in the empty freight cars, opening the big doors on both sides for the view, and to chase out the stinging odor of pine resin that no longer reminded them of home, but made them think of boys dead.

"Watch that cigarette in that straw."

A soldier with a tint of Quebecois in his accent said that in his company they were made to gargle salt water every morning against the flu.

Elated to be moving and off to another ball game, Steve almost said that gargling salt water was what killed his Uncle Pete when he drowned in the Eggemoggin Reach, but he stopped himself when he remembered that the same thing had killed Henry's father John when he'd drowned off the Sheep Ledges in '09.

Not one of the men and boys in the freight car that morning wanted to think anymore of their fellow soldiers who were dropping dead by the dozens; not one of them believed that it would or could happen to him; not one of them thought of anything but the glorious Boston Red Sox when the train had pulled out of sight of Camp Devens.

Steve Robbins guessed that a fifth of the twenty-eight thousand people in Fenway Park that afternoon were in uniform. There were soldiers and sailors and marines in blocks of a hundred or more in the stands, in pairs and clusters on the edges of the field, perched among the civilian men and boys on the far rooftops and stealing kisses from the few girls among the audience. Whole rows of drunken soldiers stamped their feet and clapped their hands in unison when a Boston player hit one into the outfield or took a walk. Clusters of tipsy sailors shouted encouragement to Carl Mays and called for Sad Sam Jones to have another inning. Squads of beery marines on the outfield fence howled in pain and shame when poor Flack dropped a line drive and let Whiteman drive in two runs.

Henry "Number Sixteen" Coombs heard his friend's assessment of the military makeup of the crowd, but he replied with only a grunt and did not look around to confirm or dispute the guess. Henry had a choke hold on the neck of the beer bottle in his lap; he had one eye on Babe Ruth, who was warming up in the hole with three bats, and the other on Lefty Tyler who for three consecutive innings had been consistently throwing a breaking ball on two strikes and was about to do the same to Hooper, whom Henry hoped had caught on by now and would take the walk.

In the bottom of the fourth Henry did not notice the boy to his right front, who was coughing so violently that he was bent over onto his knees, his arms wrapped around his rib cage, because Henry was straining to hear the insults and catcalls that the Boston dugout was hurling across the plate at the boys from Chicago. In the top of the fifth, when Carl Mays helped himself and his team by taking his fourth walk, Henry did not notice that Steve and a corporal from supply trains had found a pair of young lovelies in the fifteenth row and were immediately unsuccessful in winning their hearts.

When they stood in the seventh inning for "The Star-Spangled Banner" Steve noticed that Henry was still holding a half-empty bottle of beer, and the three other bottles that Steve had bought and fetched stood between Henry's feet still full and sweaty.

In the top of the ninth Henry did not notice a pair of soldiers making their way up the aisle with a lifeless young man draped between them, because sidearmer Carl Mays was two pitches away from a three-hitter, another World Series for the Red Sox, and twenty-six hundred dollars apiece for the winners. Henry had passed from amazed to mesmerized by the speed of Mays's sidearm.

Leaving the park with a corked beer bottle in each pocket of his tunic, in the din of cheering fans, car horns, and a bedraggled brass band across the lot, a joyful Henry did not notice four Red Cross nurses in uniforms and masks loading a soldier on a stretcher into an ambulance, because he was engaged in loud argument with an infidel from the signal company who held that if the two teams had gone out on strike after the third game as they had threatened they should be banned from baseball—every single son of a bitch of them. Henry whooped in reply and, with his famous arm, winged an empty beer bottle far over the crowd and beyond onto a distant ash heap, a distance even Mays might not manage.

His shoes in hand, Amos descended the dark staircase, stepping over the next-to-last step that would squeal under his weight and perhaps waken Leah. Clytie had slept fitfully most of the night, waking him up several times by heaving from one side to another, shifting and moaning, but now, just before daybreak, she was deep in a laudanum sleep. The morning house was damp and cool; the breeze through the open windows was southeasterly, carrying moisture and patches of fog from the open sea. Walter would certainly want to haul their traps today unless it got too foggy, which Amos doubted would happen with a steady breeze like this one.

In the kitchen he heard Maggie splashing in the washbasin just around the corner; he set down his shoes just loud enough for her to hear that he was there. She had not lit a lamp, and he thought that he would not, either; in the soft partial darkness that would soon lighten to gray, a light, even an oil lamp, would be harsh, and, he thought, it would show their silhouettes in the kitchen window.

Maggie emerged from the washroom and whispered good morning. He was surprised to see her in her robe and nightgown, but then he remembered that it was Saturday and that she and Leah had stayed up late reading aloud. When Maggie raised her arms and lowered her head slightly to tie her hair up, he thought that he had never wanted so badly to touch her as he did now.

"Did you finish the book?" he whispered.

"Not until nearly eleven." She smiled at him, or at some thought. "She slept in my bed. She wanted to hear the clock strike midnight."

"Did she?" he whispered.

"I don't know; I fell asleep. How's Clytie? I heard her once."

"She had a rough night. I gave her four drops about an hour and a half ago; she'll sleep heavy, and late."

Next to her at the counter he breathed in the smell of her soap, her sleep; when he took a plate of biscuits from the bread box, his arm brushed her shoulder and he lost two of the biscuits, but managed to hold on to the plate. She held a hand over her mouth to stifle a laugh and shook her head at his clumsiness. He ate one of the biscuits he had dropped and watched her set the breakfast table without a sound; she even caught the teapot before it started to whistle.

"You finished the first week of school already," he whispered. "Are you sorry you signed up for another year?"

"No, I'm glad I did. I've become attached to some of the kids, Leah especially, and I'm beginning to feel that the schoolhouse is mine, the board notwithstanding. Do you want butter?"

"Last spring I thought you were going to leave. That night walking home in the rain you were almost crying. You missed Ruth; you missed civilization, you called it. You were pissed off and fed up with Cecilia and Tessie and Clytie, too, though you never mentioned her. That's when you told me about that guy, your beau."

"Richard," she whispered. "And I remember telling you that I am not sweet on him anymore. I was never serious about him. What I did not tell you that night is that I was angry but I was also scared, and it was because of him, or in part at least, that I was scared. I got pregnant by him, Amos. I had an abortion. We did not want to get married; neither of us did, and I did not want a child. I hated myself afterward; I was ashamed, and still am. But I am no longer afraid as I was then that people down here would find out somehow—once I thought that Tessie had—and I would have to leave the school in disgrace and maybe even the island because they would judge me and condemn me. They would never understand; they would not even want to try."

She scooped oatmeal from the canister and poured it into a pan of boiling water, stirring rapidly.

"Who else knows about it?" he asked. "I mean down here on the island. Does Clytie know?"

"Only Rachel." She studied his face. "You're not shocked? You're not disgusted? Not angry?"

"No. I'm sorry. I'm sorry you've been worried that

people would find out; I'm sorry you had to have that operation. Don't be ashamed. It doesn't make me mad; it doesn't change the way I—"

"The way you feel about me?" she whispered. "How do you feel about me?"

"I can't say that, Maggie. I don't know how to."

"Can you show me?"

He reached out to touch her face, her hair, her neck, but his hand drew back. When she did not move, but only watched his face, he reached out again, touched the hair above her ear, drew her to him, her face against his neck and shoulder, and held her while she sobbed quietly.

He held her face in his hands and wiped her tears with thick callused thumbs.

"I'm sorry," he said.

"No," she whispered. "I'm crying because I'm happy. I've wanted this for months, and I've wanted to believe that you did, too."

"Oh God, Maggie, you don't know."

"Yes I do."

She kissed him timidly at first, then harder as he drew her closer. When she felt him becoming aroused, she pulled him even closer, her hands in the small of his back.

"Oh," she whispered. "Oh Amos."

With her rag doll Jenny hanging by her arm from one hand, and the other steadying her against the door frame as she leaned ahead and around the corner to see into the kitchen, Leah watched the lovers from the shadowy foot of the stairs, breathing through parted lips and thinking how much she hated Cecil Barter.

Chapter 13
Going Home

"She can't move out, not now. Amos can't take care of Clytie and the girl by himself. Pretty convenient, I'd say."

Cecilia Barter, September 27, 1918

Dr. Rufus Cole sat in the front seat of General Hodges' car and turned slightly to his left to address the distinguished guests in the back. The larger of the guests, Dr. William Henry Welch, was revered nationwide in the medical community and often referred to as the dean of American medicine; next to him sat Colonel Victor Vaughan, the eminent epidemiologist. The pair had come to Camp Devens at the request of Dr. Rupert Blue, the U.S. surgeon general, who was eager for expert opinions on the gravity of the situation there.

"I would begin with pleasantries, gentlemen, but I'm afraid that there are none," offered Dr. Cole from the front seat. Dr. Cole, chief of medicine at the Camp Devens hospital, was host to the distinguished guests, and he was visibly cowed by the great Dr. Welch, who intoned his reply.

"Au contraire, Doctor, au contraire. Our boys have taken the Saint Mihiel salient, with a little help from the French, and have done so in just four days, supported by fourteen hundred American aircraft."

"Ah." Dr. Cole looked at the general's driver for a reaction, but Corporal Robbins, who was on loan with the car, kept his eyes on the road.

"*And,* Doctor," the eminent Welch continued. "*And* there are rumors from substantial sources, sources that I am not at liberty to divulge, that the German chancellor has sued for peace."

As they passed camp headquarters and the well-kept central parade ground—the only patch of living color on the entire post—Dr. Welch tapped a cigarette on the thin silver case he'd taken from his coat pocket, lit it with a burnished lighter, and blew a bored cloud of smoke at the back of Corporal Robbins' head.

"I think Dr. Cole meant that there is little or no good news here at Camp Devens," said Colonel Vaughan, who would very much have liked to have been offered a cigarette, and who was not in any way cowed by Dr. Welch: not by his reputation, not by his bulk, not by his white mustaches and goatee, not by his supercilious tone.

A grateful Dr. Cole unfolded a sheet of paper and to Colonel Vaughan read the current statistics, leaving it to the experts to decide whether this was an epidemic or not.

"To date, in the three weeks since September second, we have had over seventeen thousand sick. Seventeen thousand. This means, for example, that twenty-nine-point-six percent of the Thirteenth Battalion is sick; seventeen-point-three percent of the Forty-second Infantry is sick; and twenty-four-point-six percent of the trains and military police is sick. To date we have had seven hundred and sixty-eight deaths, sixty-three of them yesterday. Our hospital, built for two thousand, is trying to accommodate as many as eight thousand; we are losing doctors and nurses at an appalling rate, and more and more soldiers are sick every day."

"Hence the term 'alarming' in the surgeon general's telegram." Dr. Welch rolled down his window and nodded imperiously to a trio of soldiers, who saluted the two stars on the general's license plate.

"I suppose so," said Dr. Cole. "You will see for yourself in a few minutes."

"We'll want to do an autopsy."

"Of course."

"I see that the windows in all your buildings are open, and that everyone is wearing a mask," Colonel Vaughan said.

"We have forbidden formations and gatherings of any kind, even to the point of staggering feeding schedules, yet it spreads. I don't know what else to do."

"Nor do I," the epidemiologist said. "It is nearly as bad in Boston. The death rate in the hospitals there is fifty percent. We will do everything we can to identify this infection and kill it, to keep it from spreading farther if we can. Won't we, Doctor?"

"We shall."

The distinguished guests, who had many mutual friends and had not seen one another in years, talked amiably until Steve slowed as they approached the hospital. There the guests fell silent. In the open area beside the hospital and between buildings countless men and boys waited in lines in the morning drizzle; they lay under blankets in rows, sat alone or in small groups against the buildings with their heads on their knees. Among the thousands crowded around the hospital compound in the gray light, the only motion was a man crumpling to his knees here, a boy curling into the fetal position there; among them all the only sounds to be heard were scattered muffled coughs and piteous soft moans.

Steve pulled around to the front door of the hospital, where a deputation of exhausted doctors in white coats waited.

"My God." Colonel Vaughan broke the silence. "I had not . . ."

"Undique ambulavit mors," whispered Dr. Welch.

A little after five that evening, in a persistent light rain, Steve found Henry sitting on an apple crate underneath a tarp outside his barracks. On another crate, this one upturned, he was writing a letter to Claire with a stubby pencil. He was bare-headed and had replaced his homemade surgical mask with a government-issue mask that he had received that morning. Though he was wearing a mask himself, and hadn't seen anyone who was not wearing one in days, Steve found the sight of Henry in a mask amusing, but only briefly.

"You brought the car," Henry said when Steve ducked under the tarp. "You'll get your ass in a sling for that."

"Probably, but no, I don't care." Steve took off his hat and pushed back his hair.

"What's wrong, Steve? There's something wrong, isn't there?"

"Are you blind? How many guys you got lying sick in your squad bay?" Steve asked.

"Four. Your fever has to be a hundred and three to get admitted to the hospital, and anyway there's some of us that think they're better off here."

"Well you're probably right," said Steve. "I just spent the day at the hospital following around three doctors, two of them sent by the surgeon general himself to figure out what's going on with this flu. The one, a Doctor Welch, was a high-toned snob when I picked him up at the train this morning; when I dropped him off at the officers' club just now he was a scared old man. I'm getting the hell out of here."

"Yeah, right. Let's take the general's car and go for a ride to Stonington. Take Claire for a spin."

"Fuck you. I saw men black in the face, men with faces like a mackerel's belly, men with blood coming out of their noses, men spitting up blood, men drowning in their own blood, healthy boys dead in an hour or two. Shit. These two doctors, who are supposed to be the top men in the country, maybe the world, they did an autopsy—I didn't watch—and said they've never seen anything like it—blood-soaked lungs so heavy they sank like a stone in the basin. One called it a mixed infection; the other one called it a plague. Neither of them had any idea of what it is, what kind of germ, or what the hell to do about it or how to stop it. It's killing a hundred of us a day and it's going to get worse. I am getting out of here, and if you had any sense you'd go with me."

"Well you can't just *leave*. We signed on. We took an

oath. If you leave you'll be a deserter. They'll hunt you down and lock you up for good." Henry shook his head. He folded Claire's letter and buttoned it into his breast pocket. "People will think you're a coward."

"We signed on to fight the Hun, to fight a war, not to die in some bunk bed with our lungs full of blood without even getting a chance to fight. Die for nothing." Outside the tarp two soldiers were examining the general's car.

"Get the hell away from there," Steve shouted, and they ambled away, hands in their pockets. "Jesus Christ Henry. I'll take you to the hospital so you can watch a few die. I'll take you to the morgue, I'll take you to where they have Negroes digging grave trenches and filling them with bodies and quicklime. Then you'll see."

"There's a war on. I'm a soldier. We still might get to go overseas." Henry was unmoved.

"That's just it. That's why I came over here right away." Steve looked around. "That Doctor Welch told the colonel here that the surgeon general himself told him the German chancellor has sued for peace. The war will be over in days. You're not going over there. And I'm not going to die in a bed in Massa-fucking-chusetts for nothing. I'm getting a weekend pass and I'm getting on the train and going to Boston and changing stations and riding to Bucksport. I'll walk home from there."

"They'll find you," said Henry, thinking that they would not find him; if they did go looking for him, it would be for John Clair from Portland. "It's desertion."

"I hope you don't think I was dumb enough to give them my real home address. And it's not desertion. I'll be AWOL, sure, but I'm going to Deer Isle. When they find a way to cure this flu and stop this plague—if the entire fucking army and half the world, it's worst in Spain, isn't wiped out before they do—then I'll come back and take the Article Fifteen in punishment. If the war is still on, that is. Let me show you. Come on."

"You don't have to show me."

"I'm going to anyway. Come on."

WESTERN UNION TELEGRAM
Camp Devens, Mass. September 24, 1918
Mrs. John Coombs, Barter Island, Maine
STAY ON THE ISLAND STOP DON'T LET STRANGERS COME ASHORE STOP FLU KILLING THOUSANDS STOP ME AND STEVE OK END
Henry

During the Friday arithmetic test in the hour before lunch, Maggie and the children looked up in unison, surprised by the frantic yelping and howling coming from the alder swamp beside the school. They often heard the Greenlaws' hound dog Slack plowing through the swamp baying after a rabbit, but this morning the sounds coming from the dog were almost childlike; they were high-pitched, confused, and fearful, and he seemed to be running in circles among the shrubs.

"Father says when a hound goes haywire like that it means there's a storm coming," said Cecil Barter.

"Shush, we're taking a test." Leah erased her last answer.

Maggie walked to the door and stood inside the screen.

She pushed her pencil into her hair and stood perfectly still. The air seemed sullen; not a leaf or stem of timothy stirred. The water in the thorofare was flat calm, and the smell of the exposed tidal flats was exceptionally ripe, though no breeze blew it toward her. She wondered why they had had no storm warning or news of a hurricane, and thought that perhaps it would be coming on the mail boat, which she had seen steaming into the thorofare a few minutes before. Not a single gull was in flight; the few she could see were perched quietly among the big rocks on the shore. The sky to the south was heavy with clouds, piled high, thick and white above, and far darker below than any fog bank, as dark and black as the inside of a dead man's mouth. She would send the first to finish his test—that would be Ethan—on an errand to the landing for any news or warning. Amos and Walter were out bringing in their traps, as was Virgil; she prayed that they were done on the southern end, and that they were either inside the Battery or back safe in the cove by now, chased home by the frightful sky.

Around the bend in the road by Town Hall she saw Cyrus Weed and Rachel in Tessie's dogcart. Cyrus was driving old black Tink hard, swatting her rump with a willow switch; in her lap Rachel's hands lay as calm as the sea.

"Hurricane coming, Miss Bowen." Cyrus did not dismount. "You ought to send the kids home. It struck Camden around ten; it's a bad one—a hurricane, not a gale. Miss Tessie sent me to take you and Rachel home, and Leah, so you can get boarded up. We ought to hurry."

"If Amos hasn't come in yet—God help us if they're still on the water—I might ask you to take us all the way down to Head Harbor; Clytie is so afraid of a storm."

"No problem."

Maggie looked at Rachel, who smiled back bravely. Maggie knew that Rachel would be so concerned about Virgil out on the water that she would not suffer her own fear of storms.

When Maggie dismissed the children, they cheered wildly and scurried past Cyrus and Rachel, heading home with their hopes set on a natural disaster of mythic proportions.

Two hours later Virgil told Ava and Walter that he was going to go walk down to Rachel's house to check on her and make sure her house was battened down proper. The storm was upon them, the wind keening in the treetops, the sea making up, with thick patches of foam blowing past the mouth of the cove. The darkness was not utter, but it was as thick as it could get in near daylight; the windblown rain was horizontal and biting cold. The little man in Ava's weather house was so far extended from the house that it looked as though he would drag the sunny little girl out his side with him.

"Good." Ava used a spatula to push rags into the cracks around the kitchen windows to shut up the wheezing noise the wind made there. "I don't like her being in the lee of that big oak; a limb or trunk could break off and crash down on her house and crush her to death."

"Don't be so goddamned optimistic," Walter said.

"Watch your language. And Rachel hates storms, she always has. Tell her to come up here and stay the night; tell her I said please. Tell her she can sing to Little John so he doesn't hear the creaking and groaning of the house."

Virgil was not gone forty-five minutes. He found Walter thumbing through the Sears catalog at the kitchen table, seemingly oblivious to the storm outside.

"Did you see the boats?"

"They're all right." Virgil dried his face with a dish towel. "They're straining, but they're all right."

"I don't even want to guess what's going to happen to those three strings we still have out by Green Ledge; I don't want to think about losing traps again this year."

"No."

Ava's voice came from the parlor. "What about Rachel for heaven's sake? Why didn't she come back with you? Is she safe?"

"She's drinking tea." Virgil sounded so far away that Walter looked up from the harness page to make sure he was there. "She's fine. She's sitting by the big vase lamp reading. She said yes."

Walter simply stared, his forefinger frozen beneath a price listing. Ava appeared in the doorway, wearing the same look on her face that she had worn when her rooster won the blue ribbon at the Deer Isle fair.

"Well," Virgil said. "What do you think?"

"What do I think?" Ava took three steps forward, kissed Virgil on the mouth—something she had never done before—stepped back, and with her hands on her hips said: "I think it is altogether fitting and proper that you proposed to her in what sounds like the storm of the century, the Big Wind itself, and she accepted you under the same conditions." Ava beamed.

"I hope she's prepared for a lifetime of misery," Walter

said. He stood and shook Virgil's hand.

"Go to hell, Walter."

"Later; hell's for later. Right now I'm going to go down to the fish shack and have a drink or two with you to celebrate."

"Oh don't go down to the water," Ava asked. "It's blowing so hard, and it feels like it's getting stronger."

"The wind's easterly isn't it?" Walter reached for his slicker. "If it gets that much stronger, it'll blow us back up here into the dooryard, dead or alive, and you won't have to come looking for us."

"You come back in half an hour; I want to go see her and tell her how happy I am."

Outside, holding his collar clamped under his chin and leaning into the wind, Walter asked Virgil why the hell he hadn't stayed down at Rachel's, spent the night there, bundling and snuggling and all that.

"She said I couldn't."

Sunday morning
Sept. 27, 1918
Ruth Dear,

Thanks for the news clippings about this "flu" epidemic. It sounds awful for Boston, even more frightening because the nature of the germ is an enigma. I pray that it doesn't spread to places like Camp Devens, though I cannot imagine that it wouldn't, with all the movement of troops that goes on. We try not to worry about Henry and the other boys. I'm glad there have not been any cases in Bangor; I certainly don't think that we will see its ugly face down here on the island. We are so far away, and as of three days ago so well protected. Tessie Wedge (who I believe secretly loves other people's infections) has drafted her reverend into service and the two of them meet the mail boat every day to keep strangers from stepping ashore and to paint the mailbag with a concoction of vinegar and camphor that may not kill germs but certainly clears the sinuses of the poor man who has to shoulder it to the P.O. Dr. Banks has put a quarantine sign at the dock in Stonington, warning off any visitors to Barter Island. If that doesn't scare them off, Tessie surely will, so we feel pretty snug down here.

The good news is that we had little or no serious damage from the hurricane. This one was a doozy and for the first time I was in the eye of a storm. The skies cleared, the winds abated, and except for the angry sea we spent ten minutes or more in a magical stillness. It came back with a vengeance and howled all night long.

The *really* good news is that Virgil proposed to Rachel and she accepted. None of us was too surprised, and we are all delighted for both of them. Walter told Amos that Ava quoted Abraham Lincoln when she heard the news. What do you make of that? Now lovely Rachel will have no more "wild nights"; she will be "moored" in Virgil, who is truly, if I may belabor the conceit, a safe harbor. The talk is of a spring wedding, and the speculation is that Rachel will move in with Virgil and the baby, leaving her house empty for Henry should he bring home a bride.

Clytie is still very sick, I'm sorry to say. At Dr. Banks's insistence, we are giving her a little laudanum to make sleep easier. Amos and I take turns tending to her needs and trying to comfort her as best we can, but she is so miserable and so cruel to Amos especially. The finest time of the day is early morning when Amos and I are alone in the quiet kitchen, he making up and packing his dinner pail, I getting breakfast for us and Leah when she gets up. A few days ago I confided in him about Richard and the abortion, and his genuine sympathy and understanding nearly melted me. I am surprised and even a little embarrassed that until recently I did not notice that for one so clumsy with words, he is often very funny, and for one so strong and clumsy of hands and feet, he is ever so gentle.

I am off to church this morning, eager to see the aftermath of the storm on the road to town and to ply Rachel with terribly personal questions on the way.

Love, always,
Maggie

P.S.: Speaking of confidences, Ava surprised me after the christening by telling me why she so loathes and distrusts Tessie. It seems that when the reverend first came to the island, he and Ava were sweethearts and Tessie was green with jealousy. When Tessie discovered them sparking in the carriage seat in the parsonage barn, she ran home to tell her father, the fearful Captain Ulysses Wedge, that there were strange noises in the reverend's barn and the reverend was not at home. When the captain burst in on them, Ava was bare to the waist. Captain Wedge would not let her cover her nakedness; while he berated the lovers, especially Ava, whom he called a harlot, he and the reverend gawked at her breasts, onto which her tears fell. Tessie watched the whole thing through the door. Ava did not speak to Tessie or the reverend for years and years, and has not set foot in their church since. I admire Ava for being civil to them now and for not stirring up talk about their smarmy little trysts, which would be very easy to do down here.

As they traveled north of Boston, Henry noticed that fewer and fewer of the passengers boarding the train were wearing masks. In New Hampshire people began closing their windows against the chilly evening breeze off the ocean. Soon Steve and Henry, two elderly couples, and a solitary forlorn soldier—all that were left of those who had boarded at Boston's North Station—were the only ones in the car still masked. At sunset, as they crossed the bridge over the Piscataqua into Maine, Steve untied his mask and dropped it out the window, and Henry did the same with his. Among the sailors and soldiers and travelers who slept on benches and the floor in the Portland terminal that night, there was no sound or sign of sickness. While Steve snuffled in a deep sleep on the bench next to him, Henry sat awake in the dimly lit station, watching the doors for the military police or shore patrol that might come through asking for passes, rounding up deserters. He would tell Claire and the rest that they had been sent home on a special extended leave until the epidemic had passed, that they would only have to return if they were to be shipped out.

It was the middle of Sunday afternoon when they arrived in Bucksport. The streets were puddled and the eaves of the depot still dripping from the rain that had just passed, leaving the sky overcast; in the west were signs of more rain.

"Doesn't look like we're going to find a ride, does it?" Steve looked down Main Street, where three cars were parked in front of the Jed Prouty Inn but no other cars or wagons or pedestrians were to be seen.

"Everybody's gone home for Sunday dinner," said Henry. "I guess we'll be walking. I was thinking about it on the train and I think I'll like walking home."

"Let's us have a Sunday dinner of our own before we start out. I'm so hungry I could eat the ass off a charging skunk."

Steve told the waiter in the Jed Prouty that they were heading home for leave prior to going overseas, and as a consequence they ate for free and ate so much that they had to loosen their tunic belts. For a good mile on the empty road out of town Steve released one rich and resounding belch after another, and Henry, laughing, had to hold his breath to suppress his hiccups. At the bottom of the long hill in the little village of Orland, Steve pointed across the pond to show Henry where he and Amos had left the flivver, and wished aloud that it was still there to take them home.

"We should have written Amos ahead of time and had him drive it up here to meet us," Henry said.

"Well look at this. Our prayers are answered."

A bearded man in a broad-brimmed preacher's hat and his wife beneath her shawl were coming down the hill behind them in a small freight wagon drawn by a beautiful pair of bays. As the wagon approached, it began to drizzle. The boys lifted their campaign hats to the lady and the farmer pulled in his reins.

"We're going to Penobscot," the man said. His wife did

not look at them; she sat still and slightly bent, a scarecrow lashed to the seat.

"We're going to Deer Isle. Mind if we hitch a ride to the turnoff?"

The man nodded, and three drops fell from his hat brim onto his hands. The boys rode in silence in the light rain, their legs dangling from the rear of the wagon, until Steve, who did not seem able to make himself comfortable, got up and sat leaning against the low side, his legs drawn up under him, his chin on his knees. At the turnoff at the cemetery on the top of the hill, the farmer slowed to let them off, wishing them good luck. Henry waved his hat at the couple's backs as they drove away.

"If it wasn't so overcast, we could see Blue Hill and Barter Island from here, the mountain at least. Jesus, Steve, what's wrong?"

Steve stood ghostly pale, one hand on the broken iron cemetery gate, the other slowly patting his chest. He swayed forward once and shut his eyes.

"What is it?" Henry shouted, thinking to himself: *No, no, no.*

"It's pain is what it is. It's pain like I never felt. It's all over. It's behind my eyes, my neck. It's in my spine and my legs, too. I got to lie down. Oh, Henry Coombs; I am fucked."

"No you're not. Not here, not in this rain. You've got to walk. I'll help you. There's a house down there; I can see it through the trees. Hold on to my shoulder."

Supported by Henry's arm around his waist, Steve walked with uncertain steps like an old woman afraid of falling. "Christ I am burning up. I feel like I am burning up, Henry."

Henry encouraged him every step of the way down the road, saying that it would pass soon, it was maybe something he ate back there, he could lie down and get some sleep, he'd soon be dry and feeling better. On the granite doorstep of a large, sprawling house and connected barn, Henry knocked on the wide blue door while Steve tried to build himself upright.

A man in his midthirties, with a linen napkin tucked into the second button of his shirt, opened the door cautiously; behind him a woman's voice ordered a child to come back to her. Before Henry could speak, the man shut the door.

"What the hell?"

The door to the connecting building to their right, the woodshed, opened and the man stepped out, napkin still dangling, shotgun leveled at the boys on his stoop.

"You got to move on, boys. That's that influenza. I got a wife and kids in here." He raised and lowered the barrel of the shotgun and Henry, without reply, helped his friend away, cursing under his breath. He could see smoke from a chimney across a far field and started toward it, Steve getting heavier and warmer every second. Before they reached the path by the stone wall, a thin voice hailed them and Henry turned to see a skinny pigtailed girl of about thirteen running toward them from the barn, pushing a wheelbarrow.

"Take him in this," she said, breathing hard. "Take him to Major Small down the road. About half a mile down there, on the top of the next hill on the other side. He was a soldier, too. He'll take you in. There's a dory planted full of onions gone to seed by his road."

Henry thanked her. He reached out to take her hand, but demurred lest he infect her, too.

"There's a blanket in it to cover him with," she said, and sprinted back to the barn.

The dory with the onions growing in it had a fresh coat of dark green paint; the front door to Major Small's house was painted from the same can, as was the trim on the house.

Steve knocked and waited, knocked and waited, glancing anxiously at Steve, who was crumpled in the wheelbarrow, coughing under the damp blanket. Around the side of the house came a tall man with watery blue eyes and a shiny bald head. He was wearing a clean blue cotton shirt that reminded Steve of Virgil.

"What can I do for you, Corporal?"

Steve thought the man might be sixty, might be seventy; whatever his age, the man's tall frame did not have in it an ounce of frailty.

"My friend's Christly sick, sir. I'm looking for a place, a shed or a barn, where he can lie down and I can take care of him."

The man did not reply. He lifted the blanket from Steve's head and shoulders and with one hand under Steve's arm looked to Henry for assistance.

"It's the influenza, sir. It's the flu that's killing so many people. It is real contagious; you might not want to get too close."

"Help me take him inside, for Christ's sake. Get him the hell out of this wheelbarrow and into a dry bed. I'm alone here. I'm not afraid of disease; I've had them all and weathered them just fine."

"Thank you, Major. We can pay you."

"No you can't. And call me Abner. Here, take this arm."

As he hung Steve's wet uniform and underwear on the rack by the kitchen stove, Major Abner Small thought that suddenly and quite completely a very large cycle in his life had come to a close with the arrival of these two boys. He put a kettle on, brought out a jug and lemons, and talked to Henry through the bedroom door as he fussed over his silent companion.

"I came home the same way, more than fifty years ago, only I was the sick one, with the fever and the shits. We were cousins and we were corporals; it was the fall of eighteen sixty-three; we were pooched and we were afraid we would never get home. I thought you were us when I came around the corner of the house; maybe you are. Go to the springhouse out on the hillside and fetch some cold water for his brow; I'll mix up some toddies."

Abner Small liked to keep his house well lit, with as many as four lamps for each room in use, and the windows open to the outdoors, with screens. He made up a thick mutton stew and rolled out dough for biscuits, then coaxed Henry away from Steve's bed.

"He's asleep. You can't do anything for him. Come take care of yourself."

Henry thanked him; he raised his toddy in a grateful salute and flatfooted half of it.

"If it turns into pneumonia, it will kill him," Henry said.

"Most likely."

Abner Small did not question the young corporal while they ate except to find out that he was from Barter Island and his friend was from Stonington. He would let him tell his story when he wanted, and as he wanted. After they had eaten and he had changed the cloth on Steve's brow, Henry told Abner that they were going home on special leave because of the epidemic; he said that they both had been cheated out of a chance to go overseas with the Seventy-sixth Division because of the same goddamned general—Steve to be his driver, he to pitch for his baseball team.

"You ought to be grateful to him, not cussing him. Have another toddy. That guy saved your lives, you know; he at least saved you months of certain misery, something no man needs."

"I wish he hadn't; I didn't need saving."

"You'll look at it differently one day. I know why you boys seemed so familiar. A general saved my life, too, in a strange sort of way. Robinson of the First Corps. He sent the Sixteenth Maine, us, to hold the Mummasford Road against Ewell's entire damned Rebel corps, God knows how many thousands of them coming in two lines at us from both sides. Colonel Tilden had the sense to surrender after we'd held them long enough for our people to get regrouped. It was chaos pure: The Rebels yelling, our wounded screaming. He tore the Maine state flag into little strips and gave one to each of us to take with us and keep it alive; I still have mine someplace around here, all blue. I know I would have been killed in the next two days—that was Gettysburg—but instead

I got exchanged in Maryland and we made it home soon after. Sick as dogs, we were, but alive."

When Steve was conscious, however briefly, he was still far, far away. He moaned softly, and his cough was childlike, coming in little spasms. He responded to Henry or Abner with grunts when they asked him something, or assured him that he would be well. They took turns sitting up with him, in four-hour shifts in the night, bathing his forehead and neck with cold cloths, forcing him to take water and broth when they could. His fever hovered at 104 at noon on the first day of their stay with Abner, and held that temperature for forty-eight hours, cold compresses and icy springwater nothwithstanding. Steve would later say that when he awoke in that bed, the pain behind his eyeballs was so intense that it hurt even to grunt in reply; it hurt to listen; it hurt when he tried to comprehend what they were saying.

That afternoon, in the sunny aftermath of the night's rain, Abner went on horseback to Blue Hill in hopes of finding quinine. He returned at dusk with an armload of sweet corn, a folded paper packet of the drug, and three baseballs.

"You're driving me crazy pacing back and forth," he told Henry. "Find an old bushel basket, prop it up in front of a gunnysack stuffed with straw, and practice your pitching. Set up where he and I can see you from his window. It's not true that Abner Doubleday invented baseball. When I was a kid, I was the third generation of Smalls to play first base. Christ."

Henry arranged the stuffed sack and bushel basket against the outhouse, paced off ninety feet, saluted to the major who sat in the window by Steve's bed, and began to pitch. He threw fastballs; he threw breaking balls; he threw inshoots; he threw wild pitches that struck the outhouse, arousing the flies inside. While he threw, concentrating on his form and accuracy, he felt his fear for Steve recede and on the second day, in the chilly late-afternoon sunlight, he began to compose a letter to Claire.

He would tell her only generally where they were—south of Bucksport—and that Steve's fever had peaked and he was on his way to recovery. He would not stop to see her in Stonington because he was afraid that he might be contagious, but would go home to the cove for a period of quarantine, then come to see her. He would beg her to avoid strangers, especially drummers and rusticators from the Boston area. He would tell her how he ached to be close to her, to touch her soft cheek, to lie with his head in her lap under a big old tree.

Abner, in slouch hat and coveralls, stopped at the mound on his way to the pasture.

"I'm going to fetch the cows and milk; you ought to go in," he said. "But first: There's two outs, the bases are loaded, the count is full, and he's their best hitter. Let's see what strike you throw."

Henry leaned forward, the ball in his hand resting on the small of his back, frowned, and threw an inside changeup that raised a puff of dust from the gunnysack.

"Nice one. By the way, he was saying 'Rose' over and over. Is that his girl?"

"No, well, maybe. There's a Rose Eaton in Stonington but I didn't know he had his eye on her. I wouldn't blame him if he did; she's a beauty."

"Maybe he doesn't know it himself."

The next morning Henry was awakened in his chair by the distant thunder of an armload of firewood tumbling into the kitchen wood box. A noisy squirrel ran along a near branch of the oak tree, leaving a wake of falling brown leaves behind him.

Henry stood suddenly, crying out: "Major! Oh Jesus Major!"

Abner gripped Henry's upper arm and shook him violently, to calm him. Steve's hair, matted and mussed from his ordeal in bed, had turned a grayish white, the color of cobwebs.

"It happens," Abner said. "Get ahold of yourself. Next it will fall out. He must be over a hundred and five degrees, and we are out of quinine. All we can do is keep him cool and pray. Pitch. His hair will grow back, if he recovers. All of it."

"I'm scared, sir. I am scared shitless." Henry wiped his own forehead with the damp cloth.

"That's all right, son. It doesn't matter. You have to keep control of yourself. Change his bedclothes; he's bound to have sweated through them. Soon now the fever will either break or kill him."

It broke late that morning. Henry found Abner at his workbench, weaving rawhide onto an ash snowshoe frame; Henry had the thermometer in hand to show him.

"A hundred and two," Henry said, his lower lip quivering. "It's dropped to a hundred and two; it's broken."

"Praise God," said Abner. "That part is over with. Now I can rest."

Chapter 14
The Mooring

"I guess I'm not too surprised. I've thought several times since he was here that that one was uncommonly clear."

Huldah Cain, October 16, 1918

Virgil set the lantern on the stone next to Gladys's grave more out of habit this time than as a precaution. This time he did not creep through the spruce and shrubs to his old watching place, but stepped quietly out into the open dooryard in front of Rachel's house and walked around to the kitchen door. The windows were so thoroughly fogged over that they barely shed enough light to cast his shadow on the lawn, and though he did not try, he knew that he could not see her if he looked. In the dark outside the kitchen door he hesitated, wringing his hands, then with a deep breath and silent prayer he rapped twice, quickly, with his knuckle and opened the door.

Standing naked in the steaming washtub, Rachel cried "No!" when she saw and heard the door opening. With an arm across her breasts and a hand at her groin, she tried to cover herself just as he had always imagined she would, but instead of the shy, amorous smile that he had imagined, she turned bright red from crown to shoulders and said firmly, angrily:

"Turn around."

Virgil obeyed, and stared in confusion at the flour sifter. Rachel stepped out of the tub for her towel and covered herself, pinching the towel tight under her shoulder with her left hand.

"You could have knocked," she said to his back.

"I *did* knock Rachel. I didn't know you were—"

"Bathing? You didn't know? You didn't? You scared me half to death, embarrassed me. No, don't turn around."

"I'm sorry. I didn't mean to scare you, Jesus."

"Didn't you notice that the kitchen windows are steamed over?"

"Well, I did I guess, but I thought you were doing the dishes," he tried.

"At eight-thirty at night?" She shook her head. Virgil raised his shoulders to his ears in all innocence and to see such a childlike gesture made her smile at his back.

"I just wanted to see you, Rachel. It's been so long, I mean I've waited so long—for years, like I said, and that's the God's truth. Now I just wanted to see you." He hunched his shoulders again, slightly, and dropped them quickly.

"Oh Virgil," she said.

He turned around and gazed at her before he took a bashful step forward with one hand outstretched.

Rachel took the hand and held him at arm's length.

"Not here," she said. "Come upstairs."

She led him to the staircase, released his hand, and followed him, barefoot and damp beneath the towel, up the steps toward the yellow-gold light from her bedroom door, hardly daring to believe that there would be comfort in her life again.

Amos sat on the boulder where the road passed over Bridge Creek and waited for Maggie and Leah. The late sunlight that dappled through the trees over his shoulder was unusually warm for early October, though it had that bright autumn quality that was so dazzling on the water. Amos was tired and hungry and eager to see Maggie. He and Walter and Virgil had gotten both boats out of the water and into their cradles and he had gotten a splinter buried so deep under his callused forefinger that Maggie would have to dig it out with a needle when they got home. She would hold his hand in hers and take great care trying not to hurt him; when he winced, she would look up, her face inches from his, and say she was sorry, she'd be more careful. He slid down the stream bank and, on his knees on the mossy stones, brushed aside the bright fallen leaves and took a long drink of the cold, iron-dark creek water. He waited another fifteen minutes, then began to walk.

They caught up with him at the narrow bend in the road called the Needle's Eye. He put his dinner pail in the back where four large squatty pumpkins sat in a bed of straw.

"I kept Fuddy after school," Maggie explained.

"Cecil made them do it," Leah said.

Amos settled on the seat next to her and kissed her forehead. "Do what?"

"Well, Cecil didn't really make them do it, but I think you're right that he was the instigator. Who else would have thought of such a thing?"

"What'd they do?" Amos insisted.

"Fuddy and Skippy picked their boogers and put them in Vin's sandwich," Leah explained.

Amos laughed. "Did he eat it?"

"No, he did not," Maggie said, irked at his reaction. "Good God, Amos."

"Vin knocked Skippy's lights out." Leah punched the air with a little fist. "He went home with a bloody nose."

From its resting place on the seat back behind Leah, Amos's hand found its way behind Maggie and to the dimples above her buttocks, where it rested. Maggie shot him a glance that said *Stop that, you sweet devil,* and the hand retreated.

On the flat stretch of road along the pond, Hortense sensed that her stable was near and picked up her gait. The broad carpet of hay-scented fern on the slope to the pond was littered with thousands of little gold leaves shed by the huge old birch that stood inclining homeward amid the green.

When Head Harbor came into view—their white turreted house against the startling blue of sea and sky—Maggie wondered if she would ever be able to live anywhere else, having been this close to Paradise for so much of her life.

While Amos and Maggie unloaded the pumpkins and a bushel of apples onto the side porch, Leah ran through the door to find her mother, her footsteps sounding in the kitchen and parlor, then scampering up the stairs.

"Amos, we can't do that, things like that, in front of Leah," Maggie whispered.

Amos set the bushel down. "I know it. It was my damned hand; he struck out on his own."

Leah emerged onto the porch from the kitchen door, looking here and there anxiously.

"She's not here," she said.

Maggie suggested that Carla Wilson must have come by and taken Clytie for a ride in her little trap, as she'd been promising to do. Amos took Hortense's reins and walked her and the wagon toward the barn. Leah ran down the porch steps and around the house to the cellar entrance, where she found the bulkhead double doors wide open. She leaned in, bent over with her hands on her knees, afraid to go down into the blackness, and when her eyes adjusted to the dark, she began to scream: "Mama! Mommeee!" frozen in position until Maggie came up from behind, put an arm around her, and pulled her away gently, still screaming.

Amos started down the steps tentatively, saying, "Clytie? Clytie are you all right?"

Clytie sat collapsed on the cellar floor, her back against the canning shelves, her legs splayed in front of her. Resting in a fold of fat on her chest, her chin was slubbered with blood and her mouth was clearly the source of the river of blood that had spread down the front of her dress and since hardened. Her skin was a paler gray than the linen smock she wore, and her eyes were closed. Beside her, on the hard-packed floor, her white palms lay faceup, open and lifeless. When Amos raised her near hand to find a pulse, he saw a Mason jar of raspberry preserves nearly empty, and by her right hand a soup spoon smeared with jam.

Amos stood up and covered his face with his hands.

"She's gone," he said to the two heads framed in light at the top of the stairs. "It's not blood. It's vomit. It was the diabetes. She was eating jam. Oh God Maggie. Oh Leah, I am so sorry."

Leah's angry and fearful yelling had subsided to single syllables: "Ma. Ma." When Amos said that it was not blood, she dissolved in tears, wailing as Maggie lifted her into her arms to carry her into the house.

"I'm going to take Leah in, sweet girl. I'll come back in a little to help you move Clytie up. You can't lift her alone."

"Yes I can." Amos's hands opened and closed at his sides. "I'm going to bring her through the front door and carry her up to her bed. Perhaps you can find something for Leah in the kitchen while I do."

Maggie could not think what to say as she carried Leah inside and set her in a kitchen chair. She wetted a towel, put a plate of cookies on the table, sat down, and lifted Leah into her lap, where she washed her face slowly and murmured words and sounds of comfort. They heard Amos come through the front door then slowly, heavily, begin the stairs. They heard the bed creak beneath Clytie's weight, and the cane in the seat of the chair at bedside squeak as Amos sat down with her.

"I need to go to toilet." Leah let herself down from Maggie's lap and hurried out the back door. Maggie sat staring after her, thinking that she must be brave, must not fall apart, for Leah's sake.

When Leah returned, Maggie held out her hand to bring her back to her lap, but Leah sat in the chair opposite, picked up a cookie, and examined it.

"Mommy wanted to die because you and Daddy was fustin'."

Maggie's eyes snapped open. She breathed, so as not to faint, and stared appalled into Leah's dark eyes.

"What did you say?" she finally asked.

"You and Daddy was fustin' and she knew it and it made her so sad that she wanted to die."

"My God, Leah, that's rubbish, that's wrong," Maggie shook her head violently to throw off something that she knew would not let go. "Did she tell you that?"

Leah was motionless. "I saw."

"What did you see? Surely you did not."

"I saw you hugging in the kitchen in the morning. I saw you."

"We were hugging, it's true. But only hugging, Leah, not the other. We would not. Hugging for comfort, like I hug you."

"I'm a little girl. He's a man." Leah broke the cookie in half.

"You mother did not want to die. You must not believe that, dear one. I promise you that that is not true. Please believe me, say you do."

Leah was silent. She nodded slightly and did not look at Maggie.

Henry and Steve found Isaac Thomas at the town landing in Stonington and asked him if they could rent his peapod for the day, for a sail down to Barter Island. Even now, eleven days after his fever had broken, Steve was pale and fragile. He wore his overseas cap low to cover as much of the peach fuzz that was growing out on his head as possible. Isaac said he would not take money from men in uniform. Steve shook Isaac's hand and Henry, who would have done the same in normal circumstances, merely nodded and thanked him. Afterward, on their way out of Stonington harbor, Steve said that he was surprised that Isaac had taken his hand—the man must know that they had come from around Boston and could be carrying the infection. Henry said that perhaps Isaac knew that once you had it, you weren't contagious and couldn't pass it on.

"How would he know I had it?"

"He would look at you."

Steve sailed the little boat down the bay toward the early-morning sun; Henry sat in the bow, the sun at his back, and watched the mainland grow lighter as it drew away, the distant hills a tawny red. They sailed in silence, Steve adrift in thought, Henry suffering a healthy confusion of feelings about coming home: eagerness mixed with fear of infecting his family; the sheer joy of being in the cove, among his family, mingled with a gnawing sense that he might not be welcome, that he might be an inconvenience somehow, or, worse, an embarrassment. It was a little after nine and flood tide when Steve turned into the cove and let go the sail in the lee of the high ledges.

Henry's intention had been to hullo the cove from the boat, roust them out so he could see their surprised faces, then call them down to the water, and there explain from the boat how he had to maintain a distance from them. But now the thought of such theatrics seemed foolish, so he asked Steve to let him off at the wharf. As Steve rowed in, Henry saw Walter and Ava and Virgil with the baby leaving their dooryards, starting down the cove road toward him. They were dressed in the same funeral clothes that they had worn last fall when they buried Gladys, and his mother was not among them—she was nowhere to be seen.

His back to Henry and the scene on the shore, Steve said that he would come down with a barge in a week and when they got the flivver up to Stonington, they could take Claire for a spin; maybe Rose Eaton would like to go, too, though he would probably be made to sign a written agreement that he would not touch her and have that notarized. Henry did not reply; he could not. He climbed the wharf ladder, waved Steve away, and turned to search the ledges and trees and buildings for his mother.

Ava stopped dead in the road; Virgil bumped into her from behind.

"I do not believe in apparitions," she said. "I don't. I won't even believe in them when I become one."

"What the hell are you talking about, sister?" Walter stopped.

"I would point, but I might offend it. Look at the end of your wharf."

Walter saw Henry and laughed. Henry was waving, not to Walter and Ava, but to his mother who had come down the road to meet the others. She stood with one arm raised, did a little jump straight up as though struck by lightning, then broke into a run on the narrow meadow path along the shore, holding her skirts up and calling Henry's name over and over.

Henry thought that he had never seen his mother run, at least not like that. He clamped his jaw shut to keep the sob from escaping and fought back his tears.

When she reached the wharf, he shouted at her to stop, to please, please stop there and not come closer. When she did stop, or shift to a slow walk, he said:

"I've been with Steve while he had the influenza. I might be carrying it from camp or from him. It's horrible and real contagious; it's killing thousands and thousands of people, not just soldiers. Doctor Banks said if I stay apart from people, not touching them or breathing on them for a week, then it will be safe. I'm going to stay in the barn for a while to be sure; animals don't get it."

Rachel did not stop, nor did the others who were a hundred feet behind her coming across the meadow.

"Please, no, Mother." Henry held out a raised palm, but Rachel did not stop. She walked straight into him and threw her arms around him, telling him, her face against his tunic, her shoulders heaving, that he had grown two inches at least. When she kissed his cheeks and forehead, he held his breath, then held her at arm's length.

"Who has died?" he asked.

"Clytie, I'm afraid," Rachel said.

"It wasn't influenza, was it?"

"No, it was her diabetes."

Henry looked over his mother's shoulder to the others who had come up behind her.

"I really mean it. I'm so happy to see all of you, God, look at Little John, but I have to stay clear of you for a few days. I'll be home for a while; they let us go because of the epidemic. For your sake, and for mine, too; I would die if one of you got sick because of me."

"From the looks of that uniform, and your hair, which you must have rinsed with motor oil, it will be a favor to us if you stay away at least until you get a bath and some clean clothes," Walter said.

"I don't think I have ever gone to a funeral feeling glad," Ava said. "I don't suppose I ever will again."

October 13, 1918
Dear Ruth,

I am sorry that you have not heard from me of late, but I have lost my sister, and as a consequence, a great hope has fallen.

Last Friday we were tardy coming home because of me, and found poor Clytie sprawled dead on the cellar floor. Dr. Banks has since declared the cause of her death to have been insulin shock. The sight of her where she had fallen was fearful (I'll spare you the details), and an agony for Leah. Amos cleaned up our little family plot and dug her grave at Mother's and Father's feet, where we placed her, with a small but sufficient funeral service. I am worried about Leah, who has said almost nothing since the day of her mother's death.

And the consequence, you wonder? It is that I have lost Amos, too. Yes, you were right to guess that our mornings alone in the kitchen were more than platonic though I did not admit it to myself for a long while; at the time I smiled happily when I read your teases and your request for a more "active" definition of *contentment*. The truth is that we were falling in love in a most gentle and private manner, and I think I can safely say that neither of us thought or cared about much else, or about others. I won't mention the sensual parts, nor will I mention the hurt we have caused. We cannot be open with our affection now any more than we could be when Clytie was alive; indeed, it would be even more offensive now. Amos spent the first few nights in the cove after her death and Rachel stayed with me and Leah. She did not say it (she never would aloud to anyone), but I inferred from our talks that she believes as I do that the island will believe that our love, for some a mortal sin, was the cause of Clytie's demise. Amos, whose face has lost its color and his eyes their animation, suggested that we leave the island with Leah, marry, and settle elsewhere, trying new occupations. He made the suggestion for my sake and he would have gone through with it for my sake, but he would not have lasted away. He might make it through one week as a grocery clerk in Ellsworth before he escaped for open water and the island. In a "wild night" of my own, alone at the kitchen table, I realized that I, too, am rooted here. I miss many things about the city, but I do not want to live away from this island. It is my place, and Amos is here, and I will remain wedded to both, in whatever form the marriages take, for better or for worse. Amos moved back to the cove for good on Sunday, and Leah and I are going to stay here. (We are not alone, as I have taken on two boarders: Guilt and Shame, who keep quiet rooms.) Amos will visit for Sunday dinner when Leah is awake and alert to keep us from temptation.

Your poor eyes are tired; close them for a moment and think of me and realize that I waited to write to you until I had recovered enough to be able to assure you that though a great hope has fallen, it is not dead; it still exists.

Reading her poems for solace, I found this:

"Somewhat to hope for,

Be it ne'er so far

Is Capital against Despair"

If that is true, as I believe it is, then I am a wealthy girl, and my immediate goal is to find a way to share my wealth with Leah, so that she can build her own Capital.

Thank you for listening, dear Cousin. I wish I could see you in person and have you see me to know that I am not despondent. I am on my feet, and I will prevail.

I'd almost forgotten! Henry came home last week. He says that they let him and many others go home until the flu epidemic has passed. I wonder. There were some who were outraged that he had come back to the island perhaps bearing the infection, but he quarantined himself in the barn for five days per Dr. Banks's instructions and there has been no sign of disease, so those who were grouching that he should be sent away have gone silent. I've only seen him once. He is taller and as impetuous as ever, in his charming way.

I love talking to you. My wrist and forefinger cry out for a rest.

Love, always
Maggie

The sea was so calm that afternoon, and the cove so quiet, that the steady lisping whisper of Walter's plane inside the fish shack made it seem as though the shack itself was breathing in and out. Amos and Henry sat on upturned traps at the end of the wharf knitting bait bags on nails driven into opposite pilings. Amos was silent, lost in the same fog of thoughts that he had been trying to navigate since Clytie died and he moved back to the cove. In the rockweed beneath them, a yearling gull caught a green crab in his beak and flew upward with it to dash it onto the rocks for easy eating; but the furious crab flailed and pinched so that the gull dropped him into the tidal flat and flew off disappointed.

"You're right," Henry said. "The only place for my mooring is going to have to be right on top of Great-Grandfather's. My boat will ground out in any other place when the tide is this low."

"You might find that his mooring can still be used. It might not have rusted too bad. Nobody's checked it since the ice tugged it and broke the buoy line."

"It's there. You can see it at low tide when the eelgrass parts," said Henry. "Let's take a look now. You bring the gaff; I'll get some buoys and a line in case it's usable."

"We'll have to lug the skiff through the mud to get it into the water," said Amos. "Why don't we . . ."

But Henry was gone. Amos pulled on his boots, loosened the skiff line, and climbed down the wharf ladder. Henry met him at the skiff with three of his buoys and a coil of line. Together they carried the skiff through the sucking mud out to the waterline.

"The tide doesn't get any lower than this." Amos pushed them off with an oar.

Kneeling in the bow with the gaff, Henry held a hand under water. "And the water doesn't get any warmer than it is at this time of year, after all summer under the sun."

When he thought they were over the old mooring, Henry leaned over the bow and, with the gaff, combed through the eelgrass that waved gently in response.

"Be careful, goddamn you; this skiff is tippy," Amos said.

"There it is, hah! Pull a little on your starboard oar."

Henry gaffed the chain in what appeared from the surface to be its end and tugged at it, to no avail. He braced himself against the gunwales and heaved again, harder. Frightened by the commotion, a small school of mackerel rippled and flashed as it fled the entrance of the cove for deeper water.

"Stop it, goddamnit. You're going to sink us."

Henry made a noise of disgust and turned around to sit in the bow seat. He slipped the gaff into the skiff, pulled off his boots and shirt, and with a hand gripping a gunwale on each side vaulted himself butt-first over into the water. The skiff pitched and Amos let loose a horrified shout that resounded through the cove and brought Walter out onto the wharf. Henry surfaced, bellowed something, took a deep breath, and dived.

On his feet now with an oar extended, Amos shouted again. "You can't swim damnit! Come up out of there!" And this shout caused Rachel and Virgil, who were walking around the bend in the road, to turn down through the grass toward the ledge that overlooked the cove.

Henry surfaced, splashing, holding the gunwale of the skiff as Amos leaned away. "It's there!" he breathed. "And it feels like it's in damned good shape. Reach me the buoys and line; I'll have it secured in no time."

"You can't swim!" Amos cried.

"I didn't say I could." Henry sucked in a breath and left the buoys bobbing on the surface as he dived again, the end of the line in hand. Amos could see the flailing bottoms of Henry's feet, but little else of him but a churning shadow.

"What the hell's he doing?" Walter called out. "He's been under too long."

"He's frigging with the old mooring," Amos called back. "I know it. Henry! For Christ's sake come up!"

Henry emerged at the bow of the skiff and held on, breathing hard. "I got it! It's not done yet, but I got it secured." He pulled up on the gunwale and the skiff tilted precariously, bringing another yelp from Amos.

"Shit," Henry said. "I got to get out of this water before I freeze to death. Row me in to where I can touch bottom."

Amos pulled hard, twice, toward the shore, cursing Henry as vigorously as he rowed, until Henry said "There" and let go of the skiff. Up to his neck now, Henry walked through the water and eelgrass, propelling himself toward the shore with his arms. On the high grassy ledge in front of her house, Rachel left Virgil's side on the run to fetch a blanket for Henry. Walter gasped, staring gap-mouthed at Henry's progress.

"It's exactly as Huldah predicted it," he said aloud to no one. "He's wet; he's walking in eelgrass, walking home; his arms are waving; and his parents are watching him. My God. Wait till Ava hears this, and Virgil, who called Huldah a hoodoo."

But then Walter thought that he would not tell Ava because he knew that she would say *They aren't his parents yet,* and she would tell him to watch his language. He would not tell Virgil because Virgil would say he'd made it up. He had to tell Huldah, though. She'd want to know how clear she had gotten it. Walter promised himself that he would go to Burnt Island again; he would take Henry with him this time so she could see him in the flesh as well as in her imagination, if that's what it was.